ABOUT THIS BOOK...

As we wrote the World War II Islands Series, **Far On The Ringing Plains, The Scepter And The Isle** and now **Men Who Strove With Gods**, Murray and I have been fighting our own battle—a battle to bring real, gutty, authentic writing back to not only the Christian Market but to published works in every market.

Now with **Far On The Ringing Plains** winning a **First Place Award** in the 2021 CIBA Hemingway Awards for 20th Century Wartime Fiction and **The Scepter And The Isle** taking a **Finalist Award** in the same competition, we feel that we may have made some progress in our efforts to upgrade our writing to the level of such authors as Ernest Hemingway, Zane Grey, Gunter Glass, William Faulkner and others.

So we give you **Men Who Strove With Gods**—book three in The Island Series. We hope you will find it not "christianese" ... just two Jesus guys writing from the heart and the gut, and that it will be a book that will take a remembered place on your bookshelf.

Patrick E. Craig & Murray Pura

MEN WHO STROVE
WITH GODS

MURRAY PURA

PATRICK E. CRAIG

"Cover by Cora Graphics Cora Bignardi—www.coragraphics.it

This is a work of fiction. Names, characters, places, and incidents are products of the authors' imaginations or are used fictitiously. Any resemblance to actual persons, living or dead, is entirely coincidental.

Copyright © 2021 by Murray Pura and Patrick E. Craig

Islands Publishing P.O. Box 73, Huston, Idaho 83630

Library of Congress Cataloging—Men Who Strove With Gods / Murray Pura / Patrick E. Craig

ISBN 978-1-7347635-7-7 (pbk.)

ISBN 978-1-7347635-8-4 (eBook)

Printed in the United States of America

 Created with Vellum

Dedicated to Judy Craig, for her tireless editing work and her unflinching support of this project.

ACKNOWLEDGMENTS

We wish to acknowledge Simona Cora Salardi for the amazing covers she has created for the Islands series. Her patience and kindness are only rivaled by her brilliance as an artist. Thank you, Cora.

ISLANDS

A series by Murray A. Pura & Patrick E. Craig

Three friends, four years, six islands and a war that demanded from all three the ultimate in faith, courage, honor & sacrifice.

CONTENTS

When Johnny and I left Saipan, we left Billy behind. Billy didn't want to go home. But even if he did go, his dad had disowned him for going to war and he wasn't welcome in Montana. So, Johnny and me sailed home without him—me to stay at my folk's place in Ritzville and Johnny to find out if the Marjean of those letters and the real Marjean were the same girl.

I'm at my folks' place a couple of days and I get a call. It's Strange, and he's so excited he can hardly talk.

"She loves me, Bud, she really does. I went to the house, and it was just like I imagined it. I got there early, and she wasn't prepped to see me, you know, all calm and everything, gussied up. Instead, she has this little housedress on and no makeup and by everything that's holy, she was the most beautiful thing I have ever seen. She comes the door and sees me and the next thing I know she's in my arms and she's crying and I'm crying and... Bud we're getting married in ten days. Can you come? You gotta be my best man!"

Well, Johnny said all of that without taking a breath, but I already knew what would happen. See, all along I've had an inside track on J. Strange, Esq. I've known what would happen sure as the sun rises. Johnny's all set and he'll be a married man in a few days, just like I said. Now I got Billy to worry about.

The last time I saw Billy, I had a bad feeling. When this man's war started I used to think that Strange was the twisted up one, wound as tight as a baseball. But war has done something for Johnny. It put things in perspective somehow. I think he found the faith he lost a long time ago, and he's got Marjean and John Albert. He's okay,

Billy Martens is the one I worry about now. Strange came over to the Islands to fight for all the wrong reasons, but Billy came with all the right answers. Somehow, somewhere, those answers slipped away, and since Cactus, he's been asking the wrong questions. When I get back to Saipan, I hope Billy's still alive. I hope he didn't swim out into the ocean and just keep swimming, headed for Japan.

Because we still got a war to fight. The scuttlebutt is that we're going to Okinawa. But I think we have to clear off Iwo Jima first. The Japs have three big airfields there and their fighters harass Lemay's bombers going out to Japan and coming back. I think we have to take it first if we are going to stage an attack on the Japanese mainland. And that's what has me worried. We've pushed the Empire back, but the Bushido spirit is still alive. Those people will never quit and I think it will cost us a million men to subdue them.

What are the odds that me and Billy and Johnny all come back alive? I don't know about that, but I know this: we are Marines. We fight hard; we take ground and we hold it. We won't stop until we're raising the stars and stripes over Tokyo. We may survive, but I'd say the odds are long... very long.

Why did we come here? What are three guys raised Mennonite doing in a fighting war? We took an oath, that's why. We agreed to it, just between us, when we met up at boot camp. It wasn't in words. It was just us, the three Mennos, being together, going to fight, living through it. The oath was about doing something, not rusting away somewhere, but standing in the front lines of life, together. We couldn't pause, we couldn't just end it. Something called us to do something, and that something is here and now. We had to come. And the call was bigger than what we were doing with our dinky, insignificant lives back Stateside. As the poem says, "Some work of noble note that may yet be done, not unbecoming men who strove with Gods."

I think we are all here looking for that noble work not unbecoming us... us, the men who strove with Gods.

I

THE LAST BATTLE

1

HOME

BUD, THE CORPSMAN

EARLY SEPTEMBER, 1944. RITZVILLE, WASHINGTON, US OF A.

They harvested the wheat in July and the dry hills of the
Inland Empire look like D.I. Butterworth's Marine buzz-cut.
Wheat cut short to stubble but unburned so the pheasant will
flock after the fallen grain. My dad and I are out hunting. It's
strange to hold a shotgun in my hands and not be pointing it at a
tidal wave of Japs.

"Did you kill anyone, Bud?"

We walk awhile and I can tell my dad is not as spry as he used
to be. Funny how when you spend every day with someone, you
don't see how time is roughing them up. But I've been gone a long
time and I see it in him. He's getting old, and I missed it.

I let the question ring in the air for a long time.

Finally... "Yeah, Dad, I did."

"You want to tell me about it?"

We walk along in silence. How do you tell your Mennonite
dad about the last Banzai of the battle of Saipan, when five
thousand desperate Japanese soldiers armed with sticks and
shovels and the Bushido code came out of the dark like a
human tsunami? How do you tell him about your best friend

throwing himself on top of you and taking the full brunt of a grenade to keep you alive? How do you talk about the American soldiers going down all around you, heads blown off and guts spread like huge slimy worms on the ground? How do you...?

"Sometime, maybe, Dad..."

The breeze picks up a little and I feel the first hint of fall, biting at my cheeks like a tiny terrier dog. Ahead the field rises toward the endless sky, gold, blue and white the only colors. It's home, but it's not. I've been away too long. It's like another planet. I've walked this field a hundred times, but I have never been here before. Ahead of us a pheasant flutters up out of the stubble. My dad's shotgun goes to his shoulder and blasts. The bird tumbles out of the sky. Good thing dad didn't see me jump. My shotgun is still pointing at the ground. It never moved.

My dad glances over at me, but lets the old rebuke slide.

Hey boy, we gotta get some birds for Sunday dinner. Gotta be quicker than that...

Now he just looks, then looks away. I'm not the Philo he raised anymore. War has cut me up, skinned me alive, and stretched my hide on an outhouse wall. He wanted Philo, the inventor, but he got Bud, the Corpsman. What he's going to do with that, I don't know. But he's kind about it and that's helpful. The war has changed a lot of things and my dad is at least big enough to take it gracefully. And, don't mistake me, he did his bit. The government was more understanding about the Mennos in this war. My dad headed up rubber drives, was an air raid warden, and visited wounded vets at the hospital. I guess when your only son is out there in the middle of it, you take a long, hard look at how you are reading the Book.

My mom is the same, though. She will never change. Weathered, brown, face like the hills of home, food as good as always—she's just glad I made it home alive. Asks about Kalasia a lot, really wants to meet a genuine Tongan princess. Excited for me that something fine and noble came out of such a FUBAR situation.

If I eat much more of her cooking, I'll have to get new togs before I ship out.

I want to talk to my dad, just get a few things straight so he can relax. But every time I start to say something, he shifts the conversation. I know it's because he's torn.

He's lived all his life believing that men don't kill each other. He didn't fight in the Big War because of it, and the Mennos got a raft of crap from the over-zealous jingoists back home. Never mind that they weren't out getting turned into mud in the trenches of France. Never mind that they kept their boys working in an "essential industry." They loved to beat down the folks who had something they stood for and wouldn't budge. Just to keep people looking away from their own hypocrisy.

When you fight a war, you discover words don't mean a hill of beans. The heroes just shut up and dig the trench. There's no strutting and fretting their hour upon the stage.

The talkers are always the walkers.

So, when you come home and sit in a bar and listen to the loudmouths telling how if it was up to them, they could win the war in a week, you just look around until you see a guy sitting quietly in the corner, nursing a Pabst. You catch his eye, and he smiles and gives a nod. You raise your beer and he raises his, and you know the guy has been to hell and back. He's watched his best friends blown into nothingness, or held their hand while they bled out in a cruddy jungle somewhere. You know the guy has done his duty, and he sees the same in you. And if you ain't been there, you haven't got the faintest idea what I'm talking about.

I guess I grew up a lot out in the Pacific. It's like all the days of my youth are gone. I can't seem to see them anymore. Combat takes all that and turns it into a meaningless pulp. I don't remember my school, I don't remember any girls I dated, all that has disappeared behind the steel wall of fifty caliber slugs taking down a hundred guys at a time in the Tarawa lagoon. The memories have drained into the muck of Cactus along with the blood of a thousand comrades, the guys Billy kept looking for, the ones he wanted to take home, like Joseph out of Egypt.

I remember something I wrote to Kalasia after Cactus.

When the sun paints the weary west with golden light and the ship sails into safe harbor, we will disembark, but we will not leave the bones behind. We will carry them—rattling mementoes of another time.

If I live to be an old man, on the day I die, I will still have the bones.

They are still with me—the bones. They hang in my memory like Spanish moss on a southern oak. They block the way to my past and grin at me if I try to push through them.

"How are you, Bud, whaddaya know? Did ya just get back from a vaudeville show?"

Eddie Kremer, Sharples, Molina, Rudy, Amina...

Sometimes the bones have names and faces. The flesh comes back on them like Ezekiel's vision. But that only happens in my sweating dreams and I can't prophesy the rebirth of Hot Lips or Teacher or the rest of them, or restore them to their land of blessing. They are gone; they don't exist anymore. They took Charon's barge to the land of the shades and they wander wailing in the dark.

I'd like to explain that to my dad, but where do I get the words to give flesh to the feelings, the visions, the faces, the voices in my soul? Does every man who has taken up arms struggle like this for the rest of their life? Somebody once said that war is the great separator. It separates heroes from cowards, the noble from ignoble, men from boys. There is no second chance and no going back.

War is the great decider, the last chance café, the non-refundable offer. It is also the wall between then and now. For the ones who stayed home, life is an expressway of current events, going from one day to the next with nothing important to mark the passing of time. And then they bump up against their own mortality and it's a complete surprise, for they have no warning, no one to tell them, "Get down, you fool!"

And they run out their lives remembering everything and nothing because they never put their feet into the sucking mud of Cactus, they never danced with the girls of Wellington, they never climbed the high mountains, they never waded one thousand yards chest deep through the blood bath of Tarawa. They have nothing to mark the end because they never expected it.

But war, battle, the enemy—these are all push pins in the map of life—each one showing you that life is precious, and each second is to be lived to the fullest and death is waiting just there, or just there, in that tree, or behind that dune, or on the shore of that river. And when you face death like that, life stops meandering like a stream on flat ground, but it rushes forward like a cataract down a narrow, rocky canyon, and every moment is eternity and yet still flashes by like a lightning bolt.

And, oh God, I wish I could tell my dad... or anybody.

THE DRIVE to Sand Point is beautiful. Once you leave Ritzville, you travel through the sere hills for a while and then you top a rise just past Keystone and the Columbia River spreads below you. It's not as wide as it is down by Wallula Gap, but it's the Columbia. I borrowed my dad's '37 Buick Roadmaster Sedan, and she's a hummer. Black, with that narrow grill, overhead valve, eight-cylinder engine and 130 horsepower. My dad may be provincial, but he's one of the few people on the east side of the state who has a television set. And he always has a good car. No flies on my dad.

Anyway, I'm going to Sand Point to stand up for Johnny

Strange and Marjean. My buddy is marrying the girl of his dreams and I tell you, she is some kind of special. She must really love him because she waited three years for him and never looked at anyone else. At least that's what her letters said. And I believe her, because she is gorgeous and probably could have had her pick of the slackers who stayed home, but she waited. And that's good.

Around Cheney, the pine trees have pushed across the Idaho border and line the roadway. All along the way are clear lakes and streams, green fields and these wonderful pine trees. Heading on into Spokane, you drive past the falls of the Spokane River. My dad and I used to come over when the salmon were running and catch a ton.

I talked to my dad before I left.

I sat him down and gave it to him straight. I know it made him uncomfortable, but he sat through it, and when I was done, I felt better and I think he understood me a little better. He was really quiet for a whole day and then last night when I was getting ready for bed, he came and knocked on my door.

"Can we talk for a minute, Bud?"

He hardly ever called me Bud, so I'm wondering what's up. He comes in and sits down beside me on the bed. He looks around the room. I've still got my model airplanes up on the shelf, some posters from the Ritzville Fair and Rodeo, and a picture frame with a bunch of baseball cards in it. You know—Jimmy Foxx, Lou Gehrig, even one of the Babe. He hesitates for a minute.

"You know, son, I didn't know what to think when you enlisted. It was a big surprise for me. I mean... well, you grew up as a pacifist. It was hard for me to see you as a warrior. You never even fought in school..."

"Dad, I..."

"Let me finish, son, I need to say this. I've been thinking about what you told me, about what you went through out there in the Pacific. It kinda shook me. I never really thought about it before.

Here I am in a church that says you shouldn't kill other men and I think I just saw that two-dimensionally."

My dad is a thinker. Did I tell you that?

"Anyway, I just listened to the preacher and read the Bible and kinda went along to get along. But I didn't do my homework. I didn't look at history and see that almost every generation has a savage race that rises up and takes on the entire world. The Babylonians, the Persians, the Romans. And in our day, it's Hitler, and Tojo, and Stalin. And it came to me, after our talk, that if somebody didn't stand up and knock these bullies down, there would be no Constitution to protect my right to have a stand on killing other men. Somebody had to do it, and if it was my son, who went out there to stand up for me, then all I can say is, I'm really proud of you, Bud. I really am. I think you did the right thing, and I'm proud of the man you've become. And that's all I have to say about it."

Well, we both stood up and then I hugged my dad, and he hugged me back, and when we broke the clinch, we both had tears in our eyes.

So, I'm driving up to Sand Point, and I'm feeling as free as I have for a long time, because me and my dad are good.

2

THE SURVIVORS
BILLY MARTENS

BILLY WAS ALWAYS UP BEFORE THE SUN.

The habit had been ingrained since Guadalcanal in the late summer and fall of 1942.

He couldn't sleep in. He needed to be up when there were still stars.

"Take it easy, Sarge," the other Marines would say. "The war on Saipan is over."

Billy would shrug. "The skinny is we're headed to some place called Iwo Jima to knock off the Jap fighter base that's been shooting up our bombers on their runs into Tokyo. Maybe the war's over here, but it ain't done by a long shot."

"I heard we're headed to Okinawa," another would say.

Billy would nod. "Yeah, I heard that too."

"Or maybe we'll skip them both and head right on into Japan."

Billy shook his head. "Japan will be a butcher's shop. If they can get the Emperor to surrender by any other means, that's what they're going to try first."

"So, you think this Iwo or whatever it is, Sarge? Or that other island?"

"Yeah, one or the other."

But, in the end, the war wasn't over on Saipan, anyway. There were Japanese troops hidden in the jungle who refused to surrender. Sniping at Marines, looting from Marine and Army stores, eluding patrols sent to kill or capture them. They even attacked Isley Field, an airstrip built for the B-29 Superfortress. When Billy was commanded to handpick a squad and "go gung ho" on these survivors, he glanced to the east where the sun rose out of the sea, and where America rose out of the sea too. That's where his best friends were. Bud and Johnny. He wished they were in his squad of hunters. But who knew when they'd be back? Or if they'd ever be back?

Billy didn't want a sizeable group smashing their way through the jungle. He wanted stealth. Marines who had learned from the islanders how to conduct ruthless and efficient guerilla warfare. He chose five men. Jack, who'd been nicknamed Jack B. Quick because of his speed in combat. Thad. Bricks—he never responded to his real name, Alphonse, which Billy couldn't blame him for, and he did come off as a stack of bricks, rugged, hard, massive. A Marine who'd known Alphonse on Guadalcanal told Billy the man had been called Toothpick then, he was so scrawny: "War put the beef on him, Sarge."

To Jack, Thad and Bricks, Billy added Darian and Player, Player being another nickname foisted on a freckled kid from Iowa whose parents had him christened Ichabod. Parents, Billy acknowledged out loud, did oddball things, and thought briefly about his father back on the ranch in Montana. Ichabod was popular with the island women, so Player he became and had settled into his new name with a grin and a modest brag: "I have dates every night of the week."

"Ice blocks under the armpits, Player," Bricks had warned. "Any islanders complain about you being Don Juan and the MPs will lock you up in the four-holer."

"I'll be careful."

When Billy picked Player up for the squad, he told him: "I'll help you stay away from the brig, Marine. You're going into the jungle with me for an indefinite period. No love life there."

"What does indefinite mean, Sarge?"

"It means forever," Bricks told him, deadpan.

Player got the BAR. Darian was the sniper and went with his modified M1 Garand. The rest drew Tommy guns, Thompson submachine guns, Colt 1911 side arms, and what Billy called their "New York Knives", Ka-Bars stamped Camillus.N.Y. on the cross-guard. Billy also threw in machetes for each man, CASEXX survival machetes he begged off the Army Air Force, trading all his cigarettes for six with their walnut handles and leather sheaths. They had blued ten-inch blades that did not fold into the handle like some other versions Billy had seen the bomber crews sharpening.

Darian swung his using a stroke Billy hadn't seen.

"What do you know, Darian?" he asked.

"My parents were missionaries in the Philippines. I grew up there. We moved back to the States in '38. This is the bolo, Sarge. The machete of choice. These ones by CASE are well-made. I wouldn't mind a few more inches, though."

"Well, they're made to go in the air crews' survival packs."

"Yeah, but these bolos need to be like razors."

"Okay. Show your buddies how to do them up right."

The squad drew ammo, C-rations, extra socks, whatever they thought they needed. The quartermaster was authorized to honor their requests without argument. He did what they ordered him to do, but with plenty of reluctance and hefty cuss words. Billy had a quick chat with him. "We're still fighting the war and you're still sitting on your ass. Give my boys whatever they ask for or meet me at midnight. Your choice."

That fall of 1944, they were just hearing about Merrill's Marauders who had been operating in Burma as long-range jungle fighters. They were quickly becoming the stuff of legend.

This meant the squad wanted a nickname. Martens' Maulers is what they came up with, Bricks leading the charge. Billy rolled his eyes and lit a cigarette. "Come on, guys, give me something better than that."

"Martens' Mechanics?" one of them suggested.

Billy grunted. "What? We're opening up a garage with my buddy, Johnny Strange?"

"Martens' Monsters." This from Thad.

"Oh, sure, that's swell," Billy groaned. "We're beasts and monsters, huh? How about Martens' Mummies?"

"You mean it?"

"No, Thad, I don't mean it. Come on. I don't want K-rations names. Give me something that fits. You want island girls to look at you instead of the pilots and GIs and officers? Give them a name they'll brag about: *I'm dating one of Martens' Marines.*"

Player shrugged. "You're from cowboy country, right, Sarge?"

Billy nodded. "God's Country, more like. Montana."

"So, those rattlesnakes…"

"None of them have names that go with my M."

"What about an African snake?" asked Jack.

Billy began to smoke. "Such as?"

"I've read about the mambas. Cousin to the cobra. I had a teacher who was into snakes. They call it herpetology. He assigned me the mamba. I had to write an essay. Saw one in a glass case too. Mortality rate is one hundred percent if the docs don't treat you in time. It's nicknamed 'the kiss of death'. What do you think?"

"I like the nickname. But Marten's Mambas sounds like a chorus line."

"Makos," Bricks said.

"What?" Billy stared at him.

"When we were in New Zealand, the family I got to know took me out on their boat. We saw some Makos. Sharks. Going so fast the boat couldn't keep up. Over forty miles an hour. Fast, strong, deadly."

"A shark is great. But Martens' Makos? This is not working out, men."

"Then let's just be that," Jack responded.

"Be what?" grumped Billy, exhaling a stream of white smoke.

"Martens' Men."

They stuck around to watch the first B-29 land on October 12th.

"She's a big baby," said Darian, mesmerized by the plane's size and the roar of its four huge engines.

"A big beautiful baby," oozed Bricks.

"Those are Wright R-3350 radial engines," Jack announced.

"How do you know?" snapped Bricks.

"I just know, okay? Dad works for Boeing. That's all I'm going to say."

"What the heck? You afraid they're going to stick you up against a wall and blindfold you?"

"And cram a final cigarette between my lips? Yeah, who knows?"

They went on their first patrol the next day. No helmets, faces and hands fully darkened, Billy telling them to use their knives and machetes over their Thompsons or 1911s. Unless it turned into a firefight. Then they were to blast away.

Always a terrible month for rainfall, October drenched them to the bone day after day. A week later, they were back at the base. They had found some sign of Japanese troops. A fire-site. A latrine close at hand. Empty rice bags. That was it.

Martens' Men were still at the base when the first bombing mission took off from Isley on the 28th—fourteen B-29s headed for the Truk Atoll and Japanese fortifications there. The noise, Darian exclaimed, was "glorious heavenly thunder," and didn't take cover from the dust that boiled over him. A few days later, Japanese aircraft attacked the base early in the morning. A few bombs struck, but there wasn't much damage to Isley or nearby Kobler Field. There was another early morning attack against Isley on November 7th. Again, the bombs accomplished next to nothing. But Player spotted Japanese soldiers on the strip trying to sabotage a B-29, yelled, and opened fire with his BAR. Billy thought the kid was seeing things until he got a good look at the blood trail in the morning. He threw his squad together and they were on the move in an hour.

"We'll never catch them now," Thad complained as they slashed through a thick stand of bamboo with their machetes. "They've had all night."

"They're out there," Billy replied. "This isn't a race. We need to outmaneuver them and ambush them."

"Maybe we should just set up that ambush back at Isley."

"There are other Marines doing that. This is our mission. You with me?"

Thad glared and swung his CASEXX bolo. "I'm one of your men, ain't I? Turning fungal and rotting in my boots. Again. At least Tarawa was dry."

"Dead dry."

The rain did not let up.

Billy pushed them deeper and deeper into Saipan's jungle.

They found no trace of the Japanese saboteurs.

"Maybe they're just ghosts," Jack murmured. "Maybe it's what we think we see."

"I shot a real Jap," Player argued. "Ghosts don't bleed."

"We probably imagined the blood, too."

"Shut up, Jack." Billy spooned out his last can of C-rations, rain dripping off the spoon, the can, his face, everything. "We'll keep coming out here till we bag something. If there're ghosts, we'll bag them along with the rest of the Japs."

Darian killed an IJN, an Imperial Japanese Navy pilot, once they'd returned to Isley. Others claimed to be on it, but Darian, nicknamed Bolo, knew he caught the Jap dead center and watched his chest split open while shots from other rifles threw chips around him. B-29s were burning, three or four of them, thick black smoke pouring into the Saipan sky, the Japanese attack sweeping over the airfield at noon November 27th. Why the naval aviator landed on the airstrip in the middle of all this, no one could guess. Fuel? Damage? Bravado? He fired his Nambu pistol at his American enemies until Darian and others cut him down, or as Thad muttered, cut him in half.

"That's a hell of a thing," rumbled Bricks. "Why'd he land his Zero on top of burning B-29s?"

"Because it's a hell of a thing in Tokyo," Billy responded. "What would you be doing if the Japs were bombing LA or San Francisco or Milwaukee?"

"What would I be doing? I'm doing it, Sarge."

"Same with Kaji. He's here doing it with his A6M Zero because we're doing it to him in his home country."

"Who the heck is Kaji?"

Billy pointed at the pilot's body with his chin. "That's Kaji. The ghosts in the jungle are Kaji. The ones burning up on a Tokyo street we B-29'd the crap out of are Kaji."

"You feeling okay, Sarge?"

"Let's get out of here. The stink of this burning rubber and fuel is making me loopy. Draw your ammo and C-rations. We're heading back into the jungle at 1800 hours."

"To do what?" Bricks grumbled. "Catch raindrops?"

Billy ignored the provocation. "Maybe we can win the war without blowing up another city or another housewife or another kid."

"Boy, you really are screwed up today, aren't you, Sarge? What do you think Tojo did to China or Bataan or Hong Kong?"

"I know what he did. I'm not gonna do it."

3

ITHACA
JOHNNY STRANGE

JOHNNY STRANGE PUNCHED DOWN ON THE GAS PEDAL AND FELT THE
235 cubic inch engine in his '42 Chevy Fleetline jam the car
forward into another dimension. He glanced down at the
speedometer. Sixty-five miles an hour and purring. The trees on
either side of Highway 2 flew by in a solid wall of green. The tires
made a roaring sound through the open window.

Danny kept this baby humming. I sure am glad I left it at his shop.

Johnny Strange was going back to Bonners Ferry, but he didn't
want to. It was the last place he ever wanted to be. He was going
to see his father for the first time in three years. Their parting had
been angry, bitter, acrimonious, and he suspected not much had
changed. As far as Johnny knew, his father was still a legalistic,
religious hack who valued public opinion far more than doing
what was right.

HE'D BEEN HOME A WEEK, and he had put this trip off the whole
time. Finally, this morning, he drove over to the Langston house
from his motel and when he came to the door, Marjean pulled

him inside and kissed him for a long time. John Albert came downstairs, Johnny picked up his son, and they all went into the front room. He sat with Marjean and his boy, and Marjean put her arm around his shoulders and ruffled his hair. He told her about hating to go see his dad.

"It's gonna be okay, sweetie. You need to go home. Who knows, maybe your father has changed."

Johnny looked at Marjean. She was so beautiful. The cornsilk hair, the funny little wolf's teeth when she smiled, the perfect face. He didn't want to go anywhere, he just wanted to sit and drink her in, inhale her, absorb her into his very being. He saw the look in her eyes and he knew she felt just like he did, but he kept looking at her. It was okay that she asked him to stay at a motel until they got married. It had been hard for her to ask. She was so shy, but as soon as he figured out what she wanted, he pulled her close and laughed.

"I love you, Marjean."

He wanted to do that for her, make her feel like a bride, make their wedding night special...

She blushed. "What?"

"My God, you are so beautiful."

* * *

Johnny Strange had lived in fear for a long time. Every night in the steaming jungles of Cactus, or dug into a bloody beach on Tarawa, or climbing the mountains of Saipan—every night he had been afraid—afraid that his dream of a life with Marjean would evaporate like a white puff of cloud over a blazing Idaho desert, disappear like Kremer's arm, vanish along with his childhood into a dark stinking place that sucked the life out of hope and crushed the heart of things not yet seen.

But when he came home, when she opened her door and he saw her face and her eyes, and then felt her in his arms, her heart thumping like a Thompson and her arms squeezing him so hard he could not breathe—then he knew that Bud had been right. God had loved him enough to give him the most beautiful girl in the world.

THE MORNING he arrived on the plane from Spokane, he went to Danny Carrabello's garage first thing, and picked up his car. He was in his dress blues with his campaign ribbons, unit citation and purple heart spread across his chest. Danny's eyes got big. He whistled and then said something strange.

"Ulysses home from Troy, eh?"

Johnny stared at him for a long moment, a moment in which he was back on Cactus and Bud was extolling on the warriors of Greece and their long voyage home. "What makes you say that, Danny? Do I have trouble at… at home?"

"With Marjean? Not a snowball's chance in hell that girl would step out on you. What did you do to her, hypnotize her?"

Johnny shook his head. "I wasn't the one doin' the hypnotizing my friend. I'm serious. Has Marjean been dating anyone? Why did you say that?"

"Naw, she's a one-man woman. I just said that 'cause I read it in a book somewhere and here you are home from the sea. And Marjean? Are you kidding? She's got that little boy of yours and he's her whole life."

"Anybody trying to put the make on her?"

Danny paused. "Oh, I guess Gerald King still has a case on her and I've heard he called her up a few times, but she laid it on the line with that slacker. Told him she wanted to see him in uniform shipping off to war and then she'd know he'd grown up and wasn't hiding behind his daddy. She told him she had a real man already. I guarantee you got nothing to worry about, buddy boy."

"How about you, Danny? Why didn't you go?"

Danny shook his head. "Don't laugh, okay. Promise? Nobody knows this."

Johnny raised his hand with thumb and the two far fingers touching. "Scout's honor."

"When I was a kid, I put a bean in my ear."

Johnny stared at Danny, trying not to crack a smile. "What?"

"Yeah, go ahead and laugh. I did. I put a bean in my ear and it sprouted and grew through my eardrum. I'm deaf in my left ear."

"You are kidding me, right?" Johnny burst out laughing.

Danny shook his head. "Nope, God's truth. I couldn't get in the Marines because I put a bean in my ear."

Johnny couldn't stop laughing.

Danny frowned at his doubled-over friend. "Yeah, yuk it up." He paused, with an injured look on his face, until Johnny took a breath. "Well, I did my duty here as best I could. I'm in the Civilian Air Patrol, ya know. I'm the local Commander. I'm not mad at you for laughing or anything, but think about this. Since I've been in charge here, not one Japanese aircraft has gotten past Spokane."

That's when Johnny lost it.

After a while, he pulled it together, stood up straight, wiped his eyes and put his hand on his friend's shoulder. "Okay, ol' One Ear." They both grinned. "I'm headed over to School Street to meet my boy and see my girl... If she still wants me."

Danny stuck out his hand. "Aww, Marjean is a real peach. She's waiting for Johnny Strange, and let me tell you, nobody deserves a girl like her more than you. God's truth."

HE DROVE up to the big house on School Street and sat in his car for a long time. It was like the dream he had on Tarawa. He could feel the sweat under his arms as the day warmed up. He wanted to turn the key and just drive away.

Die here or die somewhere else. Might as well be here.

"Yeah, right, Lieutenant."

He opened the door and climbed out on the asphalt, his dress shoes the same color, shiny and black. Down at the end, about a block away, the Pend Oreille river flowed by, level, dark, swift. Not the sparkling blue of Tarawa Lagoon or the cruddy green of the streams of Guadalcanal. No. Smooth, deep, clean Idaho water flowing down to the Columbia, headed for a Pacific Ocean that was becoming less and less dominated by the Empire of Japan.

Johnny took a deep breath and pulled himself ramrod straight. If she was gonna kiss him off, he would be a soldier about it.

Then his white gloved hand was on the bell. Deep, melodious chimes rang somewhere back in the house. The door cracked open, and she was there, her eyes wide, her face white...

Her mouth opened, her hand covered it. She pulled the door open, stepped toward him, her hand now reaching... "Johnny, I didn't expect you until tonight..."

"I got an early flight. Marjean, I... I..."

And then she was in his arms and he felt the aliveness in her, the pure living being of her, he smelled the sweet scent of her, felt her body against his, a thousand dreams rolled into one, and in that moment, death was purged from his soul and it was all right. Everything was good to go.

He opened his eyes, saw a little boy over Marjean's shoulder. Dark hair, enormous eyes, standing at the end of the hall. Johnny pulled away from Marjean and crouched down so he could look the boy right in the eye.

"Are you... are you my daddy?"

He looked up at Marjean. She nodded.

"Yeah, John Albert, I'm your daddy."

And then John Albert came running down the hall and he

wasn't one bit afraid and he leapt into Johnny's arms and then the three of them were embracing and Johnny was crying and Marjean was crying and all the days and all the hours and all the killing and all the dark nights and the dead friends and the dark dreams vanished like campfire smoke in a brisk Idaho wind and Johnny Strange was home at last.

<hr>

AND NOW HE was going to Bonners Ferry, but he wasn't really going home. He was making a courtesy call. He was going to see a man he had almost forgotten, a man who meant nothing to him, except for the fact that he was his physical father. A sign ahead—speed zone, forty-five miles per hour. He reluctantly tapped the brake pedal, and the car pulled back from its headlong rush. Evergreen Street. He was almost in town. The long straightaway where he used to drag Matt Hollins in his Bucket Ford Roadster. He always beat him, but then everyone knew Johnny Strange was a pounder. Carter Country Farm & Feed, Labrosse Hill Street off to the right. Hit the bend going forty-eight, passed a cop car. The guy looked up, a look of recognition on his face, pulled out with lights flashing, siren going.

Johnny pulled over. The cop didn't pull in behind him. He passed and slid in right in front. The door opened, and the cop got out, walked back to the Chevy, leaned in the open window.

"Howdy, Strange. Thought you might like an escort into town."

Johnny smiled. "Jimmy, Jimmy Richards. You the town clown now?"

Jimmy grinned. "You bet. You and I spent so much time leaving local cops in the dust, the town council figured they better give me the job so they could keep an eye on me. How are you Johnny?"

"Good, very good." Johnny reached out and they shook hands.

Jimmy looked at the blue uniform jacket full of medals and ribbons. "We heard you did real good out there, Johnny, and Bonners Ferry is proud of you." He paused. "You going to see your pop?"

Johnny nodded. "Yeah."

"He's not doing so good, you know. Their church folded, a lot of dirt got around."

"About Jenkins?"

Jimmy nodded. "Yeah, some parents caught the guy naked in the back seat of a car with their twelve-year-old son. He beat it out of town before we could arrest him. I hear he's over in Spokane. Then some more kids came forward, and the town found out he'd been molesting boys for years—pretending to be a Christian—and the church had been covering up for him. After that the church folded."

"It's not like I didn't warn my dad, Jimmy."

"Well, he's up at your old place. Kinda run down now. His hardware store ain't doing so good. People found other places to buy. But I'll let him tell you the rest. I gotta run. Just thought I'd say hello and welcome back."

"Thanks, Jimmy. Good to see you."

"Always, Johnny. Always."

Down the long straightaway past Carquest Auto Parts, the big curve, and then the bridge over the Kootenai River. Off to the left, the Community Hospital and then the right turn onto District 2 Road. A mile, right on Ball Park and then the house. Set back off the road.

Johnny turned in the driveway and the gravel crunched under the wheels. The place had a run-down look, like a bush that hadn't been pruned in a long time, or an old dog that had been living in a field somewhere.

Someone was sitting on the front porch. Johnny focused. It was his dad. The old man looked up, saw the car and, for a moment, Johnny thought he saw the face brighten. Then the mask came back down and the face went stiff.

I should have known! Nothing's changed.

Johnny got out and walked up the path. He looked up at his dad. Overweight, sloppy, two-day growth on his face.

"So! The killer home from battle, eh!" But there was more of a question in his words than a statement.

"For gosh sake, Dad. Can you give it a rest? We haven't seen each other in three years. I came to say hello, not to get one of your famous brow-beatings."

The old man looked away. "Yeah, sure, sorry. Sit down."

Johnny pulled up a chair. "How are you, Dad?"

"Medium, Johnny, medium. And you?"

"I'm getting married in three days."

"To that girl over in Sandpoint that you knocked up?"

A familiar twist wrenched at Johnny's guts. He stood up and looked down at Peter Strange. The man was old, shrunken, twisted, and his failure was written on his face like someone had carved it with a knife. In that moment, Johnny saw the truth, the bottom line, the *denouement* of his whole life.

"Okay. I'm gonna say this once and then I'm done." He took a deep breath. "I left here twisted up, a mess. I always thought it was Jenkins. But it wasn't him, Dad. It was you. I was twisted up because you were supposed to be a Christian, a good dad, an example. But you weren't. You were always a jerk. Now that I think about it, I think mom died just to get away from you."

"Now, look here." The old man started to get up, but Johnny stood over him, fists clenched tight, and he sank back.

"You're a hypocrite, Peter Strange, and a liar, and, basically, you're just a rotten, mean man. I'm getting married to the most wonderful girl that ever lived. She's got my boy, your grandson, a grandson you will never see because I don't want you poisoning him like you poisoned me. You can sit here with your phony world fallen down around you and rot for all I care."

Johnny started down the steps. He stopped and turned. "One more thing. You were my dad, but you're not anymore. You're just Peter Strange, a man whose house I grew up in and a man who made my life miserable until I left home and found out what genuine love is."

He took another breath, spread his hands, and then the words dropped like rocks into a mine shaft.

"We're done."

Johnny went down the steps, got in the car, and drove away.

He never looked back.

4

CALENDAR GIRL
BUD THE CORPSMAN

Man, oh, man! What a peach this girl is! I mean, Strange is a handsome guy, but Marjean standing beside him makes Johnny look like brown shoes with a tuxedo. And their little guy, J.A. they call him. He could be in movies right now. This whole deal is like a Norman Rockwell painting. And I get to be the best man.

Being in Sandpoint, Idaho, for this wedding makes all of it worthwhile—the misery of Cactus, the grim reaper reality of Tarawa, the caves of Saipan. I only wish Kalasia could be here. Then there would be no hope for any man on this planet, those two gals standing together. Marjean and Kalasia. Oh, thank you, Lord—from me and from Johnny.

I told you how me and my dad are really on the same wavelength now, and that's great. But I guess it didn't work out so good for Johnny. I didn't really expect it to. I knew from the first time I met Johnny in basic, and especially when he spilled his guts about Jenkins, that there was something deeper in his makeup, something that got him off the road and into the deep mud long before his camping trip with the church pervert.

And when he told me what his dad said about Marjean, I knew. Peter Strange is one of those men who was born with a short soul, a man who, despite his claims of religion and piety, is broken and dark inside. I don't blame Johnny for walking away. I wouldn't want my kids in the hands of a guy like that, either.

But you know what? Even though it was a tough day for him, when Johnny got back from Bonners Ferry, he was a new guy. Oh, believe me, I think he hates the reality that things didn't work out with his dad. But I could see that something had released inside, that last bit of twist that kept Johnny Strange up nights. That place of turmoil that made him love killing Japs and beating the peawadden out of guys in the boxing ring.

Yeah, Johnny is a changed man. And after tonight he's gonna be changed in ways that he can't even imagine. All the dreams, all the longing, all the urgency that dwelt in the heart of a guy that has never known genuine love—all that will find its fulfillment in the arms of the doll standing next to him. I can just tell. A girl doesn't look at a guy that way unless she is crazy in love with him. And I know, because my Kalasia looks at me like that and I know what it means. *Kapish?* Do you know what I'm talking about?

After the wedding, we are going over to Al's house, that's Marjean's dad, and we are going to have a private little party. Just a few friends and some great cooking. I know it's great because I was over there for breakfast. Cecelia, she's Al's cook, and she was stylin' it this morning. Ham, eggs, biscuits, gravy, orange juice, cantaloupe, and coffee, pots and pots of coffee. Woof! When I finally shoved myself away from the table, I felt like my center of gravity had radically shifted.

Al has asked Johnny to move in to the big house on School Street. There's an entire wing that isn't being used, and Johnny and Marjean will take it over. And I think Al would hate living in that great big house by himself. I can tell that little J.A. loves his grandpa, so it's the perfect setup. Johnny Strange is going to be living the life of Riley. He's got Marjean, J.A., a great grandpa and a friend in Al and, to top it off, Cecelia in the kitchen. What a fricking deal.

———

AFTER THE PARTY, Johnny and Marjean got into his Fleetline and headed for Priest Lake. Al's got a cabin up there, right on the water. I don't know if there's a more beautiful spot in the world. And I don't know if there is a more beautiful girl in the world, except maybe a certain Tongan princess I know. Marjean's face was like a sunset over the Rockies, all lit up and glowing, and if happiness could be scraped off, bottled, and sold, I would have made a fortune today.

Marjean is special, one in a million, every soldier's calendar girl. And now they are married and they are going to get a mulligan on a love affair that started in a little boathouse over on the lake and got sidetracked and tested by an inconvenient war and a young man's fear.

But Marjean? I can tell by the way she looks at him she knew exactly the way it was going to work out from the first minute she saw John Strange, Esq. And Johnny? A new man, a real man, all the twists and kinks worked out and I'm thanking God for doing the job that only He can do.

———

J.A. IS STAYING home with Al and Johnny told me to stay for a couple of days and check out the neighborhood. I said I would. J.A. and I hit it off pretty good and me and Al are both in the medical field, so to speak, and there's nothing happening back in

Ritzville, so I'm staying over. Besides, I have to file a behavior report with Kalasia.

JOHNNY AND MARJEAN are gone and the three of us are sitting in front of the fire. Al has cracked a couple of cold ones and J.A. is all ears as me and Al talk doctor talk.

"So, Bud. What are you going to do with all this medical training once you get home?"

"I don't know, Doc. I'm a little up in the air with it."

"Well, Bud, you're a Navy Pharmacists Mate First Class. That takes a lot of experience and a heck of a lot of training. A lot more training than the interns I work with at the hospital get, that's for sure." He took a pull on his Miller High Life. "Do you want to be a doctor, Bud?"

Boy, Al dug right into my secret cupboard with that one. I cocked my head and looked at him.

"I think so, Al. But I don't want to be a doctor that sits behind my desk in Spokane listening to some fat old woman telling me about her imaginary female problems when she's too old to even have female problems. I love medicine, I love healing people, I love learning about the body and how it works. But this war has trained me in a different school, a school where I have to do my best in five minutes or less, and it isn't somebody complaining about their backache, it's a buddy with his guts shot out by fifty caliber machinegun shells, screaming for me to do something... a buddy I can't save no matter how much I know."

Al Shook his head. "My God, what a school."

"So, I don't know exactly where that puts me as far as being a stateside doctor. Seems like it would be pretty tame."

Al keeps probing and pretty soon I've laid it all out on the table. Yeah, I want to be a doctor, but I'm not sure where to start with it.

We keep talking and at the end of the conversation Al is telling me I'd make a great doctor and when I get back from this next tour, he'll do everything he can to help me get into a decent med school and give me all the recommendations I need. Which is very encouraging.

But there is a caveat, one dark cloud in all of Sandpoint, Idaho, this special day—thinking about the low probability of getting back from this next tour. Me and Johnny gotta go back to the Pacific. And when we do, we'll get in a transport ship with a bunch of gyrenes, some we know and the rest will be a lot of fresh meat full of big words and at the same time packing their pants. We'll go to Iwo, or Okinawa, or Formosa and there will be a *tsunami* of crazy Japanese maniacs on every one of those Islands and their entire focus will be to kill as many Marines as they can. They'll kill us with machine guns, tanks, grenades, artillery, and if they run out of that stuff, they'll come at us with knives and swords, and their teeth if they have to.

And I'll be hanging plasma bags on rifles stuck in the dirt, and there will be more fields with rows of white crosses, and some guys I know, and a lot of the newbies, will never come stateside again.

And if we get all the way to Japan and wade ashore on the beaches of Tokyo, there will be 70 million Japanese waiting for us —men, women, kids, old people, soldiers, civilians. And they will kill us with guns and rocks and knives and bombs and suicide charges...

We'll send a million body bags home before we capture those Islands. And then we'll occupy and they will still be crazy and there will be samurais running around killing Marines and soldiers and it will be one hell of a show.

And I'm afraid for Johnny. He's got a life now and of the three of us, he's got the most to lose. Oh, yeah, Kalasia would be sad if the Japs kill me, but we're not married yet and it wouldn't be the end of the world. And Billy, he dumped Cham, and he really doesn't know which end is up.

But Johnny, he's sitting on top of the world and I feel like I'm maybe the only thing between him and a real snafu. So you know what? I'm going to be busy from now until that little slime bag Tojo is dangling at the end of a rope and the Empire of Japan crawls back inside those three little islands and forgets their dreams of conquest.

But there are a lot of bullets between today and peace. So, I'll be praying overtime for my buddies.

JOHNNY AND MARJEAN got back today and boy, if Marjean was beautiful when they left, she is incredible now. She's hanging on his arm and she's smiling, and Johnny is as relaxed as I've ever seen him. I'm getting ready to go back to Ritzville and I'm loading my bags into the car and Marjean comes out. She comes up, and she takes my hand and looks up at me with those icy blues and I'm telling you, if I hadn't bought a one-way ticket to the end of the rainbow with Kalasia, it would be extremely easy to fall in love with this girl, especially when she reaches up and plants a kiss on my cheek.

That's it. Stick a fork in Bud, I'm done.

"Thank you, Bud."

"For what, Marjean?"

"For being Johnny's friend and praying for him, and believing in me. He told me how you walked him through a lot of stuff, well... when he didn't think that I really loved him, and when you guys were in battle and how he was expecting a Dear John letter every day, and how you told him you knew I was his girl forever."

Tears came into her eyes.

"I know Johnny had his troubles when he left here, but I think God knew that too, so he sent you to be Johnny's friend. And I want you to know, Bud Parmalee, that as long as I live, you will be my friend too."

Marjean just kinda slipped into my arms and, for a long moment, we shared the day and love and a warm embrace. And I tell you what. It made everything we've been through since basic worthwhile. And I swore to her that day I would do everything in my power to see that Johnny got home to her.

And by God, that's what I'm going to do.

5

———

GHOSTS

BILLY MARTENS

THERE HAD BEEN THREE SUNNY DAYS IN A ROW AND THE JUNGLE steamed.

Their wet uniforms steamed.

The white mist drifted around them.

"It's like San Francisco," complained Thad, "with its damn white fog."

"That's a cool fog," Billy replied. "This isn't."

"No wonder stuff grows so fast. Look at the bamboo."

"One day this will be a nice resort. Bars, hotels, drinks on the beach."

They heard the rumble of B-29s taxiing and lifting off from Isley.

"Yeah," grunted Thad, "with a nice airport made to order."

"Count on it," replied Billy. "We just need to live long enough to fly back here in fifty years, lie on the beach and get waited on."

That night, the stars were uncountable. Billy was crouched by a palm and staring up at them through the fronds. He thought about riding the ridgeline at the ranch and how the stars gathered there too. For a moment, dreaming about it, he held his breath. He felt that was the only reason he heard the footstep behind him. He threw up his hand in front of his face just before a fast wire lopped around his throat. The wire stopped against his palm. He gripped it and yanked forward as hard as he could. The man holding it did not let go, and Billy threw him over his shoulder. Then he pounced, using elbows, knees and fists. His assailant went limp. A Japanese officer.

There was a struggle going on behind him. Bricks had another Japanese soldier pinned. But Billy quickly saw Thad was laid out and cut open from his throat to his waist. Anger burned its way through him. He felt like putting his Ka-Bar through the officer beneath him. Somewhere off in the dark, another fight was going on. He sprang towards it, pausing to kick Brick's soldier in the head with so much force he knew he might have killed him. It didn't matter. *The Mennonite boy,* he thought, *is a long way from home, and the way is getting longer every year.*

Darian, Bolo, was wrestling with a soldier much taller and heftier than the usual Japanese man. Jack was laid out beside them, not moving. The tall soldier got the best of Bolo and choked him from behind, grinning savagely at his triumph, spitting words into the Marine's ear as he killed him. Billy kicked the big man in the head with his boot just as he had with Brick's fighter, which didn't affect the Jap as much as Billy expected. He jumped on the man's back, encircling his neck with his arm and applying his own choke. The muscular soldier, also an officer, growled and threw himself backward, smashing Billy into the jungle floor. He smashed Billy into the dirt again, and again, trying to dislodge him.

But Billy had fought a lot of fights like this since boot camp, even against other Marines. He refused to unwind his arms from the officer's thick neck, squeezing as hard as he could while the man hurled his bodyweight against Billy. Thad was dead. Maybe Jack. The ghosts had emerged from their haunts to terrorize and destroy the hunters. Billy was not going to be their third victim.

He choked the officer until the man suddenly fell limp and stayed that way.

There was a gun flash, painfully bright in the jungle dark, a loud report, another gun flash, another explosion. A Colt 1911 pistol. Not a Nambu, or M1 Garand, or Arisaka Type 99, 7.7mm. He heard Player cursing his head off and there was a third shot. It took away Billy's night vision, and he had to stumble over bodies to find out who was dead, who was alive, and if they were still under attack. Another Japanese soldier, naked and wearing only a *hachimaki*, a warrior's headband, rose out of the earth, screaming, and swiped at Billy using a *tanto*, a short, curved samurai knife. It ripped open Billy's combat uniform and sprayed blood. Billy threw a wild punch that missed and the soldier lashed out at him again, trying to connect with his throat and failing. Player loomed out of the darkness and used his BAR on the warrior, swinging it like a baseball bat and striking the naked man's head with a sound like chopping wood. The Jap fell at Billy's feet. Player and Billy stared at one another.

"That's it," Player said.

Billy had his night vision back. "That's it?"

"Bricks and Jack went off after the others."

"Jack's okay?"

"Okay enough."

"Bolo?"

"He's guarding the prisoners. We've got three."

"Thad?" asked Billy.

"Covered him with his poncho," Player replied.

"Did Bricks and Jack have any idea who they were chasing?"

"Ghosts. Like the ones we bagged here. They came up behind us. Or down from the trees. Who knows?"

"Did anyone try to talk to them?"

"There's only one awake. The one you fought with, I guess. Then you got the one Bricks was fighting and this one here I smacked with the BAR. Both out. You're cut across your chest, Sarge."

"It's not deep."

Billy went and stood over Thad's body. Player watched his lips moving but heard nothing.

"What's that?" Player asked.

"Lord's Prayer," Billy responded. "Tie those other two against a couple of palms. Let me see if I can get Kaji to talk."

"Who's Kaji?"

"The Jap that Bolo is watching."

"How do you know that?"

Billy nodded to Bolo and crouched by the officer he'd fought who was bound to a palm with rope. He took out a package of Camels. He had picked up enough Japanese over the course of the war to say and understand a lot of things. He shook the cigarettes loose.

"Do you want one?" he asked in Japanese.

The officer, his face lean, almost sharp, like a knife, did not move and did not speak. But his eyes remained on Billy's eyes.

Billy lit one up and began to smoke. "I'm not going to kill you and I'm not going to torture you. You're going back to the base, what used to be your base, where you've been stealing supplies and attempting to sabotage aircraft. You'll be questioned. But again, you won't be tortured. There is not much you can tell us. The war is over on Saipan."

"Not over. Never over."

The officer's reply was sharp but quiet.

Billy shook his head. "Your men who are still out there can steal supplies and remain uncaptured for a hundred years. You are magnificent warriors. Banzai. But it will not change the outcome on Saipan or anywhere else, no matter how long you live or elude the Marines and GIs. Tell me this: if the Emperor asked you to return to Japan and rebuild the bombed cities and make a new empire, wouldn't you obey him?"

There was no response.

Still, the man kept his eyes on Billy's.

"I don't know where the Marines are going from here," Billy continued. "But if we have to take Iwo Jima, we'll take it. If we have to take Okinawa, we'll take it. If we have to take Honshu and Hokkaido, we'll take them too. We will take Japan if we have to."

The man spat in Billy's face and bared his teeth. "You will never take Japan. Not in a million years. Never, *gaijin*. Do not think you can seduce me with soft words and tobacco, you devil. I will escape and keep fighting. All of Japan will keep fighting. There will be no ending."

Billy wiped his face with his sleeve.

Then he resumed smoking.

"Saipan is an ending," Billy said. "So was Tarawa. So was Guam. The others will be too. You can knock off the bravado. You will do what the Emperor tells you to do. And one day he will tell you to surrender."

"Never."

"When he does, you will obey. Or do you plan on disobeying Tenno, the Emperor of God?"

The officer glared at Billy.

"I recommend you stay alive," Billy told him. "Instead of dying for your Emperor, try living for him. A year from now, two years at the most, if you decide to keep breathing, you will return to Japan and honor him by making everything over. That is what your Emperor will need. Healthy men to rebuild and restore the cities. Make up your mind to be one of those men and serve Tenno. The dead cannot help him. They cannot sow crops, or put up sturdy walls, or repave streets. The dead cannot erect buildings for a new Japan. They cannot become doctors, and lawyers, and professors and Shinto priests. Only the living can do that. Make up your mind to be one of the living. Make up your mind to serve your Emperor in peacetime, not just when there is a war."

Billy stood up. "Keep an eye on him, Bolo. I'll see how Player is making out with the other two. One of them had a strange *hachimaki*."

"Why strange?"

"The kanji, the words, they're saying something different."

They were both conscious, both tied to palms, watched over by Player with his BAR, rigid in their facial expressions, both silent and defiant. Billy squatted by the naked one with the *hachimaki* bound to his forehead. It was dirty, blood-smeared and torn. The entire headband was handmade and crudely rendered but readable. There was the kanji for *kami,* which meant maybe spirit or god or something close, then the red sun, what most Marines and GIs called the meatball, then the second kanji for *kaze,* which was wind. Billy stared into the man's impenetrable eyes.

"So, god wind? Or spirit wind? What's that about?"

The man said nothing. He did not even glare.

"Well, to tell you the truth, I have one in my pack back at the airfield. But I could do with another. You know Americans and their lust for souvenirs, right?"

Billy went to peel off the headband. The soldier yelled and jerked his head away. Then he tried to head butt Billy.

"My brother's!" he cried out in Japanese. "His eternal gift!"

Billy lifted his hands away. "What the hell are you talking about?"

A stream of words burst from the man's mouth. "He was an aviator before you came. He made this and left it with me. He had talked for months about flying his aircraft into American devil planes whose only purpose is to kill our women and children and civilians and burn our cities to the ground."

"That is what you did in China and the Philippines!" Billy snapped back.

"And now you are just like us, yet act superior. Your god is a bloodthirsty god. We fight for our people and our homeland. You fight only to butcher and destroy." The soldier lifted his chin. "My brother did what he said he would do. He flew into an American warship and destroyed it in the Leyte Gulf in October. *Shikishima no Yamato-gokoro wo hito towaba, asahi ni niou yamazakura bana.* This is Motoori Norinaga. Do you understand, gaijin? *If someone asks about the Yamato spirit, the spirit of the old and true Japan, yes, of Shikishima, Japan,—it is the flowers of yamazakura, the mountain cherry blossom, that are fragrant in the Asahi, the rising sun.*"

Billy stood up and stepped away. An odd feeling was running through him. It was as if he had heard a sincere prayer or walked into a sacred space. It caused his entire inner being to quiver. The soldier said nothing else. He returned to being his implacable self.

"How did you know what happened at Leyte?" Billy asked him. "You have radio communication with Japanese forces, don't you? Where? Iwo Jima? Okinawa? Honshu? Hokkaido? And what's with this *kami* and *kaze* stuff on the headband your brother painted?"

But the soldier had withdrawn into his fortress of silent strength.

"I heard about this, Sarge," Player spoke up. "We all did."

"Heard what?" Billy demanded.

"This crashing into our ships. Suicide attacks, right? It's called *kamikaze*. Our guys have been broadcasting about it."

"I never heard a thing."

"Then you weren't listening. Hey, skipper, what's eating you, anyway?"

"Nothing's eating me. Or maybe this damn war's eating me."

"We're winning."

"Swell. Bombing the heck out of Tokyo is winning, is that it?"

Jack and Bricks returned from their chase into the jungle empty-handed. Billy told them all to get some shuteye while he watched the prisoners. They moved out at dawn, the hands of their prisoners tied behind their backs but their feet free. Darian and Player carried Thad's body in his poncho, making for a hard slog. Just before sunset, the squad showed itself to the sentries at

Isley and emerged from a stand of wild bamboo. They handed their prisoners over to G2, military intelligence, and Thad's remains to graves registration. Then the squad grabbed some hot chow and hit the sack.

In the morning, Bud and Johnny showed up at Billy's tent, all smiles, slapping him on the back, asking how his girlfriend was, chatting up their trip stateside. Billy shook their hands, thanked them for the jars of honey and bars of chocolate, told them to grab a seat. He even smiled back. But not much.

6

IF I EVER LEAVE YOU
JOHNNY STRANGE

JOHNNY STRANGE WAS NOT HAPPY, NOT HAPPY AT ALL. IT WAS TIME to go and if ever a man had a reason to stay, hide out, or run away, it was Johnny Strange. It was time to go back to the war, and his guts were churning—fear, anger, love—each one had their own separate hole in his heart. He walked alone down to the river.

I could take Marjean and J.A. and go across the border to Canada. We could lose ourselves in a big city, I could get a job as a mechanic...

"Hey, Strange."

Johnny jerked around.

"Bud, when did you get back from Ritzville?"

"I went home after the wedding, hung out with my folks for a week, went hunting with my dad one more time, caught a bus to Sandpoint early this morning, and took a cab out to the house. Marjean said you were down here. What's going on?"

Johnny looked at Bud.

How the hell does he do that?

Bud grinned. "If you're wondering how I get inside your head, it's a gift."

Johnny turned away. "I don't like it, Bud, and I want you to stop it."

"Hey, Strange. I don't have any magic seeing eye, and I'm no prophet. The thing about you is, you might as well take a branding iron and burn how you're feeling right on your face. It's easy to see when you're wound up."

Johnny looked at the ground and said, almost in a whisper, "I don't want to go back, Bud."

"I know you don't, pal, and neither do I. But I'm going."

"I want to run, Bud. I want to take Jean and J.A. and go to Canada. I could be across the border in an hour."

"Yeah and you could go to Calgary, or Vancouver and get a job as a mechanic and hide out for the rest of the war…"

"You got that right, Bud."

"… and hide out for the rest of your life. Hey, Johnny, Canada's in the war too. They got agreements about returning deserters. Eventually they'll find you and if they don't shoot you, they'll put you in Leavenworth and you'll see Marjean on visiting day, and she'll have to get a job in that crummy town and live the rest of her life as a deserter's wife in a crummy little apartment raising J.A. by herself. Not something I'd wish on a girl like that."

"Aw, Bud. What am I going to do? My life is finally working and now this…"

"It's a test, Johnny. It's like Abraham and Isaac."

"What are you talking about?"

"God promised Abraham that he would have a son that was the father of many nations, Isaac. And just when it was all going great, God says to Abraham, 'take Isaac up to the mountain I will show you and there offer him to me as a burnt offering.'"

Johnny furrowed his brow. "You mean like kill him like a sheep or something and put him on the fire?"

"Exactly."

"Why in the world would he do that?"

"See if he really believed the promise."

Johnny shook his head and turned away. "That doesn't make any sense, Bud."

"Sure it does, Strange. And don't kid me. You know exactly what I'm talking about."

"What, you're saying God is testing me?"

Bud put his arm around Johnny's shoulder. "He made you a big-time promise and I know you believe it because I saw your face when you got back from your honeymoon."

"And now he's asking me to put it all on the line, to prove that he's real?"

"Nope."

"What then?"

Bud sighed. "He's asking you to put it all on the line to prove that you're real."

"Real what?"

"A real man, a real husband, a real father. A man who lives up to his responsibilities and is accountable to his given word no matter what the cost. A real man who, even if you don't come back from this tour, will leave a legacy of honor."

"What, Bud? Semper Fi and all that crap?"

"Bigger than Semper Fi, Johnny, way bigger."

"What do you mean by that.?"

Bud turned Johnny loose. "Walk with me, Johnny."

The two Marines walked down the trail along the river bank. Their khaki service uniforms blended in with the tall brown grass along the trail. The Indian Summer had left its kiss in the deciduous trees along the banks. Their red and gold flames stood like fire among the tall pines and firs that filled the Idaho forests. There was an icy wind blowing down the river and in Johnny Strange's heart.

"I feel it too, Johnny."

"Feel what, Bud?"

"The fear."

Johnny looked out across the river. "How did we get here, Bud? What is the world coming to?"

"Look, Johnny. For you, it started a long time before Jenkins and it wasn't a good start, but it got a fresh start in a moment of love the day before you left for Dago. Think about it. You were a messed-up kid who struggled with a lot of stuff—your dad, your manhood, your faith. And then you met Marjean. How do you think you got to the King's cabin just in time to meet the girl of your dreams? If you had made one more loop around the lake, she would have gotten in her car and gone back home and you would have missed her. Or if the Kings had come early, you never would have gotten that two-hour window of time alone with Marjean. How does that happen, Johnny?"

Johnny looked over at Bud. He felt tears running down his cheeks. "Yeah, I know how it happens..."

"So, I know you're afraid, I know you're mad, I know you just want to stay here and enjoy what God has blessed you with."

Johnny nodded.

"One problem, good buddy. The war's not over. We signed on and we gave an oath."

"You mean the swearing in oath?"

"No, Johnny. The one you and Billy and me gave each other when we met."

"I don't seem to remember that."

"Sure you do Johnny. It wasn't so much in words, or signing a piece of paper, we signed it in blood. It was about us loving each other enough to make sure we all got home. And it wasn't in words. It was just us, the three Mennos, being together, going to fight, living through it. The oath was about doing something, not rusting away somewhere, but standing in the front lines of life, together. We couldn't pause, we couldn't just end it. Something called us to do something, and that something is here and now."

Johnny nodded slowly. "So, we gotta go back... and finish it, or the promise God made to me doesn't mean anything. Is that what you're saying?"

"Yeah, Johnny. There's something noble left to be done before you inherit the kingdom."

The two friends were quiet, walking with their thoughts. Then Bud stopped Johnny and looked him right in the eyes. "I made another oath, Johnny."

"What oath?"

"To your wife, to Marjean. I promised her I would do everything in my power to make sure you get home."

"In one piece?"

"That, I can't promise."

The two friends looked at each other and then burst out laughing.

Finally, Johnny took Bud by the hand. "Okay Bud, I'll go. But stick close, will ya? This whole thing gives me the heebie-jeebies."

"Like white on an egg, Johnny. Like white on an egg."

WHEN JOHNNY and Bud were down at the river, Marjean had walked out to the small gazebo at the bottom of the Langston property. She had her Bible. She sat down in one of the Adirondack chairs and opened the book. She bowed her head.

Speak to me, Lord. I'm scared for Johnny. I'm scared that he'll get killed and everything you gave us will vaporize. I love him so much and J.A. needs him. Please God...

She waited in silence...

A bird sang a brief song...

The leaves in the aspen trees along the river bank rustled...

An infinitesimal breeze sprang up...

... and the pages of her Bible rustled as they flipped over to a new chapter. Marjean Looked down. Like a small brook running through a meadow and tumbling over tiny stones, the words came into her eyes and then into her heart.

'For I know the plans that I have for you,' declares the LORD,

'plans for prosperity and not for disaster, to give you a future and a hope.'

Marjean put her head down on the arm of the chair, tears running down her face.

Thank you, Lord.

NOW SHE LAY ALONE in the bed. She could hear Johnny brushing his teeth in the bathroom. So many things to get used to, sharing her life with someone. Giving up her secrets, opening her heart, deciding which side of the bed to sleep on. A glorious adventure.

Johnny came into the room. She could see the two scars, one below each shoulder. One round and one triangular, his wounds, his reminders. His body was powerful, the muscles of his shoulders and chest rippling as he came to the bed. He walked around to her side and knelt down so that his face was close to hers.

She could see his eyes soften, and something began to rush through her.

"I'm going back tomorrow, Jean, and I'm okay about it. Are you?"

Marjean turned and drew him to her breast. She ran her fingers through his hair and pulled him tight. She whispered low in his ear.

"Johnny, these last days have been like heaven. Everything I have been dreaming of since the day you left has become real. You're my man, you're my husband, you're my... my lover, everything I need and want. If I just have these few days for the rest of my life, it will be enough for me."

Johnny put his hand up and touched her face, so softly. "I wish we could have more time, my darling girl."

Marjean pulled his hand to her lips and kissed it softly. "We will, Johnny, we will. I'm trusting the Lord. I believe he has promised me you will come back to me. So, I'm going to rest in that and know that someday soon, I will see you walking up to the front door, and you'll be home forever."

She smiled. "So, yes, I'm okay. Now just give me this night and then go. I'll be waiting. You'll always be my man… I will never leave you."

"Marjean… Marjean…"

JOHNNY AND BUD lined up to board the C-53 Skytrooper at the Army Air Force Base outside Spokane. They had their duffle bags and their gear. There was a line of gyrenes and doggies behind them, all heading for the Pacific. Johnny glanced back at the gate. Marjean and J.A. and Al waved. Bud's parents stood beside them. He waved and smiled, but his heart ached.

"God, she's so beautiful, Bud."

"Got that right, Strange."

They mounted the steps and climbed into the plane. Johnny found a seat on the side looking toward the gate. Bud slid in next to him. He could just see Marjean through the square porthole window. He waved, but she didn't see him. The door closed with a thump and the plane taxied out of the boarding area. He watched and watched until he could not see her. Then he turned and slumped down into his seat. A voice interjected itself into his thoughts.

"Johnny, hey, Johnny Strange."

Johnny turned. Standing in front of him was Gerald King. Gerald was dressed in army gear with a 10th Army insignia.

"Gerald King, what in the world are you doing here? I thought you had an important job at your dad's plant."

Gerald turned red and looked at his feet. "I did, Johnny… I did."

"What happened?"

Gerald looked up at Johnny. "Can I be honest with you,

Johnny? I mean, you and Marjean are married now, so everything's settled, right?"

Johnny nodded without speaking.

Gerald took a breath. "Well, I always, I mean, I used to think
that Marjean was my girl, but I guess that was just a dream I had.
When you went off to war, I still didn't get it. I mean, I didn't get
that she was your girl. Even after she had, I mean even after your
son was born, I tried to get her to go out with me. Pretty lame,
huh?"

Johnny could feel how uncomfortable Gerald was.

"Go on."

"Well, one time I dropped by the Langston house and she
gave me my walking papers, no lie. Told me pretty much that I
was a coward hiding behind an 'essential' job. She told me she
was your girl and as soon as you came home she was gonna
marry you. She said if I ever wanted her to even say hello to me
on the street, I'd better get off my butt and get over with the real
men and do something about defending our country."

"That was good advice, Gerald."

Gerald nodded. "So, all the guys were gone, and I was the
only one in our crowd that was still home, and believe you me, it
got pretty uncomfortable. So I joined up. My dad didn't like it, but
here I am. And say, congratulations on getting married. Marjean's
a swell gal and you're a heck of a lucky guy. And I mean it, Johnny.
I do."

Johnny stood up and took Gerald by the hand. "Thanks for
telling me that, Gerald. Good luck to you over there. Make some
buddies and keep your head down while you're watching out for
them. It's the only way you'll survive. See ya when I see ya."

Gerald nodded and moved back toward his seat at the rear of
the plane.

Johnny sat down.

"Penelope." Bud said.

"What?"

"Your gal is like Penelope, Johnny. She's a one-man woman, and if she has to wait twenty years, she still will be. And now she's waiting for her King to return and claim his kingdom."

Johnny looked at Bud.

"You know, Bud, sometimes you can be a real pain in the butt." He grinned. "But I thank God every day for you."

Bud grinned back. "Good! Now let's get over there and win this war so we can all go home."

7

MENNO HOMECOMING

BUD, THE CORPSMAN

BOY, SAIPAN IS A HELL-HOLE COMPARED TO THE MOUNTAINS OF
Idaho. Hot, sticky, with flying bugs that could carry off a kid, rats,
snakes, and Japs in the caves. That's the game Billy is playing
now. Find the Japs in the caves. He's out with a new squad
combing the hills for holdouts. Probably loving it, too. Well, I'll
see Billy Martens when I see him.

Right now, Captain Crandall has got me humping all over this
island. We got internment camps where the natives are still
penned up because we haven't got all the administration BS
straightened out. So, Crandall put me on good-will duty, visiting
the camps. I'm cleaning up kids that got their arm blown off by a
mine, and old people that got riddled with shrapnel when the
Japs held them prisoner and then tried to blow everyone in the
hostage cave to kingdom come. The hospitals are still full of
collateral damage.

Yesterday, I ran into Chamorra at one of the camps. She was
sitting in a room with a bunch of kids, teaching a history class,
when I walked in. She smiled when she saw me, but there was
still a haunted look in those steely black eyes. But she was softer
than I remembered, really beautiful and feminine. Not like the

yellow-haired Jap killer I met in Hawaii. I waited for her to finish and then we went to a local pub and tapped a Pabst. I could tell she had some questions.

"When did you get back, Bud?"

"Yesterday. Johnny and I flew in from Spokane, Washington—a miserable trip. But we're back. Johnny's married."

"To that beautiful blonde he was always talking about?"

"Yeah, Marjean. They have a son, too, and he's a good-looking kid. So Strange is set."

Cham shook her head. "If he makes it home again."

"Yeah, that's the monkey wrench in the works, isn't it? Just making it home."

She hesitated. "Have you seen Billy?"

"Not yet. Crandall's got him combing the hills for hold-outs. I guess he's been out for a week or so."

"Yeah, my people are doing some of that, like, how do you say it... freelance? Only we don't bring back any prisoners. I don't think the Japs will ever surrender, so we will just keep killing them until there are none left in our homeland."

"You still going out with your team, chasing Japs?"

Cham shook her head. "No, Bud. When Amina died, it snapped me back to reality. A Chamorran woman is not to be a leader. We are helpers. So, we are letting the men take care of the killing business now. I'm in charge of the children that are still in the camps, and I'm helping in the hospital..." She paused. "I have not seen Billy since you and Johnny left. He hasn't said a word to me since then."

Well, I decided I was going to have to speak to Martens. I don't care if he decided that he and Chamorra weren't a match made in heaven, but after all they went through together, he should at least have the testicular fortitude to speak to her like a man.

As we were talking, a big, handsome flyboy colonel struts into the bar like he's the greatest thing since toasted cheese sandwiches. He looks around and sees Cham, walks over and puts his hands on her like he owns her.

"Hey, Cham, what are you doing with this swabbie? A little below your pay-grade isn't he?"

A couple of the flyboys in the bar laughed, but I also noticed some 2nd Div boys turn around in their chairs.

Cham turned red under her beautiful olive skin and kinda shook his hand off her shoulder. "Chuck, this is my friend, Bud Parmalee. We saw action together…"

A voice came from across the room. "Yeah, while you were learning how to roast kids and old people with your fire bombs, we were actually fighting the Japs."

The Colonel turned around. "Who said that?"

All the gyrenes were grinning and about ten of them raised their hands. Another 2nd Div boy, Bruiser Johanson, stood up and smiled at the Colonel, but there was no real smile there. "You heard us. You can see by our outfits that we're 2nd Div and we own this island. And we know who you are. You are little Chuckie Vincent, famous flyboy, gets in his B-29, has his minions put a flaming X down on Tokyo and then lights up hospitals, schools and houses, kids and old women from high in the sky. A real chickenshit."

The rest of the gyrenes stood up and, as the flyboys looked around, they noticed they had stumbled into Marine territory.

Another 2nd Div guy looked at Vincent and grinned, but his grin wasn't friendly, either. "You think you're pretty big stuff because they write about you stateside, but out here, you ain't puke. So why don't you and your little bugger boys take a hike? And I would recommend that you find another bar. From now on, this one's off-limits to flyboys."

A couple of the pilots took umbrage, but Vincent, being the smart college grad we all knew him to be, wisely waved his boys off.

"Come on, Cham. Let's find another bar."

Cham shook her head. "I'll be along later, Chuck. I haven't finished talking to Bud."

Then she looked him in the eyes and for just a moment I saw the Chamorra I knew from the killing cave, the yellow-haired black-toothed Chamorran demon-princess who helped the butcher Jap General of Saipan surgically remove his intestines. And I think Chuckie saw it too, because he swallowed his tongue, did an oblique left, and slid out of the room.

Cham looked at me and Cham the woman was back. "Sorry, Bud. Chuck can be a pain sometimes."

"Why do you hang out with a stooge like that?"

"He can be nice when he's not in front of a bunch of butt-kissers. Besides, a woman has to make her way."

"But what about Billy?"

"What about Billy, Bud?"

Yeah, she had me there. What about Billy? I think my father-confessor, psychiatric analyst sky pilot role has just shifted off of Johnny Strange's shoulders for good. And I have a feeling Martens will be a much tougher nut to crack.

THE 2ND DIV boys have been doing some hard work here while Strange and I were gone and with the camps built, canvas stretched, and lots of hot chow, life back here in the steaming Marianas is not that bad. The rainy season that kept most of Saipan and Tinian floating in mud is just about over and both islands are beginning to look like Americans actually live here.

The Second Motor Transport keeps its big two-and-one-half ton trucks running twenty-four hours a day to supply the various infantry and artillery outfits. There is occasional entertainment —Betty Hutton showed up with her U.S.O. troupe and she was a class act, but while the new grunts and doggies seemed to think it was a big deal, I heard some of the old-timers muttering that it didn't compare a bit to Wellington, New Zealand. Although I'm sure they meant no disrespect to the thoroughly gorgeous but totally unattainable Miss Hutton.

There is also a lot of sickness. The Marianas have their own version of Malaria, a nasty bone-cracker called Dengue fever. I worked long hours fighting mosquitos with DDT... just like Cactus.

And I'm sure glad we got Billy and a lot of other guys out there chasing the hold-outs. Every day we find a dead Marine, or we hear about a captured civilian, or a raided supply depot. I heard about a kerfuffle 1/10 got involved in while we were gone where they were engaged by two separate groups of Japs while they were out on a routine service practice. Marines from the firing batteries killed eleven Japs, while their forward observation team killed twelve more.

We also have a plague worse than the Dengue mosquitos—journalists from American newspapers who finally got permission to come aboard. As soon as they got here they started spilling the same old crap about how the Marines had recklessly attacked a Japanese stronghold without real preparation and had needlessly sacrificed the young men of America. At the same time the papers are full of pictures of the Army marching triumphantly into Rome. Beautiful eye-talian girls kissing our GIs while spreading rose petals in their path. What a bunch of horse-puckey.

I tell you when we look down on the ruins of Garapan and remember our boys who died there, the conversation turns scatological. And every time a flight of those monster B-29s takes off from Tinian, I think of Rudy Rudebaker and a lot of great guys who are taking a dirt nap far from the shores of the U.S. of A. And it really pisses me off.

I guess MacArthur has a better press corps than the Marine Brass do. But we know the story and if I see one of those slacker newspaper guys around our camp trying to dig us some BS for a story to titillate the drugstore cowboys back home, I'll quickly forget my non-violent leanings. And you can take that to the bank.

The scuttlebutt is that we will be going to Iwo Jima next or Formosa or maybe Okinawa. My bet is Okinawa, with Iwo in second place. MacArthur is already on Leyte and so Formosa has been relegated to a backwater, something we can afford to skip. Iwo on the other hand, has an airbase that the Japs are using to harass our B-29s on the way to the main islands of Japan. And if we took it we would then be able to fly fighter cover for the big boys all the way to Tokyo and back.

But Okinawa, now that would be a chicken bone shoved down Hirohito's throat, sure as shooting. The Japs consider it sacred ground, part of the actual homeland. See, up to now, we've just been slapping their grubby little hands off of countries and islands that they have been putting in their creel since 1938. But once we step onto Okinawa, the ante goes up, way up. Then the Japs would be fighting to protect their homes, their country, and you can be sure we'll see a lot of those crazy little Samurais loading into airplanes for a one-way trip to some American fleet. Or a lot more of those Banzai charges.

And if we do take Okinawa, then it's a whole new ball game, because when we send our boys onto the three main islands, every frigging Japanese citizen automatically becomes a soldier who will die for the Emperor. Not a pretty picture, and I'm not looking forward to it. After all, I promised Marjean. I'll do my best, but the odds are against any of us coming back from a Tokyo land invasion.

So, we've been back from the States for a week when Sergeant Billy Martens walks his crew back out of the jungle. Martens' Men, they call themselves, a real bunch of hard cases. They waltzed in here carrying one of their buddies in a poncho and shoving a lot of truculent Japs in front of them. After he dropped his prisoners off, and detailed his dead guy to graves registration he went back to his tent. So me and Strange paid a courtesy call.

I'm not sure if he wanted to see us or not, but we dropped by anyway. In the end he did seem glad to see us, smiled at us, asked about Marjean and Kalasia. But he's distant. I asked him if he was going to look up Chamorra and he didn't even answer, just moved the conversation to my pack of Chesterfields. I think I'm going to have to take him out behind the latrine and slap some sense back into him. But, for now, it's good to see the Sniper.

8

NIGHTMARE
BILLY MARTENS

BILLY, ALONG WITH ALL THE OTHER MARINES AND GIS ON SAIPAN, took the news about Marines landing on Iwo Jima in early February as good news. It meant the war was that much closer to its end. He felt that way when the 2nd Marine Division shipped out on March 25—it was no great secret they were going to invade Okinawa and again, an invasion brought the war that much closer to some sort of finale. For Billy, it was not just a matter of no more island fighting. It would also mean the end of the bombing of Japanese cities, especially Tokyo, and the end of what he saw as the wholesale slaughter of Japanese civilians.

"This is not of God," Billy complained. "Bombing of nonmilitary targets was never of God."

"When was war ever of God, Billy?" Bud asked him. "What part of anything we've done from Guadalcanal 'till now can you call holy and good?"

"Yet we freed people."

"Yes, people were freed."

"We freed civilians."

"Yes, yes, they were."

"So, how does bombing and killing thousands of children, and women and old men set them free?"

"All the bloody combat from the Canal till now and you still don't get it, Montana cowboy," growled Johnny. "We can't scrub the Mennonite out of you, can we? It's war, Menno Simons, total, hard, mean, nothing-watered-down war. The Japs've killed civilians by the truckload. Now God's gonna see to it they get their civilians killed by the boatload. Just like the Nazis, Billy Boy. It was all good, so long as they were the ones wiping out other cities. All good ,so long as they were putting other countries' mommas, babies and grandpas in the grave with their frigging Stukas and Heinkels. Wiping London and Rotterdam off the map was A-okay. Different story now, yeah? Berlin is getting the crap bombed out of it, Hamburg, Cologne. Sow the wind, reap the whirlwind, buddy. Read that in church once or twice, didn't you?"

At first, though Billy never talked about it, it had been hard to see his old girlfriend, Chamorra, hanging off the arm of Colonel "Chuck" Vincent, the B-29 pilot everyone stood in awe of. Finally, he just swept it off the table and concentrated on his men and the Japs hiding in the jungle. But then it began to bug him that Chamorra reveled in the bombing of Tokyo and the slaughter of its civilians—"They murdered our people without batting an eye, so now it is tit-for-tat, yes? Isn't that how you Americans say it?" Her boyfriend was an even bigger issue with Billy. He'd heard him say to another pilot, "This is the best work we've done the entire war, burning up those Nips with our bombloads." His words took a more sinister turn with Billy after the bombing raid on Tokyo on the night of March 9 to 10.

Everyone on Saipan knew it was a big raid, and that Isley wasn't the only airfield involved. B-29 after B-29 rumbled down the strip and howled into the night sky, banking west. They all knew what the bombers were carrying, too. The five-hundred-pound E-46 cluster bombs that let loose thirty-eight M-69 incendiaries. When the M-69s ignited, they spat out streams of flaming napalm. It wasn't hard to find out what part of Tokyo had been targeted, either.

Not all aircrew kept their mouths shut. The B-29s laid out a large X of flames over the densely packed homes by the docks. Bomber after bomber made its run over Tokyo and released its stick of incendiary bombs right on the X. Weeks later, it went the rounds—wind had fanned the flames, sixteen or twenty square miles or more of the city had been razed, eighty thousand dead, a hundred thousand dead, a hundred and twenty thousand dead. No one stopped eating bacon and eggs, or listening to big band jazz, or attending the church parade.

Billy felt physically sick when he took it all in. He vomited two or three times as he learned more and more about the fire-bombing. He knew what the bodies would look like. By 1945, he had seen charred and twisted Japanese and American bodies. Flame throwers, grenades, blown up pillboxes, plane crashes. He could not sleep. But he didn't see the blackened bodies in his nightmares. He saw his father.

They were riding the ridgeline behind their home. Every now and then, his father would turn to look at Billy, his face sour. "You've shamed us, son. How many men have you murdered? With your own bare hands? You like killing. Isn't that it? You enjoy killing. You're nothing like Jesus. Stop going to church. Stop telling padres you're a Christian boy. You're not. There's nothing Christian about you. You stink like hell."

Or they were shoeing horses in the barn. His father would bang out a red-hot horseshoe on the anvil and then plunge it into a bucket of water. There would be a loud hiss. His father would glare at him. "That's you. The loud hiss of hellfire. The worse thing is, you can't take anything back. None of it. You can't say you're sorry and make things right. You can't bring one of those men you killed back. You can't restore him to his family. You can't dry all the tears you've caused. You can't do anything, son. All you can do is go to hell."

One night, they sat at the table to eat but no one was at the table except the two of them and the food was poor and sparse. His father kept shaking his head. "After all we taught you. After all the praying and preaching and Bible reading. You come back alive, but none of the men you killed did."

"A person can make the Bible say whatever they want," Billy had responded, moving around the small bit of food on his plate but not eating any of it.

His father snorted. "The island fighting was bad enough. But then you hand the Army Air Force an airfield on Saipan. What did you think they were going to do with it? Drop cherry blossoms? How many people have they butchered? More than you ever killed on Saipan, Guadalcanal, and Tarawa put together." He pointed with his knife. "It's on your head. The slaughter in Tokyo. Osaka, Omura, Kobe, all the cities the B-29s have plastered, all the screaming, burning people. You. It's all on you. And you can't wash it off, Billy. You'll never come clean."

In the middle of this was Colonel "Chuck" Vincent mouthing off about the glory and heroism of the B-29 bombings, Chamorra up eating everything he said. Billy thought about Rommel going in on the plot to kill Hitler in '44. A pastor named Bonhoeffer went in on it too and he was a pacifist like Billy had been. Billy decided Vincent was the same sort of target as Hitler—a life-taker, a warmonger. That's where his mind went after the fire-bombing of Tokyo and the nightmares of his father.

He watched Vincent's movements, bided his time, then struck one night behind one of the Quonsets. He clamped his hand over the mouth of the B-29 pilot, belted him in the kidneys as hard as he could, dragged him into the jungle, and worked him over, blacking both eyes and busting four or five teeth. Billy warned him that if he went to the MPs, he would pay him another visit. He never saw Billy's face. "This is because you murder the innocent," Billy hissed. He felt good about doing it. In the morning, he felt worse.

He watched the B-29s take off as usual. Two weeks later, Vincent was flying again too. One story going around was that he had fallen off a cliff. Another that an island man jealous of Vincent's affair with Chamorra had beaten him up. Another that Chamorra herself had beaten him up—she was strong enough to have done it. The colonel went nowhere without a couple of MPs in tow after that.

And then, it didn't matter anymore, because the 2nd Division was shipping out. If they could conquer Okinawa, Billy reasoned, perhaps that would be the final straw for the Japanese high command. And the Emperor. The second day at sea, March 26, news got to them that the fighting on Iwo Jima was over. It was up to them to put the final nail in the coffin.

For a while, some of the Marines wondered if they were heading to Japan itself. The invasion fleet they latched onto was huge, the largest any of them had ever seen. It spread out over the Pacific without an end in sight. Billy was leaning against the gunnels when Johnny shoved in beside him. He offered Billy a Chesterfield. Billy took it, lit it, and thanked him.

"You think Japan, Johnny?" Billy asked.

Johnny shook his head and smoked. "Nah. The swabbies tell me it's Okinawa where we're going. That's our bearing. The brass will confirm it in the morning. You kinda wish Japan, don't you?"

"Yeah, I do."

"That'll end the war. That'll end the bombing."

"It will."

"I don't get it, Billy. No Jap ever shed tears over our dead bodies." He looked at Billy's knuckles. "Boxing palm trees?"

Billy rubbed his hands and crammed them in his pockets. "Something like that."

Johnny looked back at the ships surrounding them as they sailed. "They could shoot you for that, you know. Never mind the brig. Firing squad, Billy Boy."

"What are you talking about, Johnny?"

"I reckon he never saw your face in the dark. Did it make you feel better, Billy? Did it win us the war?"

"You're talking oddball, buddy."

"Am I?" Johnny exhaled and the sea breeze brought it right back in their faces. They both coughed and laughed. "You'll remember my troubles back at boot camp in California, Billy. Same as yours. I squirmed out of it. I guess we can say that you did too. I learned not to make a habit of it with officers. Learn the same lesson, Billy. Keep your nose clean on board. Keep it clean on Okinawa. If we ever up end up back on Saipan, keep it squeaky clean there."

Billy was quiet for a few moments. Then he rested his hands with their raw knuckles back on the gunnels. "What'll it take to win the war, Johnny? What will make them give up?"

Johnny grunted. "I'll give them this. The Japs sure as hell are pugilists. If they were a brawler in the other corner, I'd have my work cut out for me. I'd need to pound their ribs and crack their jaw more than once. Probably have to land a few solid haymakers to do them in. Get my nose bloodied along the way and lose some teeth. One eye swollen shut."

"All that happened."

"It sure as hell did. But in the end, who's still standing? I always was. The Corps too. This round won't be any different. Gotta say though, in answer to your question. It won't end till we're marching through Tokyo, or what's left of Tokyo, and their own country's blown to crap. Even then, the job won't be finished. They'll be hiding in the hills. They'll dig in on Mount Fujiyama. Attack us while we're eating sushi, or swimming in the Sea of Japan, or while we're asking a master swordsmith to build us a katana of folded steel. They'll do guerilla warfare on us for a thousand years."

"You're a ray of sunshine, Johnny Strange."

Johnny shrugged. "That's the way the fighter in me sees it. Only one thing can ring the bell on this matchup."

"What's that?"

"The Emperor. The Emperor says stop, they'll stop. The Emperor says surrender, they'll surrender. Not before."

Billy watched a pack of sea-blue Grumman Hellcats sweep past overhead. "Are we gonna make it, Johnny? Are you and me and Bud gonna make it?"

Johnny lit a fresh cigarette off his old one. "I don't know, buddy. No point in talking about it. Talk can't change anything."

9

LOVE DAY

JOHNNY STRANGE

Hell from the skies!

Johnny Strange hunkered down on the forward deck of LST 884 with the rest of his squad. He watched as the Japanese Zero thundered out of the pre-dawn Easter morning sky and took the unarmored troop transport Hinsdale, half a mile behind them, right at the waterline. A huge fireball erupted, and the Hinsdale rose out of the ocean like a breaching whale and then settled back, dead in the water.

Johnny shook his head in disbelief. They were not even supposed to be in this fight. They were the feint, the diversion. But he guessed no one told the Japs.

Someone yelled, "Here comes another one!"

The Zero came out of the cloud cover at about twenty-five hundred feet, dropped to one hundred feet, and bore down on the helpless LST...

When Johnny got back to Saipan, the world had changed. Marjean was his wife, forever, and he had a son that crawled into his arms his first day home and hardly left that spot the whole time he was in Sandpoint. Bud had gotten some brilliant advice from Marjean's dad and was on his way to Med School. All he had to do was survive this battle and the one that was coming up —the invasion of Japan. And that was all Johnny had to do to get back to his family.

Pretty simple, Strange. Just stay alive. Just don't be one of the 70,000 that might get it on Okinawa or the 1,000,000 that will take a dirt nap on the beaches of Tokyo. Yeah, right!

Johnny had not wanted to come back. He only did because he couldn't shame Marjean and John Albert by deserting—but he wanted to.

The Canadian border was an hour away from Sandpoint and there was a moment when he had wanted to walk into the house, tell Marjean to pack a bag, fire up the Chevy and head north. But he didn't because Bud called him on it. He had sworn an oath, and now he was keeping his word. Not just the Marine oath, but the unspoken one between him and Bud and Billy, the one where they promised to have each other's backs and make sure they all got home alive.

So, it was a very pissed Johnny Strange that set foot back on the coral sand of Saipan. Pissed because if he wasn't careful, the war could take the only happiness he had ever known and suck it up into some black hole in space. Pissed because the Japs hadn't figured out they were getting their butts kicked. Pissed because so many of his friends had been killed, most of them horribly. Pissed because he had finally gotten unwound inside, being with his beautiful wife, and now he was screwed up tighter than ever.

Not even seeing Billy could cheer him up, not that Billy was cheerful himself. In fact, Johnny had never seen Billy so dark. He was gone on a ghost patrol looking for Japs that weren't smart enough to figure out *Nippon ga maketa!* So, Billy was in the jungle digging the holdouts out of caves and swamps and cane fields and from under every rock on Saipan.

When Johnny and Bud arrived they didn't see Billy for three days. Then, when he came in, he was dragging a bunch of hard cases with him, one of them in a body bag. Tough guys who called themselves Martens' Men. When Johnny heard that, he almost cracked up.

What a bunch of crap!

They were all new. Crandall was Company Commander now, Bakar was his adjutant, although they had to promote him to Sergeant-Major to get him on Crandall's staff. So they didn't see Crandall much. They had a new lieutenant over the platoon, and a bunch of new guys with names like Jack B. Quick, Bolo, Gyprock, and Carlos who made up X-ray squad. Nobody Johnny knew. And Billy himself might have been a new guy for all the friendly Johnny and Bud got out of him.

And then there was the uncertainty about what would happen next. Nobody knew for sure was going on or where they were going. Trying to find it out was like getting stock market advice from a shoe-shine boy the day before the market crash. Some guys said Iwo, some said Formosa, some said Okinawa. He had a heated debate with a doggie from 77th Army over a couple of Pabsts one night in a Saipan bar. The doggie was pretty sure he had the answers.

"MacArthur is in the Philippines, working his way up Leyte right now. He's getting ready to invade Luzon and march into Manilla. Once we take that back, the rest of the army and the Marines will go to Formosa so we can give the Chinese a hand."

Johnny shook his head. "Doesn't make sense."

"Why not, smart guy."

Johnny took a pull on his beer. "Because the Japs have a full field army on Formosa, smaaaarrrt guy, and we don't have the nine divisions we need to take them out. Our plan has been to skip the heavy lifting—island hopping—and leave the Japs isolated like we did when we jumped over Rabul. So why would we jump into a battle we don't have the men or material to win? Besides, that's not where the war is."

The doggie scowled. "Okay, what's your plan, Gyrene? Where is this here war?"

"Straight north, buddy boy, that's where it is. If we want to show the Japs what happens when you grab the tiger's tail, we take the war right back home to Japan. MacArthur liberates Manilla and then uses his forces to cut the Jap oil supply lines. No more planes flying out of Kyushu. In the meantime the Marines go after Iwo and Okinawa. If you fellas want to join us on Okinawa, we could use your help. I'm betting a bunch of guys get shipped to Iwo in January or February."

"Why Iwo?"

"Look, it's 1400 miles from Saipan to Tokyo. LeMay's B-29s fly all the way there without fighter protection. Iwo is half that distance. If we take Iwo we will have an air base where our fighters can join the Super-fortresses mid-flight and cover them all the way to Japan and back. And if our big guys get in trouble, they can land at Iwo."

The army guy nodded. "Yeah, I can see that…"

"And then, as soon as we get a lock on the situation there, we head to Okinawa."

"Why Okinawa?"

"If we take Okinawa, the Superforts are even closer. We need to be bombing their factories and warehouses, and especially their airbases into dust." Johnny went on. "By taking Okinawa, we get to rub the Jap's noses in the mud. Okinawa isn't just some island they conquered, it's their home address. We take Okinawa, it's a real kick in the teeth to Hirohito and the rest of the Jap High Command. It'd be like if they captured Hawaii and Alaska. That's how we show them they never should have taken us on. So, I say… Okinawa."

Johnny stood up and spoke loud enough to be heard over the

din. "HOW MANY OF YOU GYRENES AND DOGGIES WANT TO END THIS WAR AND GO HOME!"

Heads turned and hands raised.

Johnny sat back down. "There you have it, my friend. Okinawa is the straight shot to Tokyo."

AND OKINAWA IT WAS. Just as Johnny had predicted, MacArthur took Luzon and Manilla and the American fleet moved to cut the oil supplies to the Japanese army and navy. In February, the 5th, 4th and 3rd Marines hit the beaches of Iwo. But what was supposed to be a week-long fight turned into a bloody month-long scrap. The only good thing that came from Iwo was the picture of the flag being raised on Mt. Suribachi. And meanwhile, Johnny, Bud, and Billy got ready for the invasion of Okinawa.

Just before they left, Captain Crandall briefed the squad and platoon leaders.

"Sorry to tell you this, fellows, but we will not be in it. We're going to be a diversion, like Tinian."

Groans and curses rose from the assembled men in the briefing, but Johnny breathed a sigh of relief.

Thank you, Jesus!

Someone spoke up. "Isn't this a total waste of the best fighting division in this man's war?"

Crandall shook his head. "I know. But remember. We got onshore at Tinian, so I think once we do the diversion off the east coast, they'll swing us around to the actual landing site and send us in. Or put us ashore at Mintago once the 10th Army gets moving from the Hagushi beaches. We'll see what happens."

ON MARCH 27, 1945, most of the squad loaded aboard a troop transport and embarked for Okinawa. After a five-day trip, they rendezvoused with the rest of 2nd Div off the eastern coast of Okinawa. After a brief pre-dawn Easter service on the deck they clambered down the cargo nets and loaded aboard LST 884. A faint glow lit the eastern horizon. Easter Sunday, Love Day. Billy and Johnny sat smoking Marlboros with Bud.

Bud took a long drag. "Where'd you get these?

Billy shrugged. "Don't ask."

Bud grinned. "Did you hear Turner is bringing the 10th Army to Okinawa?"

"Asleep at the Wheel Turner?"

"The same. The guy who left us alone and unsupplied for three months on Cactus because he got caught with his pants down on D-day and the Japs snuck down the Slot and sank four of his cruisers."

Johnny shook his head. "I don't think anybody who was onshore that night can forget the feeling of waking up to an empty ocean. No transports, no supply ships, no aircraft carriers. Gone like a cool breeze."

Billy grinned. "Hey, that's how I got introduced to those wonderful Jap cigarettes, bad Saki, and terrible tinned tuna straight from the dog food factory in Tokyo."

"Yeah, Turner made a big mistake. He made his plan based on what the Japs might do and not on what they could do. When that Jap task force came tearing down the slot and caught our ships with their knickers down, it was almost the end."

Billy nodded. "Yeah, if we hadn't had guys like General Edson and General de Valle with us, we would now be part of the infernal muck of Guadalcanal."

One of the new recruits, a red-headed kid from Seattle, looked over at Billy.

"Were you guys on the Canal?"

All three nodded.

The kid's eyes got big. "What was it like?"

Bud sighed. "When I stood on the deck of the transport that first morning and the first rays of the sun touched her, she was beautiful. Towering mountains, beautiful forests, gentle waves washing the beaches, the glitter of sun and water and scoured white sand beneath groves of palm trees leaning lazily toward the sea, like paradise."

"Paradise, my ass," sneered Billy. "Bud, only you would think that.

The kid looked at Johnny. "What's he mean?"

Johnny took a drag and nodded toward Bud. "Only Mr. Dreamer could see it that way. When I went up on deck I knew we were in for it, because I could smell the stink of her. Not a paradise, but a mass of slops and stinks and pestilence. Scum encrusted lagoons and swamps straight outta hell, infested with giant Marine-eating crocodiles. Spiders as big as your fist, wasps as long as your finger, and lizards that could bite your leg off."

Bud ginned. "He's right. It was a paradise only in my dreams. Instead I got ants that bit like fire, tree leeches that fall on your neck, fasten on, and suck your brains out before you can claw them off. Centipedes that burned your skin if they crawled across it. Swarms of flies that fed on any open wound or sore, snakes, horrible land crabs..."

Billy and Johnny looked at each other. "Wilma Shottmeier!" The three Mennos burst into roaring laughter.

The kid looked at them like they were crazy.

Johnny stopped laughing and took a drag. "Then there was that Jap who tried to fly his plane into our ship."

Billy nodded. "Yeah, if Corporal Strange hadn't manned an abandoned machine gun and shot the nip down, we wouldn't be sitting here now."

"Yeah," Johnny said, "He was coming right at the ship..." He leaned over the gunwale to toss his cigarette and looked up. "JUST LIKE THAT GUY!"

Everyone turned in time to see a Jap Zero come roaring out of the low-hung clouds. The plane barreled down in a steep dive, flattened out, and took the unarmored troop transport Hinsdale, half a mile behind them, right at the waterline. A huge fireball erupted, and the Hinsdale rose out of the ocean and then settled back.

Someone yelled, "Here comes another one!"

The Zero came out of the cloud cover at about twenty-five hundred feet, dropped to one hundred feet, and bore down on the LST.

"GET DOWN!"

The Zero came right at them and dove straight into the port beam of their LST. The force of the impact sent the plane's engine hurtling into the tank deck below on the starboard side. There was a muffled explosion and then fire was racing through the entire ship.

The impact knocked Bud over on the deck, then he gathered himself and jumped up. "There are Marines asleep in the tanks down there. We got to get them!" He started down the deck.

Johnny grabbed his arm and held on. "Bud stop! that's a wall of flame. You can't get through. They're gone, Bud, gone!"

Bud tried to wrestle free, but Billy held him and Johnny grabbed on.

"All those guys in the Amtracs, dear God…"

The three friends watched helplessly as the flames ate through the decking. A few minutes later, with the fire raging out of control, the abandon-ship order came and the surviving Marines went over the side.

"Stay with me, you guys," Billy shouted. "Swim away from any burning oil and stay in a group. Head for the transport!"

Johnny Strange went over the side with Bud and Billy right after him.

Holy crap! I thought we weren't in this fight.

10

MINTAGO BEACH
BUD, THE CORPSMAN

IT WAS PANDEMONIUM IN THE WATER AFTER THE KAMIKAZE HIT. I
was fighting to keep wounded men afloat, but some panicked and
were thrashing so hard I couldn't hold on to them. We were still
by the cargo nets we'd climbed down to board our LST. Marines
and swabbies came to us to drag casualties up on deck. Marines
who weren't wounded helped bring men up, too. Whenever I
could get a frightened casualty under control, I passed him up to
others. All the time, at the back of my mind, I was wondering
what would happen when the next kamikaze struck.

But not much happened after that. I could hear a few
screaming aircraft and catch glimpses of half a dozen Zeros
streaking out of the sky at our destroyers, some hit by flak and
trailing smoke and flame, others intact. I saw gigantic explosions
as several smaller ships erupted. Then it was quiet. That was
April 1. No other attacks happened for days. I continued hauling
men out of the water, those who couldn't swim and those who
were bleeding and clasping their hands over gaping holes, crying
out with the pain. Billy was good, Johnny was good. Our squad
was good. The dead floated away.

I had been reading the papers about kamikaze attacks while

we were still stateside. Stuff had been happening in August and September, but the Japs really let loose at Leyte Gulf. I kept picking up info as we headed back to Saipan. The swabbies had old papers lying around. I have to confess it never occurred to me if we launched another invasion of another island, an island beyond Iwo Jima, that the kamikazes would be inflicted on us full throttle.

There were different interpretations of the kanji. Spirit wind, god wind, holy wind, divine wind. I chose "god wind" though I suppose that was an odd choice for a Mennonite boy who said there was only one God, his Christian God. I wondered if I'd have the guts to strap myself into a Thunderbolt, say, crammed with bombs and high explosives, knowing I was for sure going to die, and I'd die by diving my plane into a Jap battleship or destroyer. I doubted I'd do it. And that had nothing to do with my pacifism the war had chipped away at. The courage or commitment to do anything like that, for whatever reasons, didn't exist in me.

So, I could not understand kamikaze. Why do that instead of just dropping your bombs on the ship you were targeting? Why the suicide mission? But then there was a lot I didn't understand about the Japanese and its warrior code of Bushido. Like seppuku. Why knife your guts out for honor? Why kill yourself instead of surrendering to live another day? Maybe even escaping and living to fight another day? But the Japs had treated our soldiers who surrendered in the Philippines like dirt because they considered them a disgrace. The Americans should all have committed seppuku, ritual suicide. The fact that they didn't meant they were beneath contempt and should be treated like garbage. And they were.

It wasn't twenty minutes after our LST got blasted by the kamikaze that some Marine major showed up looking for us. By us, I mean the squad that had formed itself around Billy, Sergeant Martens, which included Johnny Strange and me. I forget his name because my head was so scrambled, and I was there on the deck with my gauze and morphine, helping the ship's docs, blood all over my hands and uniform.

"Martens' Mavericks! Where the hell are you? I know you were in that LST. I hope to God some of you are alive. Sergeant Martens!"

Billy stood up, soaked and bloody, but not from his blood. "Here, sir."

"By heaven, that's good news. Is your squad intact?"

"It is, sir. They all made it."

"Did you receive any special orders, Sergeant Martens?"

"Special? No, skipper. We are just part of this fake landing like everyone else in the 2nd Division. To draw the Japs away from the true landing beaches."

"You were supposed to be released at the beach. Then move inland to knock out enfilading fire against the main landing force."

"First, I've heard of it, Major."

"Someone screwed up. Get your crew together—Martens' Mavericks, right? - and climb down into the next available LST. Make sure you have plenty of ammo, water and C-rations. You're going ashore and staying ashore. Thank God I have an extra set of your orders and a map. Here." The major handed Billy a plain brown envelope. "You'll strike northeast about four miles. There's a gun emplacement there we knew would give part of our landing force a bag of trouble, and it has. Knock it out. Assign a man to follow me and pick up some satchel charges."

"Jack!" Billy hollered. "Jack B. Quick!"

"Yo!"

"Follow the major. Then double time it back here." Billy looked around. "My squad, assemble here! We're going in! We're not just doing the feint to fool the Japs! We're going in! Check your water and ammo! Make sure you have grub! Gyprock!"

"Here, Sergeant!"

"Make sure you have all you need for the MG."

"You bet, skipper."

"Martens' Mavericks! Move your butts! Fall in here!"

"Who are Martens' Mavericks?" I saw Johnny show up with a sour expression on his face. "I thought we were Martens' Men or Martens' Marines or some other corny BS like that?"

Billy grinned. "Apparently the brass has renamed us Martens' Mavericks, so that's who we are from now on." He popped a stick of chewing gum in his mouth. "You have a problem with that, Corporal?"

"Nope. Anything's an improvement on Martens' Men."

Billy looked at me. "Replenish your supplies, corpsman. You're still with us."

"We have these casualties here, sergeant," I replied, a bit peeved.

"Yeah, I was there, remember? If we were just staying on as part of the trick, you know, to fool the Japs into thinking we're part of the main landing force, I'd leave you here. But we're going to need you because we're going into combat. And there are plenty of corpsmen and sawbones on board here. So, I say again, replenish your supplies and get ready to move."

I was still peeved. "Aye, aye, skipper."

But I moved.

I needed more gauze and morphine, and now I needed powdered plasma too and extra water for it.

The major came barreling back. "Still here? Quit goldbricking, Martens, and get your men over the side. That emplacement needs to be gone yesterday. You have a radioman?"

"Yes, skipper."

"He'll be communicating with me. I'll tell you what needs to be done. My call sign is in the envelope."

"I thought we were just taking out the one gun emplacement, skipper."

"The hell you say. Once you're ashore, you're a valuable asset. The Japs will concentrate all their firepower north of where you land. They won't be looking to the southeast once they determine what we're doing here is a feint. You'll be invisible and you can come in right behind them. There's a war on, Martens, and maybe this is the last act. Who the hell knows? But you are in this one. After the gun emplacement, I'm pretty sure we'll have a pillbox for you. Get over the side and get to work. You are the 2nd Division landing force on Okinawa."

"Aye, aye, skipper."

We all climbed down into the LST, the major commandeered for us, and growled towards the beaches like the other LSTs. Except we didn't turn around and head back once we reached the shore. The LST opened up, and we piled out. We'd all expected more kamikaze attacks, but there were none. We stepped ashore and barely got wet.

Johnny and Billy stared at the map, Johnny fished out his compass, and we headed north. We could see the battleships hammering the island with their big guns, see the smoke and dirt rising into the sky in massive explosions. We could not hear any of it for several seconds and then all the noise came to us in a continuous roar. It was like all the other invasions from Tarawa on. Everything the same, everything different.

This wasn't the same bunch that had landed together on Saipan in June 1944. Some were back home, some were chronically disabled, some were down with malaria, some couldn't walk because of the jungle crud that was eating away their feet, some we'd lost to combat fatigue. There were thirteen of us making our way north and east from our Minatoga beach head. Myself, the corpsman, Johnny, Billy, Jack, Bricks, Darian or Bolo, Player, Gyprock on the MG, Carlos, Jesus, Zeph, Kelly, Brad. All, except me and Johnny, had been assigned to him as his veterans fell away for one reason or the other. Billy had taken some into the jungle to hunt for Jap ghosts. Those were the only ones he had done any fighting with. It was like we had a squad of raw recruits. Several had fought with other Marine units on Saipan.

We were going to make out all right. Which we found out pretty quickly.

Okinawa's coastline was smothered in jungle, and we soon vanished into it. The island was rugged and mountainous, with ridge after ridge to ascend and descend. There were plenty of freshwater streams, so keeping our canteens full wasn't a problem. Every man in the squad had three, Gyprock and Bricks had four apiece. They'd told us the monsoons would arrive in force in May and stick till the fall. The driest months were November through February. I hoped we'd be done with Okinawa before the heavy rains came. But in my gut, I knew better. The closer we got to their sacred homeland, the harder they were going to fight. It only made sense.

We would have done the same thing. If the Japs had landed troops on America's west coast in '42, we wouldn't have had the military in place to defeat them. They'd have taken Washington, Oregon and California, then begun to move inland. Even though it would've looked hopeless just like it did in Bataan, we'd have fought like hell, our backs to the wall, while their huge and savage army and air force, honed to a razor edge by years of warfare with China, swept over us. This was Japan's situation in 1945. If Okinawa fell, the only target left was Nippon, their nation. So, I expected the combat was going to be as intense as it had ever been. But that first day of April 1945, kamikazes absent from the skies, the main landing force and their battles out of sight on the west side of the island, it didn't seem like the island fighting was going to end with a bang, borrowing T. S. Eliot's lines from The Hollow Men, but with a whimper. Pretty dumb thinking on my part, excused only by the fact it was the forlorn hope of wishful thinking. Headline in my head: WAR WITH JAPAN ENDS WITH NO FURTHER CASULATIES ON EITHER SIDE.

We came up on what the major wanted us to find after hoofing it over the ridges for almost three hours. (His name was Krazits.) We were up high, high for Okinawa, on a rocky knoll, and the Japs had a clear field of fire. The guns were all pointing north, away from us, not south, where we were coming from. There wasn't a lot going on in this sector, but the emplacement was blazing away and Krazits cussed us out that it was still active. Troops were pinned down and taking casualties. We saw them, strung out on their own rocky promontory, unable to move because of the enemy fire. So, we got close enough, without any trouble, at least at first, for Jack B. Quick to stuff some satchel charges into whatever vents or ports he could find. This blew out the rear of the emplacement, but guns were still firing to the front.

Johnny yelled for the men to get in close and get dirty. As we moved towards the fires the satchel charges had started, several Nambus opened up on us. We flattened, but not before Bolo and Bricks and Kelly hurled grenades. The Nambus went silent, and the men rushed in on the emplacement by the back door, Thompsons shattering the Jap gunners. Brad was this wild patriot type and had about a dozen US flags of various sizes in his pack. He somehow strung one up over the captured guns. We heard some troops who had been pinned down cheering.

"Our good deed for the day," Johnny grunted, lighting up.

Carlos was on the radio. "Black Bull Two, this is Green Fox Five. That emplacement northeast of Mintago is silenced. I repeat, silenced. Over."

"Well, hallelujah, Green Fox Five. Make contact with Captain Serge Nickerson. Stay put with him and his unit. I'll re-establish communication with you when it's time. Out."

Carlos looked at Billy. "Short and sweet, Sarge."

"Short. I don't know how sweet. Okay, men, take another ten. Then we'll link up with this Nickerson. I assume he's with the forces to our front. Where are Jesus and Zeph?"

"Souvenir hunting," grunted Johnny.

Billy rolled his eyes. "Ten minutes."

I think the 2nd Division itself was of two minds. When we

first got word we were going to be a floating reserve, after we did the fake beach landing, a lot complained they didn't want to miss the action. After they thought about it, just as many took it as a gift horse, and were glad to be spared the meat grinder. Now here we were, thirteen of us, 2nd Division, and we weren't about to escape the meat grinder or miss the action.

"What do you think about where we are right now, Johnny?" I asked him.

He was methodically working his way through a pack of Lucky Strikes. "Does it matter what I think?" He looked at the squad, all of them lying flat on the ground. "It doesn't matter what they think, either."

11

DIVINE WIND
BILLY MARTENS

THE LANDINGS ON THE WEST SIDE OF THE ISLAND HAD STARTED ON
Easter Sunday. Despite the church services on deck before Billy
climbed into his LST, which moments later was hit by a
kamikaze, it never hit home until after they hunkered down with
Captain Nickerson's crew and awaited further orders. April 1.
Easter morning. Christ's Resurrection. Billy sat and had a smoke
on it, a Marlboro, a lucky find.

Back home, Easter had happened hours before. He saw, as
clearly as if he were there, the wild flowers his mother would
have placed around the church with his sisters' help. Father
would have stood behind the pulpit and declared in his powerful
bass voice that the Resurrection was what Christianity was all
about. There would be communion. The congregation would
sing *Up from the Grave He Arose*. They'd have sung *The Old Rugged
Cross* on Good Friday. Billy recalled there'd been services for
Good Friday onboard ship too, but he'd avoided them. He still
thought Easter was a true thing, something both historical and
religious, something important. But he wasn't sure if he and God
were in the same foxhole anymore. Maybe, maybe not.

He smoked through an entire pack, had some hot chow at

sunset, talked with Nickerson about nothing in particular, dug in and slept a short stone's throw from Johnny Strange like he'd done the entire war. And maybe the war was over. Maybe this was Nippon's last gasp.

Before he slipped off, he listened to distant gunfire and watched the bright parabolas of tracers to the northwest. Would the Japanese truly surrender if they lost Okinawa? *You know better, Billy.* Yeah, he did know better. Wishful thinking. He'd wanted the end so the B-29 bombings would stop and the killing stop too. But Marines landing to conquer the island of Japan would just be more rivers of blood, military and civilian. He was convinced every Jap would take up arms against them. Housewives, restaurant owners, florists, school teachers, geishas, plumbers, Shinto priests—they'd all fire rifles, toss grenades and wield katanas. The end of the bombings of cities would not end the war. There were no easy answers, there was no easy way out. Billy turned onto his left shoulder and wondered what good his father's prayers for peace had ever done, what persons his pacifism had ever saved.

The ruckus from the landings on the east side of the island woke him up earlier than he wanted. *Ruckus.* He smiled. That was mom talking to him from ten thousand miles away. He sat up, stiff and sore, as if he'd spent a rough day in the saddle. Johnny squatted by him with a hot tin mug of coffee.

"Here ya go, buddy," Johnny announced, grinning. "Rise and shine. The cook swears it's Peel the Skin Off Your Bones Coffee, a special blend he conjured up in Minnesota."

Billy barked a laugh. "Peel the Skin, huh? Any rubber tires in it or bits of Jap Zeros?"

"That's the funny thing. I thought the Japs would kamikaze us to death out here after they hit our LST yesterday. But nothing. The skinny is they don't have the planes or enough pilots with suicide on their minds."

Billy sipped. "Hey, this is swell." He took a longer drink, even though the coffee was scalding hot. "I can't believe that about not enough suicide pilots. How many suicide soldiers have we fought since '42? Bushels of 'em. How many banzais did we see? It's their code. You've reminded me of that a dozen times, Johnny. Bushido. You win your battles or you die trying to win your battles. If the enemy doesn't do you the favor of killing you, you kill yourself or ask a buddy to behead you after you begin your stomach cut and your guts are spilling out."

"And grenades. Remember how they'd let their grenades go off in their fists on Tarawa?"

"Yeah. Or take off their boots, and wrappings, and socks and squeeze their rifle triggers with their toes, shooting straight into their mouths." Billy wound his hands around the tin mug to better feel the heat. "I don't buy the skinny, Johnny. It makes no sense that we're on Japan's frigging doorstep and suddenly they're gonna fold like we've dealt them the worst hand at the poker table."

"No. To carry your idea forward, the Nips have aces up their sleeves."

"That's what I think."

"Did you see Nickerson?" Billy asked.

"I did. He was getting about six mugs of coffee and looping through their handles with his fingers. Which aren't small."

"Any orders from Kravits?"

"Just to sit tight. There are more landings to come."

And there were. L-Day plus one—Love-Day plus one—"As if we'd get D-Day and Normandy confused with landing on a tropical island off the coast of Japan," spat Johnny–and Marines were coming ashore further down the southeast coast. L-Day plus two, more landings in the southeast. On L-Day plus four, April 5th, Bud had news. The Marines and the Army had been rolling up Japanese forces in the west and north.

"Piece of cake, I've heard," he told them. "Little opposition. Ill equipped and ill trained Jap troops."

Johnny and Billy stared at him.

"That can't be true," Johnny argued. "When have the Nips ever given up without a fight?"

"Well, I think that's what is happening in the north and north-west. I've picked it up from a lot of sources. Things may change, though."

"Things may change?" Johnny chewed a stick of gum as fast as he could. "You tell us all this stuff that's hard to believe and then you tell us your BS may change?"

"It's not BS. They think the enemy is concentrated further to the south. That's why the north has been so easy. Which means with these new landings in the southeast, things may start to pop."

"Huh. I'm from Missouri on this, Bud. I'll need to see it to believe it."

On L-Day plus five, April 6, the heavens opened.

Four hundred kamikaze aircraft descended on American warships off Okinawa, sinking two hundred and damaging over one hundred and fifty. Bud, Johnny and Billy and the others watched, stunned, as the suicide planes came in waves, obviously well-coordinated, hour after hour. Dark pillars of smoke rose from the sea east and west of the island as ships burned to the waterline. Anti-aircraft fire peppered the sky. Even hit and throwing trails of sparks, kamikazes continued to their targets, their pilots pushing them headfirst into scores of naval vessels.

Billy saw one destroyer disappear in an orange ball of fire. It was there, the kamikaze struck, the explosion rocked the waters around the ship, waves raged in all directions. But when the flames fell back, there was just the blackest smoke, an agonized patch of sea, and nothing else.

"When are we going to do something about it?" fumed Billy.

"They're hitting them with AA," Johnny responded. "Our flyboys are picking them off."

"Picking them off? Then why are they getting through and deep-sixing so many of our boats?"

"Because the Jap aviators don't care if they die, buddy. And because they won't let death stop them from fulfilling their suicide missions. Shoot their Zero to pieces, fill those aviators full of tracers and they'll still keep coming. The dead man's hand on the stick will take those planes anywhere the Emperor wants them to go. Especially straight down and into one of our boats. It's the damnedest thing, Billy, but what are you going to do with people who are determined that certain death will not make them surrender but just make them fight that much harder?"

"I'm wondering how long they can keep this up."

"Long, Billy, long."

The next day was the same. And the day after. And all the days after that. Into the daily attacks that consisted of silver streaks of diving airplanes, their sparks and smoke and winding flames, US ships erupting in black and purple smoke that towered into the air, came the report the Yamato, the biggest battleship in the world, had been sunk by American naval aircraft. The assault on the Yamato had taken place on L-Day plus six, April 7, three hundred nautical miles north of Okinawa. Yamato had finally turned turtle, its forward magazine had exploded, an enormous pillar of smoke had shot into the sky and the huge battleship went under. It had been on its way to wreak havoc on US landing beaches and naval shipping, working with the kamikaze assaults to devastate American forces and thwart the invasion of Okinawa-honto, halting the US advance in the Pacific.

It was on the 10th they finally heard from Kravits. He was transferring to another vessel because the troopship was returning to Saipan. It was too vulnerable to kamikaze attacks. They would hear from him again in twenty-four hours. He would have a better idea where to send them at that time: "You've been goldbricking long enough. Never mind Nickerson and his skirmishes. You have bigger fish to fry."

Nickerson's men had been probing the jungle and inching north, taking Martens' Mavericks with them. There had been nothing to write home about. A few MG nests, even fewer snipers. But with kamikazes shrieking through the sky off their right shoulders, ships' guns banging like Thor's hammers, the action usually ending with a shattering explosion, along with the crash of gunfire intensifying several miles to their front, everyone, even Johnny Strange, was getting edgy—despite the nonchalant effect the Marlboro drooping from the corner of his mouth produced, like something from a war correspondent's ink drawing of a well-seasoned vet.

"You're not fooling anyone," Billy told him.

"Who the hell am I supposed to be fooling, Menno Simons?" Johnny snapped.

"You're smoking three packs a day. This island is getting to you. The island and the kamikazes. You know the crap's going to fly, Johnny. You know it in your bones. You just don't know where and when. Hell, you don't even know how. And it's eating you up."

"I'm A-okay, Billy Boy. Give me a stack of Bibles and I'll swear to God."

"It doesn't matter about the stack of Bibles and it doesn't matter where you park your cigarette. You've got the goosebumps just like the rest of us. We're all in the same boat."

"You stick to your boat," snarled Johnny, checking to be sure his Marlboro was where he wanted it at the corner of his mouth, "and I'll stick to mine and we'll see whose tugboat gets sunk by a suicide plane first."

Three things happened after Johnny said this. There was a louder than usual explosion from the sea when a ship was hit by a Jap suicide plane, a machine gun opened up on them from behind with the familiar staccato of a Nambu they'd heard for three years running and Jack B. Quick screamed he'd been bitten by a snake. Johnny, Zeph and Kelly immediately went after the MG, crouching and slithering and sprinting through the jungle growth, Johnny biting off, "Who the hell walked us right past these Nips?" Billy saw the snake vanish into the bushes, black and amber and a horrific seven feet long, and quickly joined Bud in bending over Jack.

Bud cut away the pant leg while Nambu bullets cut palm fronds over his head: "They briefed us on all the venomous snakes. That was an Okinawa Habu we saw beating it. The worst pit viper on the island. No slice and suck. No tourniquet. I'm just going to keep his leg immobilized and keep him calm. The more he gets worked up the faster his heart pumps blood and venom through his body. Geez. There are three bites."

"Do you have anti-venom?"

"No, Billy. Maybe Nickerson does."

"He's way ahead. A couple of hundred yards."

"Get Carlos to radio. See if they have anything."

"Carlos!" yelled Billy.

"Yo!" Carlos yelled back.

"On me! And keep your frigging head down till we silence that MG!"

Carlos came at running crouch. He got Nickerson right away, but the captain didn't have any anti-venom. What they'd had, they'd used on three of their men when the unit had first landed. One of them had died anyway. Which is what Billy watched happen to Jack, squeezing his hand as he spasmed and convulsed. The cough of the Nambu was silenced. Jack went silent too. The Marines could only hear the screech of kamikaze attacks against US vessels in the Philippine Sea.

The next day, Billy received a coded message from Krazits: *Proceed north towards Shuri Castle. We believe it is heavily fortified. Assist other Marine and Army units as you push forward. Once you reach Shuri, we will provide you with a contact in the 1ˢᵗ Marine Division. It will take you a couple of weeks. Semper fi, Marine. Out.*

Johnny shook his head, blowing smoke through his nostrils—like a dragon, Billy thought.

"Swell," Johnny snorted. "Our friends, the 1st Marine Division."

"It'll take us a while to get there, Johnny. It's a good slog. Probably the two weeks and a bit more, judging by the map." He held it unfolded in his hand. "Bricks. Brad. Player. Get Jack buried."

"Two weeks is fine by me," Johnny grumbled.

It would take them a month.

12

WALL OF STEEL
JOHNNY STRANGE

*Whoever told that major we were just supposed to move inland
and knock out enfilading fire against the main landing force had their
head so far up their backside they can see their tonsils.*

Johnny Strange hunkered down below the top of a small ridge
that ran roughly northeast and southwest. It was just dusk. He
flattened against the ground behind a bush to keep from sky-
lining himself above the ridge top. The valley below was
swarming with Japs. He could see about a hundred Okinawan
volunteers carrying ammo down a trail into the hills. Beside them
marched fully armed Japanese with what looked like at least
eighty-pound packs. From where he was, he could spot at least
four machine-gun nests, and there were several of the large
Okinawan tombs lining the hillside across the way, which no
doubt had their full contingent of concealed Japanese soldiers.

When they blew up the gun emplacement after they came
ashore on Love Day, they stirred up a hornet's nest. Not long after
their attack, a wall of steel had thundered down on the hilltop—
mortar shells and artillery fire and they knew there were a lot
more Japs in the south than the Brass believed. They had beaten
it out of there, inching north along the coast. While they were

trying to avoid the Japs, they were looking for more guns. But except for some emplacements registered on Mintago beach, they saw little along the shore. They worked their way north along the coast, but saw more of the same.

But when they did recon inland, out of the coastal forests and into the barren rangeland in the middle of Okinawa, that's when they found Japs and plenty of them. Everywhere they looked, they saw gun emplacements, machine-gun nests, fortified caves and tombs, signs of recent traffic, even horse tracks. They had been hiding under some trees for most of the day and now Billy sent Johnny up the hill to look around.

He scooted back down the slope on his butt and rolled in next to Billy.

"They are there all right. Brother, this whole end of the island is packed with Japs. They are doing the same thing they did at Iwo—not worrying about stopping us at the beaches. They've honeycombed this whole end of the island with fortified caves, tunnels, gun emplacements. They are just sitting there waiting for our guys to come get them."

Billy took a drag on his Marlboro. "Yeah, I guess our planes don't see them because they move at night. Creatures of darkness, these little Nipponese."

Johnny shook his head. "We need to find the command center and report directly to Buckner. I think the generals think this is going to be a cakewalk. But from what we're seeing, this will be no picnic."

"I just got a message from Krazits. He's going to detach us from Nickerson and send us toward a place called Shuri castle, the Jap headquarters. But if what we are thinking is right, it will be a long time until we get to Shuri."

Billy picked up a stick and made a rough map in the dirt. A central point with concentric rings radiating out from it.

"So, here's Shuri, over west, close to the town of Naha. My

guess is they've built defensive rings going out from their HQ. Remember how they fortified Betio?"

Johnny nodded. "Yeah, every nest, every bunker, every artillery emplacement was bound to the ones all around. So, everywhere we tried to go, there was a wall of lead and steel."

"That's right, and they've had a lot longer to get this place ready. They moved their army on the island a year ago, and they've been digging like gophers ever since. They've got troops and Okinawan conscripts working. You've seen the hills—limestone and sand. You could dig a cave with a spoon in about an hour."

Johnny agreed. "I heard from a guy who was on Iwo with a supply outfit for a few weeks. He said the Japs had honeycombed Mt. Suribachi with caves and tunnels, concealed gun emplacements, MG nests. He said that they would come up from underneath trenches our guys dug and just drag them down into the dark."

"They've had a year to beef this place up. We need to get north and let the guys know what's going on. They need to come down here with their eyes open."

———

THE NEXT DAY, after a hard night of scrambling over hills, moving through gullies and staying as hidden as possible while moving up the coast, Marten's Mavericks hooked up with a patrol from the Army 7th Division, who took them over to Division HQ. After grabbing some chow, Billy and Johnny were ushered into the presence of General John Reed Hodge, commander of the 96th and 7th Army Divisions. The General was real Army, trim, chiseled features, no-nonsense. They instinctively snapped to.

"At ease men." He looked up at Billy. "Who are you, Marine?"

"Sergeant Billy Martens, Sir. This is Corporal Strange, 2nd Division Marines, Sir, I company. They attached us to Captain

Nickerson's recon and demo team on Love Day. But then Major Krazits detached us and sent us up here."

"Where is Krazits?"

"The 2nd sailed back to Saipan. They took more casualties from kamikazes on Love Day than the whole 10th army. So, they sent them back."

"Smart thinking, even for Marines." The General grinned. "Now, what have you got for me? My adjutant says it's pretty important."

"Sit, we just want to let you guys know that the whole southern end of this island is crawling with Japanese, but they are not out in the open. We did a lot of recon and the further you get toward Shuri, the more massive their defensive emplacements are. They have guns and soldiers hidden in caves, trenches, abandoned buildings. They have gun emplacements and soldiers on the backside of the ridges, so they stay hidden, and we can't get to them with naval gunfire or our guns on Kerama."

General Hodge motioned for Billy and Johnny to come over to the desk. There was a map spread there.

"Show me."

Quickly they pointed out the defensive positions they had spotted and noted how they seemed to spread out in concentric rings around Shuri. General Hodge studied the map.

"Looks like they learned their lesson on Tarawa and Saipan. Don't stop us at the beaches. Let us get our men ashore and then cut us off from our supplies and wipe us out."

Billy nodded. "If I may, Sir?"

"Go ahead, Sergeant."

"I think it's more than that, Sir. I think General Ushijima knows he can't win. LeMay has been pounding Tokyo and other cities into splinters and burning down the rest. The Japs know that they have lost the war and, like I said, Ushijima knows he can't win this battle. We have unlimited supplies and control the air. Every man he loses is one he can't replace, every shell he fires, he can't replace. I think he's hoping that we will grind to a halt on his defenses here while his kamikazes sink enough of our ships that we will back off. Then the Japanese will ask for a negotiated peace that's favorable to them, including no occupation and keeping the emperor."

General Hodge smiled. "Pretty good thinking, Gyrene. Ever think of switching corps? I could use a man like you on my staff."

Billy grinned. "No, Sir, I've never even given it a thought."

General Hodge glanced around and lowered his voice. "Just between you and me, the puffed-up West Pointers they keep sending out here sit on their brains all day, so think it over, will you?"

"I'm complimented, General, but I've been too long in this outfit, Sir."

General Hodge shrugged. "I understand, Sergeant." He looked over at Johnny. "What about you, Corporal? Ever think of jumping ship?"

Johnny shook his head. "No, Sir. Like my Sergeant here, the thought never actually crossed my mind."

"Well, I enjoy working with experienced men. I think I'll try to keep you around until we get some of this kefuffle straightened out. You boys have obviously been around the Quad a couple of times. Where did you serve?"

"Started D-Day on Cactus, then Tarawa, then Saipan. I got to go home for six weeks to marry my girl."

"Congratulations, Corporal. Every man needs a good wife back home. I know. I have one."

Johnny nodded.

And I sure as shootin' wish I was back there right now...

General Hodge stood up. "All right. Thanks for the report. I'm going to call a staff meeting for 1600 hours. I want you fellas there. Go catch some shuteye or grab some chow. Report back here then."

"Sir, yes, Sir."

JOHNNY AND BILLY lay in a couple of bunks in a tent General
Hodge's orderly had pointed them to. Bud had gone off to help in
the field hospital. Johnny took a long drag on his Marlboro. "Did
you see any Marines around here? Except for Bud?"

Billy shook his head. "Not one. But the 1st Div came ashore on
Love Day with the rest of the Army. Wonder what's up."

Johnny lowered his voice. "I'll tell you what's up. 1st Div is the
best fighting force on this island and the Army knows it. My
guess is that the Army wants to be the one that gets the glory for
crushing the Jap Thirty-second Army. I hear our boys are basically on guard duty up north, sitting on their hands."

"I think your guess is good as gold. But if what we think is
going to happen happens, those Army boys are going to need
some help and need it quick. If they go stumbling into that
hornet's nest south of us, they will bite off a big chew. That's
when we'll see the 1st."

Johnny shifted on his bunk. "I also heard scuttlebutt in the
chow tent—the army wants to do a landing at Mintago."

"Unless they can clear out one hundred thousand Japs before
they jump off, they are big-time outta luck."

"You know what ticks me off, Billy?"

"What, Menno?"

"We're not even supposed to be in this fight. The rest of 2nd
Div is now basking in the tepid sunshine of wonderful conquered
Saipan. Had Krazits not sent us ashore, we'd be smoking cigars at
the local pub and talking about the USO show we saw last night."

"Ticked, Johnny, or scared?"

"Both, Sergeant Martens. I got a wife now, a beautiful wife,
and a little boy that really got his hooks into me. I don't want to
go out there with a bunch of half-assed doggies and get my rear
shot off, because they are trying to keep the Marines out of the
show."

"Well, if we were back on Saipan, you'd most likely pull ghost duty with Marten's Mavericks."

Johnny laughed. "And that's another thing, Sergeant. You haven't been one step further than me or Bud or some of the other guys from 2nd. And yet you got a bunch of newbies kissing your butt like you're the best thing since sliced bread. What a joke!"

"Well, while you guys were goofin' off stateside, I was out here winning the war."

"Why do you think we came back, Sniper? We didn't want you to get all the glory."

"Too late, Menno, I already got it."

———

THAT AFTERNOON, they sat in on the staff meeting. General Hodge rolled a wall map down and pointed to a section south of the landing beaches.

"Four days ago, we took the Pinnacle, this limestone hill, a few miles below the landing area. Our deepest penetration has been on the west side where 3rd Battalion, 383d Infantry and 96th Recon Troop moved from Isa to Uchitomari on April 4. But these ridges in the center are heavily armed and the Japs have us backed up there. We took Cactus ridge, not without a fight. And now we are looking at taking this little hill here, one thousand yards west of Minami-Uebaru. From what I've learned from Sergeant Martens and Corporal Strange, they have riddled these hills with a system of caves, tunnels and connecting trenches. We are not just going to walk through their lines."

A major raised his hand. "After we take that hill, what's next, General?"

The General pointed to a long ridge. "We have to take these strong points at Ouki, triangulation Hill and Tomb Hill. Anything to add, Sergeant Martens?"

"Well, General, from what we've seen, the hills you are looking at are just holding positions. The Japs are using them to wear us down. Once you get past them, you're going to come up against the steel hard edge of the real Shuri defenses." Billy walked to the map and pointed. "Right here. It's called..." he squinted at the map... "Kakazu Ridge."

Johnny looked at the map.

Why do I not have a good feeling about this?

13

THE RED HILLS
BUD, THE CORPSMAN

BILLY WAS RIGHT. TODAY THE 1ST AND 3RD BATTALIONS OF THE 383rd Infantry are going to attempt to seize a place called Kakazu Ridge. General Hodge attached us to Colonel May's outfit to tag along as spotters, you know, to help point out the dangerous places where the Japs might give us a hard time. He called a briefing and gave it to Billy and Johnny. Before the briefing, Billy just shook his head.

"Bud, everywhere I can point on that map there are Japs."

They drew us up in position for the attack and Billy and Johnny, who had done most of the recon on this position when we were coming up from Mintago, knew pretty much what to expect. Unlike outposts like the Pinnacle or Red Hill, which were just there to slow us up, this ridge was an integral part of the Shuri fortified zone and a bastion that could expect reinforcements and heavy fire support from the ring of positions that surrounded Shuri Castle, only four thousand yards to the south.

Johnny was squatting down with platoon leaders from the 1st Battalion, drawing a map in the dirt. It was about two hours before dawn and we were scheduled to move out in twenty minutes. I guess they thought the darkness would hide us, but they hadn't seen the gorge. If we got through or around it before daylight, we would be very lucky. Johnny pointed to the map.

"There's a ravine, a deep gorge, between us and that hill. You can't see it from here because it's hidden by trees and brush. That gorge is going to be almost impassable itself. If you get across the gorge, you got a moat right in front of you, a deep moat. Beyond that, the Japs have studded the front of the hill with natural and man-made positions. You got most of the artillery clustered on the reverse slope where we can't reach them, and their fire is going to blanket the entire front of that rise as you're going up. After that, there's a cluster of buildings with machine-gun emplacements that cover every inch of the backside of that hill."

I could tell by the look on their faces they were unhappy about what Johnny was saying. And I didn't blame them. See, I promised Marjean I would take care of Johnny, bring him home. When they told us we were just going to run a feint on Love Day and then hang out as reserves, I was feeling a lot better about the whole deal. Getting Strange home would be a cinch. Then whoever that stupid major was that sent us ashore, right into the heart of the heaviest defensive positions on the entire island, he's on his way back to Saipan and me and my two Mennos are right in the thick of it... again. If anything happens to Johnny or Billy, I won't be able to go back stateside for a long time. Not if I have to look into those steely blues and tell her Johnny didn't make it.

And me, well, I got promises of my own. I got a beautiful Tongan princess back in New Zealand, nursing a lot of guys that haven't seen a woman like Kalasia in their whole life. Can you imagine what some poor, shot-up Army boy hauled back from Leyte or Saipan in a stinking transport would think when they regained consciousness in a Wellington hospital and the nurse that's bathing their poor, fevered brow is my Kalasia? The poor sap would think they had died and gone to heaven. Must be twenty guys a day leaving that hospital who would give anything for a date with my girl. And if I get it here on this stinking hill, what's Kalasia going to do? Get her to a Nunnery? Sit in a room with the lights out for the rest of her life? I don't think so. My girl is one hundred percent woman, and she's got fire and steel in her. If I get it, she'll cry for a few days, wipe her eyes, send a pray to heaven, and get on with living. As they say, you can get busy dying or get busy living. I know what Kalasia would do.

I tell you, that's not something you want to go to sleep at night thinking about. And now we are looking over at this little ridge about a thousand yards away and these doggies think they are just going to go over, slap the Japs around a bit and then hit the chow line. But I know, and Billy knows, and Johnny knows that a lot of guys are going to die on that dinky little ridge over there.

It's not high, it's not jagged, nor is it especially abrupt. Just a stupid little red hill that has got to be one of the strongest defensive positions on Okinawa. Johnny and Billy did a lot of crawling around to check that place out.

Behind the ridge, five hundred yards south, is the Urasoe-Mura Escarpment, which to the newbies around me, seems like an insurmountable obstacle. So, they are looking there and not paying attention to the ridge in front of them. Kakazu is just an ugly, stubby little hill, covered with burned off bare tree trunks standing like skeletons against the skyline. Just below it is the town of Kakazu, a bunch of tile-roofed buildings, each one surrounded by hedges and stone walls and totally able to defilade the open fields around them. This place has got all the earmarks of death on wheels.

If we even get up there, we'll face enormous firepower. Kakazu itself has got two summits with a kind of saddle in between them. The saddle is dotted with tombs, which are filled with Japs, heavily armed Japs. The other thing Johnny is telling the doggies is about the mortars on the back side of the ridge that are zeroed in on that gorge and the forward slopes of the hills. If these guys even make it across the gorge, it won't be duck soup trying to get up that hill.

So here we are, sitting in a briefing with a bunch of new kids from Oakland, and Chicago, and New Orleans, and we're telling them that most likely today is their last day on earth. And they haven't got the faintest idea what we are talking about or what's waiting out there for them. Kinda like the Marines who waded across that bloody lagoon at Betio, not understanding that there was not one lane of fire that was not covered by Jap 50-caliber machine guns or field pieces or rockets. And so, they marched through the chest high water and the bullets came and they died in rows, like Braddock's troops marching into the French trap, or the Light Brigade riding into the Valley of Death.

I don't want to be the oracle of doom here. That's not my point. Just like us, when we hit the beach at Cactus and did not have the faintest frickin' idea what was ahead of us, these kids are all smiles and backslaps, and swapping smokes. Not that there aren't a few who get the drift. I can see them kissing their crosses or checking their ammo belts, limbering up the bolt on their M1s. I feel like Cassandra standing on the walls of Troy, looking down at the horse and getting an icy cold feeling in her gut, but for us it's a hill not a wooden horse but I still want to yell, "Don't go out there, leave that hill alone..." But I'm keeping my mouth shut because this is war and it doesn't matter a hill of beans what I want.

See, after three years fighting these creeps I know that the only way we are going to put an end to it, to all the killing and suffering and destruction is to keep going, to take our guns and our knives and our grenades and go out there and kill and slice and blow up every little yellow bastard that we see, until there are none of them left alive on this island. I don't like it; I didn't sign up for it. I remember what I told the Brass when they asked me would I fight. I said I would do anything they needed except carry a rifle and kill someone. Everyone in Boot Camp called me Hambo because I was a CO. I joined the Marines because I felt I had a responsibility to help defend the country that gives me the freedom to be non-violent. Back then, my faith told me it is wrong to kill men. But now I'm not so sure.

I became a corpsman because it was the best place for me to help. I had a knack for it. The more I found out about the human body and its miraculous healing powers, the more intrigued I became. I've seen guys get holes as big as a grapefruit punched through their bodies, patched them up, sent them to rehab, and then watched in amazement as they got out of the truck six weeks later and rejoined the outfit.

"Hey, Bud, whaddaya know?"

So how do we reconcile all this? The miracle of life and the tragedy of death. Well, first we deal with the dealers of death. After watching my buddies die on Cactus, Tarawa, and Saipan; after watching a lunatic with a rising sun scarf wrapped around his head as he dove his plane into an LST full of Americans, it occurs to me that the people who want to inflict death on everyone should be first in line to see what it's like.

As stoic as those Japs think they are, as "Bushido" and "Samurai" as they act, you can't tell me they are not afraid to die. Every man I've ever meant, no matter how noble, or brave, or honorable they are, has a place inside them that clutches onto life like a mountain climber who slipped off the cliff and dug his fingers into the rock like a vise to keep from falling. So, I say, you want to deal out death? Then you qualify to go to the head of the line to be sacrificed for your cause. And the guys around me, the veterans, and the newbies—even though I can see the fear in their eyes, the same fear that is inside of me—they know that the only way to set this whole thing straight is to go out there and kick some butt.

That said, they still have no idea...

WE KICKED OFF BEFORE DAWN. The darkness hid our movements as we moved out. They drew us up east to west, Company C and A of the 1st Battalion and L and I of the 3rd Battalion. The darkness hid us and we actually got A and C across the gorge and up the hill before dawn without being discovered. We heard a few gunshots over to the west, Company L killing a few random pickets, but the bulk of the Jap forces remained quiet.

But you know what they say, the best laid plans of mice and men. I Company got delayed in its jump-off and by daylight was in open ground around one hundred and fifty yards south of Uchitomari.

Shortly after 0600, the enemy was alerted. A lone Jap in a pillbox spotted Company A on the hill and opened fire. Almost immediately, a rain of mortar fire fell all along the front, with the staccato bursts of the Nambus punctuating the blasts. Our guys were right out in the open, all available foxholes and tombs were already filled with Japs. The saddle separated company A and C and there was no contact between them. The fire from the Japs extended all the way down the hill and into the gorge. They were pouring it on with artillery and mortars from all over the south end of the island. The fire cut off Company I in the open ground to the West and so L was isolated on Kakazu West. Me and Billy and Johnny watched as L made a run for the top of the hill. They made it with fixed bayonets and immediately the Japs poured out of every hole and came after them. It's like I said, our guys knew they had to put these Japs away, or die, so they just went for it.

But it didn't turn out good for a lot of guys.

14

MISSING IN ACTION

BILLY MARTENS

Billy hollered at his squad to move up and engage.

"Let's go! Let's go!" He pointed with his finger. "Set up the thirty over there! Gyprock! Jesus! Go!" He glanced quickly around him. "BAR men! Johnny! Player! Up front! Tear into 'em! Get in close!" He bent his arm at the elbow and pumped it up and down, bullets ripping by his head. "Double time it! Zeph, Kelly, Brad, Bricks, Bolo, take the left flank. The rest of you form a line on the right. Keep moving. This isn't trench warfare and we're not at frigging Ypres. BAR men! You gotta be the tip of the arrowhead! Lead the way. Everyone, keep our flanks tight. No one gets past you."

They rolled into the Japanese assault. The Tommy guns were sheer destruction at close range. A part of Billy's mind yelled, *I hope this will end it! I hope this will end all of it!* But the rest of his mind was blank. He'd been in fierce firefights too any times before to believe this might be the last battle.

He crouched and ran ahead. Johnny was on his right and Player on his left. A Nambu opened up on them and he heard Johnny yell "knee mortar". He dove for the rocky and rough jungle ground. Felt a sharp outcrop rake his cheek and the sudden flow of blood. It was nothing. It was not a bullet.

The bullet came a moment later. He thought a powerful man had swung a sledgehammer at his helmet. The shock ripped through his whole body, not only his head. The helmet went spinning off and his skull rang. Everything was a blazing white. Johnny yelled, "Incoming!" Billy was lifted, turned over several times, and hurled. Pain cut him apart when he hit the rocky slope. He kept rolling and rolling and then he didn't fight to stay conscious anymore. There were no dreams, no images. When he opened his eyes a half hour later, he did not know where he was and he soon realized he could not hear. It was as if his ears were filled with water. His head was pounding. He ran his hand over his face and could not hear it, only feel it. His fingers came away with blood.

He went over his legs and arms. Nothing was broken. But his ribs hurt like anything and they hurt worse every time he took a deep breath. The toe of one of his boots was ripped open.

Billy saw he was in some sort of ravine and puzzled how he would haul himself out of it. If this had been Montana, he'd have a pair of thick deerskin or moose-skin gloves on his hands or in the back pocket of his jeans. There were branches to grip. If they held, he could scale the ravine's sides. He suddenly remembered the fierce clash with Jap troops his squad was engaged in. He had to rejoin them.

He began to climb. But the branches tore away in his hands and he tumbled back. This happened three times. Sitting down, defeated for the moment, he reached for the canteen on his hip. It was gone. The cigarettes and chewing gum he kept in his breast pocket were gone too. There was part of a chocolate bar in his pocket, smashed flat as a knife blade. He ate it. Once he began swallowing, his ears popped. They immediately filled with the chatter of machine gun fire.

That's a Nambu. That's our thirty. That's how Gyprock triggers and that's how Jesus feeds in the belt, smooth as silk. There's Johnny yelling. He'll lead them well.

It all sounded far away. Several hundred yards. Maybe more. Billy glanced up at the top of the ravine again and realized the growth over its opening was thicker than it had seemed at first glance. Unless someone stuck their head through it, they'd never see him. Though he'd doubted anyone in his squad had been sent to find him or his body. Not with the fight they had on their hands.

He heard voices. His ears were ringing off and on, but the sound of language was unmistakable. It wasn't English. And it wasn't male. Female soldiers came to the edge of the ravine and talked. He could make out their uniforms and boots and rifles. When he had rolled into the ravine, his body had made something of a break among the leaves and branches growing over it. The rifles had bayonets attached. The only bayonet he could make out clearly was smeared in blood. On her hip, that woman wore a holstered Colt .45 and a USMC Ka-Bar in its sheath.

He knew enough Japanese to understand they were planning to come at his men from behind, and get in close enough to use bayonets, knives, pistols, and bare hands if necessary. He'd read briefs about how well-trained many of the Japanese on Okinawa were in karate. They could break a man's neck with a strong knife-hand chop to the throat. It reminded him of how ferocious the island women were on Saipan and how they'd overpowered Japanese troops, using only their hands and legs.

Billy wished he had a weapon. All he had was the bolo machete. It was still attached to his web belt. There were twelve to fifteen female soldiers, and he figured he could get most of them with a few quick bursts if he had a Thompson. Of course, if he missed one or two, they only had to drop a Jap grenade into the ravine, and that would be it.

They suddenly began to use English, and he saw several of them bending over two figures on their knees, their hands tied behind them. Marines. Billy could just barely make out their faces. They were bruised and badly beaten. The women kicked them and pricked them with their bayonets. Slapped them and laughed.

"So, you are American men?" Their English was good. "You are Marines? We defeated you easily. Wiped out your squad on our own. Did not even need our rifles. How weak you are. America is weak. Japan is strong. You will all die here. You will never see Tokyo."

A woman gripped one Marine by his hair and grinned, twisting her hand viciously. He yelled out. She slapped him across the face. "Coward! Weakling! Now, tell us what we want to know and you will have a swift death. Hurry! Time has run out. We need to go and kill the rest of your Marines."

He would not talk, so she yanked him to his feet by the hair, spit in his face and pushed him away. Another soldier took this as her cue to whirl in a circle and deliver a powerful kick to his chest. He collapsed. Sneering, a woman asked him again if he would tell them what they wanted to know about US troop positions. He refused to respond. So, he was dragged to his feet again, punched in the face and stomach, and positioned for another kick. A different soldier let out a yell and jumped into the air, flying at the Marine, smashing into his head with her boot, breaking his neck. Billy heard the crack and watched the man's head sag sideways. The kicker prodded his body with her boot and it flopped to the ground. She smiled and went to the other Marine. "This will be you unless you talk. If you tell us what we want to know, I will kill you quickly with the sword. You will feel nothing. I promise." She patted the scabbard at her side. "You will like it."

The angle was such that Billy could just barely see what was going on. He was certain they thrust bayonets into the Marine's arms and legs, making him scream while they mocked his manhood. Then his scream was cut off as the kicker used a rope to choke him. Finally, he watched the female soldiers bend over him, listening. Billy could not make out the Marine's words, but he saw several of the women nodding and smiling. He assumed they had tortured what they wanted to hear out of him, likely where the Marine units were most vulnerable. All but the kicker and another soldier took off running, rifles ready, and disappeared into the jungle.

True to her word, the kicker unsheathed her katana, showed it to the Marine, unbound his hands with one slash, then shaved his arm with its edge, tossing the hairs in his face. He tried to get up, but the other female soldier got behind him, clamped her hands down on his shoulders, and forced him back to his knees. The kicker lifted her katana.

"I am doing you a great honor," she said. "You Americans do not know how to fight. You surrender too easily. Women can overpower you with ease. But you fought better than the others and, once we captured you, it was you and your fellow Marine who resisted our interrogations to the end. So, I kill you as a defeated Samurai dies, by the sword. This is Bushido and I end your life by its code. It is my gift."

She swung and neatly sliced the Marine's head from his shoulders. Blood sprayed. His body remained in the kneeling position. They left it like that, placing his head beside him. Then the two female soldiers bowed to him. The kicker cleaned her blade on his uniform, slid it back into its sheath, and they both took off running after the rest of their squad. Billy grit his teeth. There had been nothing he could do, but that didn't make it any easier.

He remembered a GI telling him they'd fought a platoon of women soldiers weeks before and the women had been far more brutal and battle worthy than their male counterparts. "They fought like demons from hell, Sarge. For every one of them, they took two or three of us." Now those ruthless female warriors were hurtling into his men from the back and the flanks, hiding in the jungle and springing at the moment the Marines were most vulnerable. Billy growled and forced himself to try scaling the walls of the ravine again. He had to get back in the fight. He wished he had a dozen of the Chamorro female warriors from Saipan to fight beside him. There was no doubt in his mind they'd be able to crush the Japanese women.

He had to get out of the ravine. Fingers and toes. He'd picked that up back home when he was a teen. For a year, he did a lot of climbing without using any equipment. Just hands and feet. He tugged off his boots, stuffed his socks in them, tied their laces together and slung the boots around his neck. Then he inched his way up the wall, digging for toeholds, clawing for finger holds, feeling for the cracks and crannies that gave him the purchase he needed.

Billy fell about twelve feet on his first climb and it knocked the wind out of him. The second climb, he only got to about ten before he lost his grip. *They fought like demons from hell, Sarge. For every one of them, they took two or three of us.* Billy swore and began his third fingers and toes attempt. This time he stuck to it, made sure his holds were secure, kept moving, and finally, sweat streaking his face and soaking his uniform, made it to the top and hauled himself out. He figured it had been one hundred feet, give or take. Chest heaving from exertion, arms and legs trembling, he took a minute to catch his breath and steady his body. Then he pulled on his socks and boots, drew his bolo from its sheath, dug his Rising Sun *hachimaki* out of his pocket, bound it around his head and ran up the slope. He did not run well; he was not fast, but neither did he stop. The sound of gunfire drew closer and closer.

Suddenly, he burst into the battle zone. His men were fighting to the front and fighting the female soldiers to the back and sides. The women were yelling taunts in English and Japanese and their shots were hitting home. He saw Zeph's shoulder explode. Saw Kelly take four shots to the chest and collapse, his chest breaking apart. Stumbled over Brad in the grass, his belly slit wide open by a knife or bayonet, long dead, eyes gouged out.

Rage poured through Billy. He had his *hachimaki* tied to his head. He would do his warfare with his bolo. His blood was up. He screamed his *banzai* and struck at the female soldiers who were picking off his men, slashing with his machete. They did not know he was behind them until he killed three of them. He recognized the kicker and beheaded her. The women were sprawled behind rocks and intent on killing Marines. They did not expect a wild attack from behind.

Billy dodged left and right, twisting away from their long stabbing bayonets, their lunges with knives, their kicks. Shots snapped over his head. One woman barreled into him, screaming and knocking him flat, going for his eyes with her nails, nails he saw could only have been left that long to aid in unarmed combat. He rammed his machete through her throat, pushed her body off, jumped to his feet and squared off against another woman soldier coming at him with her bare hands.

She swirled and landed a powerful kick to his stomach. It made him stagger backwards and double up in pain, his wind smashed out of him. He watched her smirk and leap at him, hammering her leg and foot down into his back, driving him to his knees. Then she cried out in Japanese and cracked her fist into the back of his neck. He could feel himself blacking out as she grabbed his hair, pulling back his head and exposing his throat to her spear hand. A BAR suddenly banged out its staccato beat and Billy saw her break into bits and pieces of bone and muscle and blood. Then it was Johnny Strange standing over him, eyes wide.

"Holy cow, Billy," he gasped. "I thought you were dead and gone over an hour ago."

15

GOING HOME
JOHNNY STRANGE

JOHNNY SHOOK HIS HEAD. THIS WHOLE THING WAS A MYSTERY TO him. The mystery was how he and Bud and Billy were still alive. After the battle of Kakazu Ridge, which they never really won, the Army just kept climbing up and down stinking hills and trying to drive the Japs out of the most brilliant defensive network he had ever seen. Every cave, every tomb, every hillside —they all had gun emplacements, mortar stands, troop caves, machine-gun nests, connecting tunnels, hidden ammo dumps, tank traps—it was insane.

He sat with Bud over a cup of coffee in one of the few times they had rested since April 10. "Didn't they figure this out before they landed us here?"

Bud took a slug, savoring the hot black brew. "Ushijima came here with 100,000 troops a year ago. He conscripted about 40,000 Okinawans and together they started digging and pouring concrete and making tunnels and connecting everything together —it's a beautiful thing to see... well, not so much for the guys who are trying to take it."

"Like yesterday. We go to take that frickin' little hill. Only all around it are three other hills we haven't taken. And when we go up the slope, the Japs put a wall of steel down on us from the other hills that nobody, I mean nobody, could get through. So, in order to take the hill, we have to go take the three other hills that are putting fire on us. But when we try to take them, then the other hills plaster us."

Bud agreed. "Yeah, and then when we get to the top, the whole back side of the hill is filled with more guns and mortars and tunnels and they just fire at a sixty-five degree angle up over the top and blast us. Pretty sweet setup... for the Japs."

An Army lieutenant came by and spotted them. "You the Marine recon squad?"

Johnny nodded. "That would be us, Sir."

"Sergeant Martens is looking for you."

Johnny finished his coffee and stood up. "I don't know if that's good or bad these days."

When Johnny had pulled Billy out of the firefight with the Jap Valkyries, his buddy was pretty beat up. Johnny took Billy under his arm and led him down the ridge. "I swear on my mother's grve, Billy, when I saw you get blown over the edge of that ravine, I thought all I would find down there were pieces."

Billy spit some blood from a mashed lip. "You and me both, Menno. You and me both."

That was on April 10. Now it was May 1, and they had been through more firefights than they could count. Nishibaru Ridge, Item Pocket, Dead Horse Gulch, and the battle at Skyline Ridge, the Maeda Escarpment—places that made Tarawa or Bloody Ridge look like a schoolyard tussle.

Johnny and Bud followed the lieutenant, and in a minute, they caught sight of Billy. He'd been up and around for several days. His ribs were still taped, but he seemed to be pretty much back in action. He looked up and grinned that familiar Martens grin—half scowl, all teeth.

"Hey, it's the inner circle. Welcome, boys. Looks like we get to rejoin the Marine Corps. They sent 1st Div down here from up north, some island called Ie Shima. Now they are working their way down the west coast and they are sending us back over on that side of the island."

The Lieutenant interrupted. "That's right, Sergeant, but we got something for you to do on the way."

"Sir?"

"We had a real fight at the Maeda Escarpment and we are missing some men. We want you boys to head that way, but since you scouted some of that, we want you to look for our wounded or soldiers that are hiding out. There are still a lot of Japs over there, so be careful."

Johnny shook his head. "Huntin' doggies, hey Billy? Lead the way."

———

THEY WERE MAKING their way down a draw between the backside of the Maeda Escarpment and another range of hills. All along the sides of the slope above were dozens of the ornate Okinawan tombs, most of which the enemy turned into machine-gun nests or mortar emplacements. Some even had tracks where the Japs had 75mm guns hidden and when the tanks would go by, the Japs rolled them out, blasted the tanks and then hid them away again.

Billy split his squad. "Johnny, you take seven guys and work your way down that side of the draw. I'll take Bud and the rest and we'll cover this side. Be careful and stay sharp. A lot of these tombs and caves front on tunnels that go all the way through the hill, and the Japs are running around in there like rats. Don't stay inside long. We're looking for wounded or shell-shocked Americans. You may find wounded Japs, but make sure they don't have any grenades and then shoot 'em." He grinned.

Johnny led his seven guys across the flat and up the slope. He signaled for two guys to take each tomb. "One guy checks with the light, the other guy has his back. Don't silhouette yourself against the mouth of the tomb. Hold the flashlight away from your body in case a Jap shoots at the light. Okay, meet back here in thirty. On my mark, 7:15 a.m. Five, four, three, two, mark,"

The men split into their teams. Johnny took Brad and headed up the slope. Above them was a *kameko-baka,* a turtle-back tomb.

When they got to the tomb entrance, Johnny signaled Brad to cover and then slipped in the door and to the right, into the gloom. Count of three and Brad followed. Johnny held his Tommy gun in front of him. Light from the entrance outlined the abandoned machine-gun set up in the doorway. There was a corpse hanging off the gun, so burnt it didn't have enough meat left to stink. Behind it, Johnny could see another room. He flicked on his light and edged along the wall. Then he heard a sound, a soft moan. Raising his hand, he signaled Brad and pointed to the back of the room. Brad moved to the far wall, and they both crept toward the back wall.

He heard it again, behind the slab that sat upright before the door into the rest of the tomb. He signaled to Brad again and Brad crouched down, his BAR at the ready. Johnny reached around the slab to light up the area behind it and then looked. There was someone lying there, an American soldier. Quickly, Johnny scanned the back of the tomb. Empty!

He knelt at the side of the American soldier. The man was lying on his side, facing the slab. His sleeve and his pants leg were both soaked in blood. The patch on his arm read 307th. Johnny gently rolled the wounded man over. Blood covered his face. He was almost unrecognizable as a human being. Johnny tore the unbloodied sleeve off his other arm and wet it with water from his canteen. As he washed the man's face, he realized something.

I know this man.

And then he knew. It was Gerald, Gerald King, his friend from Sandpoint, Idaho. Johnny turned to his BAR man.

"Brad, jump outside and see if you can see Bud across the way. If you can, give him the signal to get over here. Fast!"

Brad moved out. Johnny gently washed Gerald's face.

"Gerald? Gerald, can you hear me?"

The eyes fluttered and then opened. "Who... who are you?"

"Gerald, it's me, Johnny. Johnny Strange."

Gerald's eyes focused. "Johnny?" Gerald gave a half-chuckle, half-moan. "What the hell are you doing here?"

"Looking for you, Buddy. Got a corpsman headed this way. Just hang on."

Johnny took his K-Bar and cut the sleeve open. There was not a lot left of Gerald's arm. Someone had wrapped a rifle sling tightly around above the wound, so the bleeding was not bad.

"How did you get here, Gerald?"

Gerald took a deep breath and gasped from the pain. "We were up there, on that stinking ridge. It was every part of hell rolled into one nasty fight. We would climb up the cargo net they hung on the cliff and take them on, maybe gain a hundred yards. Then they would come at us and drive us back off the top. We finally got a toehold up there after we blew up a big cave-tunnel-pillbox complex about two hundred yards in. It was almost night, and we were setting our lines when a big spigot mortar shell came in and blew me right over the edge. I rolled all the way down here."

"Who tied your arm off?"

"I landed right in front of this place. Our boys had been through with armored flame-throwers and cleaned it out. I knew something hit me pretty good and I could see my arm was a mess, so I crawled in here and used my sling to tie it off."

Just then, a spasm of coughing hit Gerald. He coughed and

gasped, and Johnny could see blood coming out of the corner of his mouth. Gerald got it under control and then looked up.

"That's not the worst part though, Johnny."

"What, Gerald?"

"I'm riddled with shrapnel. My chest looks like swiss cheese."

Johnny opened Gerald's shirt and almost threw up. Gerald's chest was oozing blood from fifty holes.

"I'm gonna die, aren't I, Johnny?"

Johnny took hold of Gerald's hand. "You just hang in there, Gerald. The best corpsman in the whole goshdang Marine Corps is on his way."

"I don't think I have time."

There was a moment of silence. Then Gerald squeezed Johnny's hand. "I always loved her, you know."

"Loved who, Gerald?" But Johnny knew.

"Marjean. I loved her from the first day I saw her. I... I hated you for taking her away."

"Gee, Gerald, I..."

"You don't have to say anything, Johnny. I don't hate you anymore. Marjean didn't need a little wimp like me." He coughed again. "She needed a real man, someone who would stand up and be accountable, defend the country that gave him everything instead of hiding in his daddy's factory. She needed you, Johnny."

"But you're here now, Gerald. You stood up."

"But I'm gonna die here in this stinking hole and I'll never get a chance..."

He began to cough again.

"Don't talk, Gerald. Just wait for Bud. We'll get you out of here and you'll be going home. You'll see."

Brad stuck his head in. "Bud's on his way."

Gerald squeezed Johnny's hand harder. "I... I... I don't think so. Johnny." He paused. "Do you still believe in God, Johnny?"

Johnny nodded. "Yeah, I do."

"I thought you gave up on Him?"

"Yeah, Gerald..." Johnny mulled that over for a second. "... But he didn't give up on me."

"I never really believed, Johnny. My dad and mom, well... they were too..." Gerald stopped and his breathing was ragged.

"I think I need him now, Johnny; God, I mean."

Johnny looked down at Gerald.

Lord, give me the right words. I don't know what to say.

Gerald squeezed again. "Help me Johnny, I don't want to die in the dark."

Johnny took a deep breath. This was Gerald, his friend, who was dying in a burned-out tomb four thousand miles away from Sandpoint, Idaho. Gerald, his buddy, who used to cruise through downtown with him in the souped-up Chevy. They used to pound the boat together out on the lake. What could he say that wouldn't sound phony, like a bunch of bull?

"Gerald, I'm not good at this... But I'll try. I don't know much about the Bible, but I know one thing. God loves you so much that he sent his Son to pay for all the wrong things you ever did. And me too, and everybody that's willing to believe that's what He did. He wants you to believe that."

"But how can I know he's real, Johnny? How?"

Johnny looked down at the face of his friend. A picture came into his mind. "Gerald, do you remember that time we were out on the boat in the middle of the lake and that cloud formed up over the mountains? It was..."

"Circular, right Johnny? That incredible cloud that looked like a spinning top?"

"Yeah, and remember what happened?"

Gerald closed his eyes. "The sun was going down and each level of the cloud turned a different color; gold, orange, pink, blue, indigo, and then above that, the stars."

"And while we watched..."

"The moon came out, and the lake lit up like a thousand candles shining in fractured glass."

"And the breeze died..."

Gerald smiled. "And then the lake was smooth as glass, with the cloud and the moon and the stars all doubled up like in a mirror... Amazing, just amazing."

"Gerald, do you think that kind of beauty just happens... on its own?"

"No... It couldn't. It has to be..."

"...Somebody making it happen. Someone who wants us to see that He made a beautiful world for all of us to live in—a world our sin and our rebellion has totally screwed up. But he keeps trying to show us what He made. And if we see it, I mean really see it, that's how we know he's real."

"So, he's always ready to let us see..."

"Yeah, Gerald. He's always there, waiting for us to see his hands at work in the world He created. And I think... if we see Him in his creation, then we see Him."

Gerald sighed. "You're right, Johnny. Nothing could be that beautiful, unless somebody made it."

"And He wants you to be with Him, forever, Gerald. In the heart of all that beauty."

"Forever?"

"Yeah, Gerald."

"I want that, Johnny. I don't want to die without it..."

"Hang in there, Buddy. We'll get you home. We can talk about it then. When you're home."

There was a long silence.

Then, Gerald's eyes opened wide and then an amazed look came into them. "I don't think I'm going home, Johnny—at least not back to Sandpoint." Gerald gasped and the next words were spoken through a bloody froth. "I think... I think I'm nearly there already, Johnny. Nearly home..." Gerald stared into the dark beyond Johnny and a look of wonder came over his face. "I see the cloud, Johnny, I see the beautiful cloud... He's waiting..." His eyes focused on Johnny for just a moment and his hand squeezed

Johnny's hard... so hard. "Tell my dad..." Gerald closed his eyes. He whispered, so soft that Johnny had to bend down. "So long, buddy. I'll see you when I see you..."

Gerald took one last shuddering breath and then Johnny felt the pressure of Gerald's hand relax.

"Gerald? Gerald?"

A hand touched Johnny's shoulder. He looked up. Bud was standing there. He had that smile on his face that Johnny knew so well. The sad smile that said 'another one gone and I can't help.'

Johnny looked down at his friend. And then he was crying.

16

SUGAR LOAF AND CHOCOLATE DROP
BUD, THE CORPSMAN

One thing I learned about Jap tactics from one island to the next—there will always be a counterattack.

And it will happen when you think you have a good part of the military situation sewn up.

So, it was predictable. Not so predictable we were fully ready for them, though.

But I had a special kit set aside I never touched. A big one. So I'd have what I needed when there was the inevitable banzai assault. Lots of morphine. Lots of dried plasma. Lots of clean water to mix it with and make it viable. Lots of pressure bandages. Lots of gauze. No one dipped into that kit. No matter how bad the fighting got. Because no matter how bad it got, the worst was yet to come.

That's what I'd learned since Guadalcanal.

And it came at the beginning of May like a tidal wave.

Thousands of the Japs slammed into our lines, broke through, and swept everything before them—Marines, GIs, armor, artillery. It was all overrun.

We had to fight with our fists, our nails, our boots, knives, pistols, geez, whatever we could grab, like stones, and rocks, and dead palm branches, the biggest you could lift and swing. They swarmed over our position, knocked me down, tried to use the bayonet. I killed one of them with the surgical scissors in my hand. The other I strangled with my bare hands till he stopped thrashing and gagging. I hated it.

But I hated it afterwards. At the moment I killed, I wanted to live. I wanted to help our wounded. Not just the squad. Not just Martens' Men, Martens' Mavericks. The entire unit they had attached us to. So, I killed in a blind panic as they roared through us and moved on, yelling their battle cries. Another Jap would have got me. I never saw him coming, but I heard the struggle behind me as I bent over a Marine shot in the chest. I glanced back and Johnny was gutting a Jap with his Ka-Bar, gutting him like a fish. I didn't feel a dang thing watching it. It was 1945, not 1942. I'd seen it all. I was just glad the Jap was dead, not me. However Johnny went about it didn't matter to me. No way of death was cleaner or more noble than another.

People say it was all a blur when they go through something that is harsh and that happens too fast. That was sometimes true for me, sometimes not. I held onto isolated images of violence, as if everything had stopped, and focused on that one moment of death—Billy smashing his canteen into a Jap's face over and over again, until his canteen was bent out of shape, and the Jap a mess and dead. Yet all around that image, it's just a river of bits and pieces swirling past, and I can't make out anything. The smells are there of burnt gunpowder, the stink of explosives, the coppery metallic odor of blood, the war reek no one talks about that comes from men defecating and urinating in death, everything loosening as they come to an end that began in their mother's womb. It should be a profound moment when a man passes. But there are few profound moments in combat of any kind, none when it is the most brutal of all, hand to hand. Then it is the biblical eye for an eye, tooth for a tooth.

I'd never wanted it, never wanted any of it. I'd thought it

would be so clean and neat, as if I'd be suturing in a white room in a white, pristine hospital building. And each island was worse than the one before. There were more casualties than the island before. Billy wanted to end Okinawa because then he reasoned all the fighting would end and the bombing of Tokyo and the other Jap cities would end too. But winning Okinawa promised nothing but more combat when we jumped into the surf on Japan's beaches. There would be no stopping the blood-letting.

The Japs punched through our area on the 3rd, a Thursday. Their assault wave ran out of gas on the weekend, Saturday the 5th. Then it was mopping up. Bodies were everywhere to bury. There was a short break, sure. But there were more bodies to come when the next battle started up. For me, it was always the same. I saved who I could. Let the others go in pain or peace. Left it in God's hands as I worked against the clock of death. Had to leave it there.

I had scrounged a map. It was rough, but it turned out later to be pretty accurate at assessing what the Japs had done. They'd concentrated their firepower in the south, which we'd already discovered, and strung a fortified line between Naha on the west coast, right through Shuri, an important objective, and on into Yonabura on the east coast. Shuri was the heart of their defense. We had to crack it.

I sat and smoked through a pack of Chesterfields when I heard they'd hooked us up with the 1st and 6th Marine Divisions. The skinny was we were going for Shuri. The beast.

But we couldn't do that till we cleared the approaches. I don't know. I had a premonition or something, a tap on my shoulder from God—it was going to be a rough go.

It wasn't like we hadn't had a hundred rough goes already since we'd floated away from California so many years ago. We'd crisscrossed hell times past counting and watched men die and die and die till we couldn't see it or feel it anymore. Blood was nothing. Heads without bodies, legs without a man, faces scorched to black by flamethrowers. It didn't matter to anyone.

Not even those whose first battle was Okinawa. If they were still alive on May 6th, 7th or 8th, their hearts were rock, their faces stone. They'd puked up their guts at the horror enough times, cried tears for the dead when no one could see, screamed they were losing their minds and their humanity with screams no one ever heard except God. Now they just went into combat like the rest of us who had been at war all of our lives. Shoot, strike with the rifle butt, plunge the knife in deep, punch with the first, smash skulls with a rock, choke out life with two hands that were scraped and nicked and split open. How did that poem by Tennyson put it? *That which we are, we are.*

I said it out loud. A prayer, a defiance, a fist shaken in the face of death, and Imperial Japan, and their stinking Rising Sun. *One equal temper of heroic hearts, made weak by time and fate, but strong in will to strive, to seek, to find, and not to yield.* We were going to take Shuri, we were going to take Okinawa, if we had to take Japan we would take that too, and end it. I would save as many bullet-riddled bodies as I could. And we would not yield.

We attacked a small hill guarding Shuri on May 12. No bugles, never any bugles, no flags waving, no swords. Just us with the 1st and 6th Marine Divisions. As it turned out, more with the 6th than the 1st as the fight got hotter. I immediately thought of Tarawa. Pillboxes covered other pillboxes on the hill. Nambus covered other Nambus. Hidden mortars. Hidden machine-gun nests blistered lethal crossfires with other hidden machine-gun nests. Caves everywhere, some you could see, most were camouflaged with jungle growth. The bodies fell.

Marines called it Sugar Loaf Hill. Who names these places of slaughter? Some committee safely tucked away in New Jersey? I found out later it was a lieutenant colonel named Woodhouse. The Japs called it Grinding Bowl Hill because to them it was like a *Suribachi* bowl, the kind they used in their kitchens to grind up food, like our mortar and pestle. Only the *Suribachi* bowl was upside down. And just fifty feet high. But for the casualties we took, it might have been five thousand.

I had my big bag restocked for the push into Suri. I needed everything and had to be resupplied constantly. Me and the other corpsmen would get a hundred bodies in fifteen minutes when the grunts went after Sugar Loaf. Into the middle of this melee pops Johnny Strange. Johnny, who would stay in a fight even with a Jap bayonet stuck in his skull. A nasty chunk of shrapnel pierced right through his trigger hand.

"Just pull it out and dope it, Bud," he growled, cigarette dangling out of one corner of his mouth as if was a war model for LIFE magazine, "and gimme something for the friggin' pain. I gotta get back to the guys. We're embedded with a couple of companies of the 29th Marines. We're in it thick. They need my BAR. It's a helluva fight, Bud. Bullets as thick as windshield bugs. Guys dropping on every side of me. Blood and brains all over. You'd think I'd seen it all, but I haven't."

Once I'd pulled the shrapnel out, a four-inch chunk, razor sharp, dosed the wound and gauzed it with a pad, he bared his shoulder for the syrette of morphine and was gone, smacking a fresh mag into his Browning as he ran. I barely had a moment to watch him before stretcher bearers brought in a sergeant with an open skull. I could see his brains. He was smoking a cigar and looked at me with a grin. "Something new, right, Doc?"

It reminded me of spinning tires in a slick of mud. We could not get over that hill. Marines charged up that mound and rolled down it again, shot to pieces. On the 14th, Monday morning, they shipped the squad out to help platoons battling nearby on what they called Chocolate Drop Hill. Everyone was hungry for sugar, I guess. It was only another mound, but it was cross-stitched with machine-gun nests, just like Sugar Loaf. We spun our tires there too. Out of the frying pan and into the fire.

Our squad was used to beef up assaults because we'd kind of

grown into a heavy weapons platoon. We had the Brownings that
Johnny and Player minced Japs with. We had a fifty-caliber
machine gun now, a Ma Deuce, as well as a thirty. Two
flamethrowers. And Bricks was humping an 81-millimeter mortar
with three pups they'd just put ashore—one had the bombs for
the mortar, another lugged the plate, the third hauled the tube
and loaded it up for firing.

"I can't nursemaid 'em," Bricks would growl. "They gotta
watch out for themselves. This ain't no horse and pony show."

So, with all that firepower in a fast-on-our-feet squad, we
were in high demand to shore up platoons and companies
depleted by heavy casualties. Later on, I read we took over twelve
thousand dead on that island. Too much, Lord God, too much
and too many. That's why we were where we were. There were so
many holes to fill to win the fight on Okinawa.

Chocolate Drop was a butcher's shop. A company would go
up the slopes, get cut down by Jap fire, withdraw, another
company would take its place. I didn't stay at the tent or collec-
tion point like I did at Sugar Loaf. I went up with Billy and
Johnny and the squad. I had my teams of stretcher bearers. Hot as
the fire was, this was a better place to be. I could save more lives.
War took them. I took them back. As many as I could. An old
story. A story without a final page.

17

RAISING THE DEAD
BILLY MARTENS

It rained most of the time. There were some days and hours of sunshine. Now, in the middle of May, it was raining much more. The heavens had opened.

Billy gave up trying to light a cigarette as torrents poured from the sky. He guessed the time had come to head up Chocolate Drop Hill one more time. He got up into a crouch the moment the company they were embedded with rose at their captain's command. Jap machine guns immediately opened up and cut the captain in half. The company surged up the hill, regardless. Billy joined them, waving his squad forward. "Let's go!"

The squad slipped and fell in the muck, stumbling over bodies of dead Marines, broken M-1 rifles, abandoned flame throwers, boots, canteens, over severed limbs and decapitated heads still crammed in their helmets. The slope was a quagmire of mud and rotting men and maggots and rivers of rainwater that sluiced down to the bottom of the small hill and formed pools. Despite the nightmare wreckage of men's lives underfoot, Billy was sure they would swarm the top of the hill this time. But accurate sniper and machine gun fire and pinpoint mortar bursts denied the summit to the assault forces yet again. He had to yell for his squad to pull back, as the company also withdrew, leaving dead and wounded behind.

Corpsmen ran up to survivors who were smothered in mud and slime and streams of blood, stretching forth their hands as they cried out among the corpses. Jap gunfire cut the corpsmen down. Billy seethed: "Dammit! Martens' Men on me! Hose those Jap SOBs! Cover our corpsmen! Cover Bud! On me! On me! Fire till you run dry! Gyprock, come on! Get your thirty on target! Swenson, Jambert! Make that big fifty bite! Grenades! Bolo, you have an arm like a Red Sox pitcher! Throw 'em in! Marines, give your pineapples to Bolo! Now! Not next week!"

The hammering of the fifty and the thirty on either side of him made Billy's ears ring. He ignored it, trading his Thompson submachine gun for the scoped M-1 slung over his back, kneeling in the mudslide of bones and bodies beneath him and picking off Jap heads whenever they popped. Explosions from the grenades Bolo was hurling spun broken bodies and broken guns into the air. Few of the grenades fell short. Two companies charged up the hill, shooting from the hip, passing Billy's squad and clawing for the summit. They fell back, but not all the way down the hill. Not this time. They squirmed down among the mud and filth and blasted the enemy, refusing to withdraw.

"Are we heading back down, Sarge?" asked one of the new men, who worked with Bricks on a flamethrower. "The bullets are getting pretty thick."

Billy finally got a Camel lit. "You asking me this for yourself, or did Bricks put you up to it?"

"No, Sarge, not Bricks, I just thought—"

"I'll do the thinking, private. Got it? We're not retreating this time. Get back on that flamethrower before I kick your ass from here to Tokyo. Tell Bricks we're charging in three, flamethrowers to the front. We'll cover you. Now get moving and act like a frickin' Marine."

Billy found a raw recruit he remembered was Mackenzie.

"Mack, get down and get me some dynamite. Scuttlebutt has the company using it to seal off the caves. Go. And bring someone back with you who knows how to use it without getting all of us blown to pieces."

He nodded. "You can count on me, Sarge. How soon do you want it?"

"I want it now."

The other companies rose and made for the top, shrugging off the hail of Jap bullets. Billy champed at the bit, waiting on the dynamite, but finally waved his men forward, taking them to the crest and ordering the flamethrowers to sweep the Jap positions and caves. Fire roared like a furnace and enveloped the hilltop. As soon as the flamethrowers stopped, Marine sappers moved in with sticks of dynamite and told everyone to fall back. The hill exploded in black and orange, like film Billy had seen of a volcano erupting.

Minutes later, Mackenzie arrived, panting, lugging a box of dynamite, with another grunt hauling a second box behind him. A sapper was with them. Under covering fire from the Marines, he placed his dynamite and cut it loose. Dozens of caves were buried in a towering cloud of ash and grit and black smoke. Marine heavy machine guns riddled the mounds of dirt and broken rock. Then Marine point men gingerly probed the hilltop and the rubble. A few shots rang out. There was a rattle of submachine gun fire and several cries. Then there was nothing.

Bolo returned with his blood-streaked machete in one hand and his Tommy gun in the other. "The only thing moving up there are the watches on the wrists of the Nip officers."

Billy glanced around him. "Flamethrowers! Scorch the caves that aren't sealed off. Johnny. Player, go with them. Cover them. The rest of you, sit tight."

The flamethrowers torched the caves again. Smoke rose. When Suds and Hendricks stopped burning, other platoons sent out a second wave of skirmishers to check things over. Billy watched them pick their way through the dismembered bodies and shattered rock and twisted machine gun barrels. They moved through the dark dynamite smoke like phantoms. A BAR snapped off several rounds. Another joined in, both cracking off shots together. The only sound after that was the sound of the smoke.

Billy looked around him. "Carlos."

He popped at Billy's elbow, face black with ash. "Yeah, Sarge."

"Get Black Bull Two. Tell him the Marines have Chocolate Drop."

"You bet."

Carlos called it in. "This is Green Fox Five. The hill is secured. Repeat. The Marines have Chocolate Drop Hill. Over."

Black Bull Two rumbled back. "I will seek confirmation, Green Fox Five." It was Krazits. "Stand by."

Billy lit two cigarettes and gave one to Carlos.

The radio crackled.

"This is Black Bull Two. Confirmed. Proceed to Sugar Loaf."

Billy snarled. "We've been to Sugar Loaf."

Carlos nodded. "This is Green Fox Five. Repeat orders. We have been at Sugar Loaf. Over."

"This is Black Bull Two. I don't give a flying rat's behind if you've been to the Halls of Montezuma. You're going back to reinforce Marine units. The assault is ongoing. Get your butts to Sugar Loaf and report to Major Quarrels. That is all."

"Well, okay then." Billy leaned back, cigarette between his lips. "I don't feel like hollering anymore. Tell the boys we're taking two hours to clean weapons, replenish ammo, eat C-rations and brush our teeth. Then we're heading back to Sugar Loaf. But not until then. Maybe they can grab some shuteye. Okay?"

Carlos grinned. "Gotcha."

"And take the stupid battery out of your stupid radio."

"Done."

Billy closed his eyes. Listened to Marines moving around and calling to each other. Breathed in the dynamite smoke that lingered. Felt another rain squall break upon his face. It did not put out his Camel, so he kept smoking, nodding off, waking, puffing a few moments, then nodding off again. When the cigarette burned down to his lips, he spat it out and kept on sleeping. Finally, he looked at his watch and sat up. Johnny was just nearby, sitting on his helmet and drinking a hot coffee he'd scrounged from somewhere.

"Hey, Johnny," he said.

"Hey, Billy."

"As soon as you finish your coffee, we'll head on back to Sugar Loaf. You can get the boys together."

Johnny nodded. "You know it won't end after Sugar Loaf."

"Or Okinawa. Yeah, buddy. I know."

The fighting ended at Chocolate Drop on the 16th. But the battle continued at Sugar Loaf until May 18th. It was the same sort of fighting it had been at the beginning of the assault days before and the same as the battle on Chocolate Drop. Small hill, hundreds of caves, hidden machines-gun nests and vicious patterns of crossfire that shattered Marine attacks again and again. Marines battled their way up the slope and were thrown back. Battled their way to the top and were thrown back again. They fought their way through a maelstrom of gunfire and Jap grenades and the swirling black, red and orange of flamethrower hellfire.

"Carlos!" Billy snapped on Thursday morning. "Tell them to hump more ammo up here. We're almost out. Thirty, fifty, thirty-aught-six, forty-five for the Thompsons, a bushel of grenades too. Carlos! Where the hell are you?"

Mackenzie was at his elbow. "He took a slug to the head, Sarge. They riddled the radio. I'll go down and get them to hump up what we need."

"Go, Mackenzie."

Billy squinted at the hilltop. Marines were lunging up there again. "Now there's some brave men," he muttered. "What's happened with the fifty? Fifty! Cover those Marines at the crest!"

Nothing happened. The thirty was chattering. But not the Ma Deuce, the M2 fifty caliber gun.

"What's going on over there, people?" Billy barked. "Let me hear the fifty! Swenson! Jambert! Now!"

Player ran to Billy's side in a crouch. "Fifty's gone, Sarge. Gun and operators are shot to rag dolls."

Billy lowered his head a moment and cursed. "I want the 81-millimeter mortar to blast the crap out of those caves. We hardly used the frickin' thing on Chocolate Drop."

"Sarge, every time they did, the crew was cut to the stalks."

"Get Bricks to lob the mortar bombs up there and grab whoever he needs to do it. Now, Player, now."

Player scrambled off.

A few minutes later, the first mortar bomb blasted the summit to pieces.

Then there was another and another.

Some of the ammo came. Billy yelled for his squad to grab what they needed. Then it was time to go.

"Up with the flamethrowers!" Billy yelled. "BAR men, cover them! We're heading for the top! Let's join the grunts there! Double time!"

Billy and his squad headed up the slope again, joining the other Marines. Jap bullets sliced through a fresh downpour of rain. Just Like Chocolate Drop, decaying bodies and skulls and worms were underfoot in the mud and the pools of water. Twice Billy slipped on Marine dead and fell. The second time he got up, he saw a Jap mortar blast the 81-millimeter crew to bits. He saw Bricks somersaulting through the air. He saw sheets of fire smother the hilltop. Then one of the flamethrower men was hit and exploded into a ball of orange and purple. Billy heard one short scream from the man. He couldn't remember his name and hated himself for it. Reynolds? Richardson? Rennick? What was it?

He ran again. "Let's go, let's go, let's go!"

The fighting ended on Friday.

Billy stood among the flames and dynamited caves and rubble, the mounds of black smoke that reeked of fuel and heat and burnt skin and hair. Then he headed down the hill. His men followed him. Some Marine was putting up a flag in the scorched dirt. Billy ignored him.

Bud watched them come from his tent. He looked up from a Marine whose stomach he had just finished suturing. He recognized Billy's face first. Then Johnny's. Bolo. Player. Gyprock. He squinted through the rain.

"Where are the others, Billy?" he asked.

Billy walked past him into the tent. "This is it."

"It? But where are Bricks and Carlos and Jesus and—"

Billy snapped. "Didn't you hear me? I said this is it. Don't ask me again. I don't walk on water, I don't raise the dead."

Billy sat in the far corner of the tent. There was a small pile of arms and legs and feet and hands there. He barely looked at them. He tugged off his helmet. His hair was matted with rainwater, sweat, and streaks of dark blood. A cigarette went into his mouth. He didn't smoke it. Just let it sit there between his lips. Everyone left him alone.

The battle for Okinawa stopped on Friday, June 22.

Billy was well aware the B29s were still flying from Saipan and that an amphibious assault on Japan was next.

One quiet morning, he looked out over the ocean from a hilltop.

"The last enemy to be destroyed is death," he said out loud to no one, quoting the Bible. "Dear God, when does that happen?"

18

THE BELLS OF SHURI
JOHNNY STRANGE

WELL... IT WAS OVER.

From Love Day, 1945, when they clawed their way up from Mintago Beach, to June 22, when the brass declared Okinawa secured, Martens' Mavericks crawled, inched, crept, ran and scrambled through the caves, cliffs, and gorges of Okinawa. Every inch they took was through knee deep mud, pouring rain, perfectly registered enemy artillery, hidden gun emplacements, grenade showers and mortar barrages. They left behind 100,000 dead Japs and maybe 20,000 more sealed up in caves and tombs, along with 7,000 Army and Marine dead and 5,000 Navy. The hills were alive with the reek of un-fetched corpses, and squads of men were searching the boondocks for any sign of the 10,000 missing Americans, wounded or dead.

Johnny Strange was a tough, battle-hardened, killer Marine, but the things he had seen on Okinawa had left him silent, moody, morose. He tried writing to Marjean, but the gut-wrench inside him was so deep he couldn't even scratch the surface.

Maybe someday I'll be able to tell you... but not today...

So, the letter he was trying to write was easy-to-read, life in camp, what Billy and Bud were doing kind of stuff...

Nothing to write home about...

Johnny laughed, a quiet chuckle. Billy walked in.

"You're scarin' me, Strange. Sitting in your tent, staring at a half-finished letter, and talking to yourself."

Johnny looked up. "Did I say that out loud?"

"Didn't have to. I know what you're thinking."

"Now you're scaring me, Sniper."

"Well, finish it up Johnny Boy, we're going to do body round up. We got seven to ten thousand missing guys out in them thar hills that need to be found, so saddle up."

Bud came in. "They found Ushijima, and Cho, too."

"Dead?"

"Yeah, as a doornail. Looks like they did the ol' gut slice and then some helpful aide whacked off their heads."

Johnny shrugged. "Good. The more of these crazy nips we send to their ancestors, the better off this planet will be."

"Yeah, well, you're right about the ones with guns." Billy took a drag. "I just feel bad for the civilians who are getting burned to a crisp in Tokyo by that slime-bag, Chuck Vincent."

"Doesn't have anything to do with Cham, right?"

Billy came closer. Johnny could see he was wound up tight. "I'll thank you to keep your trap shut about Cham."

Johnny shook his head. "Sure, Sniper. Semper Fi."

Billy got very close, reached over toward Johnny, and clenched his fist. Johnny just stared at him. "Listen, Sniper, you may be a crack shot, but I was All-New Zealand Middleweight Champion. I can take you easy, so just settle down. I didn't mean anything by it."

Billy's fist slowly unclenched and instead he took the pack of Camels out of Johnny's t-shirt pocket. "Yeah, I know, Strange. I just wanted one of these."

Johnny took one out too and lit Billy's with his Zippo. "This isn't a gentleman's war, Billy. We aren't lining up in ranks and going at each other and when one guy loses, he hands over his sword and everybody goes home. This is all or nothing. If the Japs were in our position, they would burn down Montana, Idaho, Washington, and the entire west coast. You know that. You came into this fight knowing that. So, what is all this crap about the poor civilians?"

Billy started to say something, but Johnny kept going.

"When we go into Japan, every one of those civilians you're crying about will have a gun or a shovel or a stick or their hands and they will stab, shoot, gut, or burn every man with a U.S. uniform they find. And if the Empire was on top in this war—if we had lost on Cactus—that same group of poor civilians would be in uniforms, marching through our streets, raping our women, killing our men, and making slaves of the rest." He put a finger in Billy's face. "You frickin' know that."

Billy sagged down on the cot and took a deep drag. "Yeah, I know, but..."

"You're still asking the wrong questions, Billy." Bud pulled out one of his ubiquitous Chesterfields and lit up.

"What do you mean by that, Corpsman?"

"When I first met you, Billy Martens, all you could talk about was the rape of Nanking and the atrocities the Japs committed in Manchuria. Then we watched them march through the Philippines and the Dutch East Indies. When they captured our boys on Bataan and Corregidor, they death-marched them to prison camps. If the guys faltered or fell out, they shot them where they lay. Then they worked them and starved them to death. If we are killing several thousand Japs a day, it's because they paid their money and they took their choice. They started this scrap, and they woke up a giant when they bombed Pearl. What were they thinking? They knew we'd come after them—all of them—with everything we had. So, I don't know what your problem is."

Billy looked up. He had a cornered look in his eyes. "I know, Bud, I know. But somehow, somewhere, this killing has got to stop."

Johnny shook his head. "It will not stop until the mighty armies and navies of the Empire of Japan are crushed into dust. That's all they understand. The day the Emperor tells them to stand down because he knows his entire country is going up in fire and smoke, that's the day when the killing stops. And what we know is, between the end of this bloody battle on Okinawa and the day he gives that imperial command, there stands a whole bureaucracy controlled by the Army. They are maniac, Bushido Samurais, and they would rather die than surrender—as proven by the hundreds of headless, gutless, armless bodies we've been digging out of caves and crevices. Men who shot themselves, stabbed themselves or blew themselves up rather than give up."

Billy sighed. "So, I guess we just keep killing them until they are all gone or Hirohito stands down, right?"

Bud nodded. "Sad, but true, Billy-boy. Sad, but true."

———

THEY HEADED TOWARD SHURI. The Japs had defended the place with animal ferocity, but now the historical seat of the Okinawan kings was a pile of rubble. Johnny reflected on the preceding two months as they walked along the road leading to the castle.

They had better leaders than we thought they did. There were more of them than we knew. The terrain was horrendous and heavily fortified, and we were thousands of miles from home. A real SNAFU!

Shuri Castle stood on a high hill of ground on the south edge of Shuri town. The walls were coral block twenty feet thick at the base and forty feet high, and they towered all around a large central area. Now, after the Battleship Mississippi shelled the place for three days with fourteen-and sixteen-inch shells, the massive ramparts remained intact in only a few places. When they walked in, they met some Army guys from the 77th Division.

The doggies were busy cleaning up and clearing the rubble. An Army captain walked up to Billy.

"These your boys?"

Billy nodded.

"Can you give us a hand? We just uncovered the main entrance to the underground headquarters. We are sending some guys in and we could use your firepower, in case there are any Japs left."

Billy nodded. "Lead the way, Captain."

A group of men gathered around an opening in the ground. A ramp slanted down into the darkness. The opening was wide enough to walk through and Billy's squad filed in one by one after the 77th guys. Inside, the tunnel widened until it was about eight feet across and six feet high and ran down into the darkness. Soldiers with flashlights walked along the walls looking for side entrances and branch tunnels.

Bud looked around at the solid rock and coral walls of the tunnel and shook his head. "Holy cow, this place is a real fortress."

The Army Captain responded. "When we took Conical Hill, the Japs knew they were done at Shuri—we had cracked their defensive wall and it was only a matter of time until we took their headquarters. So they fled. They started slipping out from the night of May 26 to the end of the month. When we got here, there were only a few dozen of them left. Most had headed south to the cliffs along the coast. But the ones who stayed were still defending these tunnels."

Johnny checked his mags. "Yeah, I got a buddy in the 1st Marines and he said that when they walked into the castle from the Naha side, that was all the further they could go. All the tunnel entrances were defended, and the gun emplacements around three sides of the castle kept them pinned in here for about three days."

The captain lit a smoke. "We had been here about four days

when we started hearing explosions under the castle. We figured the ones who stayed behind were blowing themselves up with grenades."

A voice from ahead cut through the darkness. "Up here, Captain."

They moved forward cautiously and as they did, they noticed a foul stench. Around a corner in the tunnel they came up with the point men. One of them was leaning against a wall, throwing up. In the middle of the passage was a pile of human parts. Heads, arms, legs, guts, all shredded. The pile formed a rough circle and the remains of an ammo box was in the center of the pile.

The captain took off his helmet and wiped his forehead with the back of his hand. "Holy Mother of God."

The guy who had been on point leaned on his rifle. "Looks like the Japs gathered around this box full of grenades holding hands, and somebody tossed in a grenade and blew the bunch of'em to hell."

Johnny spit. "Good place for'em."

They moved on. They spent about three hours going through the tunnels. The Japanese had done an incredible job. Some of the tunnels went down three stories. There were even electric elevators big enough to hold a squad of riflemen. Many of them opened out onto the hillsides below and around the castle. Burned and blown up machine-gun, mortars and even anti-tank guns littered the ground at the entrance to these caves.

Johnny walked over to look at the burned remains of a mortar operator. He kicked it with his foot, but the man was definitely dead. "Our guys had to climb up here and throw satchel charges inside. I heard about one guy who brought a flame throwing tank up top and then hooked up a two-hundred-foot hose. Then he climbed down here and put fire into the places our guns couldn't get to."

Billy remained silent, but Johnny could tell the whole deal was getting to him. "We done here, Captain?"

The captain nodded. "Yeah. Looks like they are all gone. Thanks for your help fellas. See ya around."

Billy and his squad headed for the fresh air. When they climbed out, they found a bunch of guys hauling two giant bells out of the rubble. Shell fire had scarred and dented them. One was about five feet high and the other about three-and -a-half. The bells had oriental characters inscribed on them.

Billy took a look. There were a bunch of guys standing around and Billy asked them, "What does it say?"

Most of the guys shrugged, but out of the group stepped a small oriental man. He looked like a Japanese, but there was something different about him. He bowed.

"My name is Takazato Iki. I am Okinawan. I can read these words. He brushed away some of the debris and dust and began.

"In the Southern Seas lie the magic islands of the Ryukyu Kingdom, serene and beautiful. The Kingdom of Ryukyu embraces the most excellent qualities of the three Han states of Korea and the traditions of the Mings of China. Though these Islands are separated from these nations by distance, still the Kingdom of Ryukyu is as close to them as lips to teeth."

He stopped for a moment and wiped away more of the dirt. Then he went on. "Behold! What is a bell? A bell is that which sounds far, wide, and high. It is a rare instrument of the Buddhist monk, which brings order to the oftentimes chaotic life of the listener. At dawn, it breaks the long stillness of the night and guards against the torpidity of sleep..."

"It will always ring on time, tolling the approach of darkness and the hour of dawn. It will startle the indolent into productive activity that will restore honor to their names."

"And how will the bell sound? It will echo far and wide, like a peal of thunder but with utmost purity. And evil men, hearing the bell... will be saved."

Billy stared at the little man for a long time and then he picked up a piece of timber lying near and struck the bell... hard. The bronze metal reverberated with a deep tone and rang through the courtyard.

Billy threw the stick down and looked at his friends. "I hope those bastards in Tokyo heard that."

He walked away.

II

JAPAN

19

THE END OF ALL THINGS
BUD, THE CORPSMAN

WITHIN A WEEK AFTER WE SECURED OKINAWA, MARTENS'
Mavericks were winging their way back to Saipan. After the hell-
hole we found when we invaded the enemy's private real estate,
Saipan almost felt like home There are nice bars where a
converted non-alcoholic Menno can drink the blues away—very
handy to blank out the thoughts of what was going to happen
when they put us ashore at Tokyo Bay. Of course, everyone in the
bar had all the answers. A lot of theories and a lot of hogwash.
Billy and Johnny and I had some long late-night discussions over
endless rounds of Pabst that usually ended up with Billy crying in
his beer about the children of Japan, and Johnny cursing the
entire slant-eyed race to hell. Didn't solve anything, really, and
mostly what we got out of those discussions was a royal headache
the next morning.

What we knew was that the minute we set foot on the sacred
soil of Japan, there would be more dying than had been seen in
all the wars of history. The Japs had proved to the U.S. military
exactly where they stood on that subject when we invaded Iwo
and on Okinawa. Before then, we were just stripping their stolen

empire. Now we were getting up close and personal with every-thing the Japs held dear. Oh, we were in for it all right, big time.

What we didn't know was that while we were dying on Saipan and Okinawa and Iwo, out in the desert of Eastern Washington State they had a huge concrete building where a crazy little eye-talian guy named Fermi had kindled cosmic fire and they were force-feeding a big hunk of uranium metal a steady stream of neutrons. At the end of this conveyor belt from hell they were collecting tiny teaspoons full of the first man-made element on earth—Plutonium.

Nor did we know that this innocent-looking dust was, via the benefit of billions of dollars of research and development, being used to create the vital heart of a new bomb that was going to really shake up Hirohito and the rest of the madmen who had been working at their war of conquest since 1931.

So, with all this information completely hidden from those of us who had been bleeding and burning and dying—doing every-thing we could do to just keep from getting shot—the Brass back in the U.S. of A. was doing practice runs out at a place called Almogordo in New Mexico, and getting ready to unleash the heart of the sun on the Imperial war machine.

You know, you think that once they knew this thing would work, they would have just stood us down and sent a telegram to Tojo and the boys. A brief note to let them know that if they didn't cut the crap, their Island Kingdom was going to get turned into smooth, shiny glass for the next three thousand years. Would have saved a lot of good men dying in the caves and mud of Okinawa and Iwo.

Meanwhile you got a lot of really uptight, cranky, worried Gyrenes and Doggies practicing beach landings and drinking themselves stupid every night to get away from the fear.

Fear. It was like a stink coming out of every tent. Like a crap game where you throw seven after seven and your pile is building into a real bankroll and then just when you think you got it made

—snake-eyes. Lots of us had been on Cactus, Helen, and Saipan. A lot of the 1st Div had survived Peleliu—a genuine fouled-up battle that was just stupid. They promised the Marines four days of vacation and gave them two months of hell.

How many times can you stand up on a hill with four thousand Japs coming straight at you and your buddies going down on all sides and you come out clean as a whistle? How many times can you wade through a bloody lagoon and the guy on either side of you gets their head carried away by a 50-caliber shell while you waltz on in and take a nap under the sea-wall? How many times can you run up a hill with your friends getting hammered by mortar shells and machine-guns and all you got was dirty boots?

I mean, Billy and Johnny and I knew the big dice in the sky were going to roll double-ones for a lot of guys on the sands of Tokyo bay and what were the odds it wouldn't be us? I'm telling you, this kind of thinking is not conducive to a happy state of mind. So, in the days between July and August, 1945, there were a lot of fistfights, a lot of guys visiting the sky-pilots and a tanker-load of beer and spirits consumed.

The Germans had surrendered in May, thirty-five days into the fight on Okinawa, and you know what? It didn't mean nothing to the guys who were still bleeding and dying six thousand miles away in the tombs. We couldn't even celebrate. It was like that war was on a different planet. The Germans may have been tough, but when the going got hard, and they got backed into an inescapable corner, at least the Gerrys had the smarts to "hande hoch," drop their guns and goosestep into the camps by the thousands, like the obedient little Nazis they were.

But the Japs? Jesus, Mary and Joseph, what is with these people?

So August 6, 1945, was just another rotten day on Saipan. Even though the sun was shining and the sky was cloudless, nobody was looking up. People were on their knees, or staring into a bottle, or losing themselves in the arms of some anonymous B-Girl in a tent somewhere. No one noticed the single B-29 that took off from Tinian, followed by a gaggle of fighters. No one noticed the plane flash in the sun, circle once and then head due-north. No one noticed, and no one cared.

But I'll tell you this. At the end of that day, many people in Japan cared. The ones who turned into toast or shadows on a wall didn't care of course, but the ones who lived through the sun lighting up twenty-five hundred feet over their heads and melting their eyeballs in their heads, or the wind of a thousand tornados blowing them into the next valley, or the radiation blast that stripped the skin from their bodies and left it hanging in sheets from their bones, or the firestorm that swept through their city, they cared.

The ones who staggered through the streets screaming for water, they cared. The ones who had to swim through a raft of corpses to get across the river, they cared. The ones who desperately dug through the rubble trying to find the family that didn't exist because they had vaporized and were now just atoms drifting on the summer breeze, they cared.

When you look at it, Billy and Johnny were both right. How could one human being do such a thing to another? How could people nonchalantly drop a bomb that killed two hundred thousand people in an instant? But how could we not, knowing that if we sent our boys ashore on the beaches of Japan, millions of young American and Japanese men would die, frickin' millions?

Somebody had to make the call, weigh the pros, weigh the cons. And somebody did, and three days later they dropped another one and that was that. Except for a little turmoil from some diehards in the Japanese military, the war was over. The war was over!

Six days after Nagasaki, Hirohito made a formal announcement and the Japanese military got the word. You're done. Knock it off.

Well, from what we heard later, there was a virtual orgy of suicides. All the big boys, all the war-machine pushers, they all took the coward's way out and started shooting, stabbing and poisoning themselves. I guess they knew that the hangman's noose was on the bill for a lot of them; but I will never, if I live a hundred years, be able to figure out the Japanese.

Were we happy? Damn straight. You never saw a happier bunch of guys. Kinda like Abraham when he's got the knife all the way back for the downstroke into his son Isaac's heart and God says, "Wait. You're good. I know you love me. Put the knife away."

And if you think we were hitting the booze before, you should have seen those guys on Saipan on August 15. Party-central. And in the midst of it, Crandall calls me in and tells me I'm going home and I'm on the phone to Kalasia and asking her to come to Ritzville and marry me and she says yes. And I'm done, I think...

<hr>

So I'm in Ritzville and I'm ten days away from Kalasia landing at the Spokane airport and I get the call. When I answered the phone, I was not expecting Crandall. The voice was scratchy, so I knew he was still overseas.

"Hey, Bud, whaddaya know?"

That question was not as easy to answer as it had been in 1940. In 1940, I was a know-nothing honyock from Ritzville, Washington, who had no plans for my life except to keep going to my dad's Mennonite church and maybe get a job selling shoes downtown. For me, there was no world beyond the dry, sunbaked hills around my little town. The closest big city was Spokane, and I had only been there a few times. Now, it was 1945, and I was just coming to the surface after a deep dive into the depths of hell. But on my way there and back, I found treasure. Kalasia, my Tongan princess, who was coming to America to marry me. Johnny Strange and Billy Martens, more than comrades in arms.

There in the Pacific, we learned a lot about death. But we also learned about living. Living was the first ray of sunlight on a crystal morning. Living was shared laughter in a forward foxhole. Living was the embrace of a mermaid in azure waters. Living was coming back to Ritzville and touching the tears on my mom's wrinkled brown face—wrinkled and brown like the hills of home. Living was walking in bare feet into a ripening wheat field—walking so far out that the wheat and the sky were all there was—the blue coming down to touch the upraised gold, nothing but blue and gold. Living was digging my feet into the earth and standing for a long time, like a planted tree.

Yes, we learned to die, and we learned to live out there in the Pacific. And now I was home on leave and the war was, except for the sweating dreams, slipping past me like the telephone poles alongside the tracks when you ride the train out of Wellington New Zealand and you are in the middle of sea and sky and mountains and forests—just being there washes you clean—and once again your God seems closer and almost audible and the whispers you hear aren't the ghosts of the ones you left beneath the mud of Cactus or bobbing in the blue lagoon of Helen or laid in a simple grave on Saipan, or shredded in a cave on Okinawa, like Gerald King.

So, when the phone rang, and I heard Crandall's voice, it jolted me back there for just a moment and I had a horrible thought… maybe it wasn't over after all. Maybe the Japs hadn't surrendered. Maybe all the Japs we had killed had come back to life and were rushing toward us, Samurai swords glinting in the blood-red sun. Maybe we hadn't bombed them into submission. Maybe the whole rotten country had thrown the Emperor out and now beckoned to the Americans, saying, "Come and get us." But the thought passed and I was back in the land of the living.

"Not a lot, Captain, what's up? Where are you calling from?"

"I'm in Nagasaki. Look, Bud, I know you are getting ready to get married..."

"You are coming, right?"

"That depends on how long they keep us in Japan. Considering that, I have a favor to ask."

"Shoot, Captain."

"I got an important detail for you before you get hitched. It entails two things. See, there are Marine POWs still in Japan and they are digging them out of the camps where the Japs kept them. They need care, Bud, good care."

"What's that got to do with me, Captain?"

"The brass sent a Special Task Force, Bud. We need to be there for the Marines. They've asked me to head up a team in the force and I need a good corpsman with me. There's only one I would take, Bud. You're the best I've ever seen."

"I appreciate that, Captain. Thank you. But what's the other part of the detail?"

"This side is a little more hush-hush. The government is sending a medical team to check out the survivors of Hiroshima and Nagasaki. The scientists want a report so they can see how successful their little invention was, if you call that successful. Once we finish with the POWs, we'll join the research team. I need a corpsman with a heart, because the Japanese civilians we interview are going to be terrified. The war-lords that ran that country told them horrible stuff about Americans—like if we came, we would rape all the women and torture all the children."

Yeah, I knew that. One of my recurring dreams was of the Jap-birds of Saipan. The women holding little children in their arms as they leaped from the tops of the tall cliffs at the north end of the island. Women with gods that whispered death in their ears; women with no hope... and I watched as they floated down,

down, down, into the cruel arms of the rocks and the sea below, their hair and the white dresses lifting like wings, wings that could carry them to heaven and safety, wings of angels taking them far away across the ocean…

Yes, I knew about the fear and the lies.

"When do you need to know, Captain?"

"I need you here next week, Bud. And I'll need you for three months, minimum. Can you come?"

And so that's how I found myself on a plane headed for the one country in the entire world I never wanted to set foot in.

20

TORRI GATES

BILLY MARTENS

I took a long time making my way up the mountain.

I paused and looked out at the view every five or ten minutes.

The harbor front. The long stretch of water where ships came into port, including the ones that had brought in the 2nd Division Marines. Ships that now floated at anchor.

Again and again, my eyes fell on the devastation the plutonium bomb had wreaked on Nagasaki.

The skinny had it that the name of the bomb had been Fat Boy. The B29 Superfortress that dropped it was Bockscar, a plane I swore I'd seen at Tinian and Saipan.

I felt a stab in my heart when I first saw the port city.

Every morning I woke up in a classroom that served as a barracks for what was left of my crew and thought: *No, it was not that bad. It couldn't have been.*

Then I went outside and looked towards the center of the city.

The second or third day, I saw my father standing amidst the ruins, staring at me, hands in the pockets of his denim coveralls: *You see, son? You see? War. The devil's pleasure. You were part of it; you were part of his poison. How proud are you of your wartime exploits now? Make amends. The Lord has afforded you an opportunity I wouldn't.*

An older woman, I put her at sixty or sixty-five, came up to me each morning with a cup of tea. She brewed it over a small wood fire, selling it to Marines. There was, after all, plenty of rubble she could use for fuel. I gave her a dollar a week for the tea. Sometimes two. Then kept my eye on her, M1 Garand on my back, to be sure no one robbed her or threatened to take her cache of U.S. coins and bills. That was our job anyway. My squad policed the district. There was to be no tolerance for crime. Or revolt.

The possibility of revolt worried me the most. Americans were not welcome here. Not welcome anywhere in Japan. The shame of losing the war was too great. Marines had been disemboweled by katanas and had their throats slit in broad daylight and at night. At some point, the Emperor would have to intervene and end the insurrection and violence Jap officers were perpetuating. To them, Okinawa had not been the last battle. Japan was, and the war was ongoing. No bomb made by American demons would bring their Empire to an end. They would drive the white devils into the sea.

I did not have my rifle on his back as I hiked to the mountain's summit. I had my Colt pistol and a Ka-Bar knife on my web belt. I was in what we considered a safe and secure area. Shinto priests had made it clear to all their people this must be so, for they had several shrines on the mountain. Their wishes were respected and honored. It did not take more than an hour for me to reach the first shrine.

They had briefed me on all things Japanese, on etiquette and culture and the history of the island, as well as Shintoism and Buddhism. It had proved impossible to remember everything. But I knew what a Torri gate was. It separated the everyday world from the sacred. One stood before me now, the path I was walking taking me right to it. I wasn't sure what to do next.

Instinctively, I unbuckled my web belt and placed it off to the side with its firearm and knife.

Then I bowed and passed through the gate into the holy.

The path led to a building that I supposed was a shrine.

A man stood in front of me.

I had no idea where he had come from.

He wore a wide straw hat that made me think of an inverted Suribachi bowl, except it came to more of a peak.

"Are you a priest?" I asked the man. "A monk?"

The man said nothing.

I remembered to bring out the five one-dollar bills I'd tucked away.

I folded them over and handed them to the man.

The man bowed, and then I bowed.

The man indicated with his hand that I should walk on towards the wooden building.

I went inside.

Felt I should remove my boots and socks.

Padded through the building, not understanding what anything meant.

Eventually knelt and tried to pray.

Our Father, who art in heaven.

"But I need a God on earth, not just in heaven," I whispered.

I knelt a long time.

Then remembered I had been told there was more than one Torri gate.

I went outside, put on my socks and boots, and followed the path past the building.

I did not see the monk—I had decided to call him that—but after ten minutes I reached a second and larger Torri gate surrounded by tall trees. Some had been knocked flat and uprooted and I knew it would have been Fat Boy. The gate was nicked and scarred and partly crushed for the same reason. I saw the monk again just inside the gate. I bowed and walked through. The monk stepped aside and nodded that I should continue.

I removed my boots and socks and entered the building. It was larger than the first, just as the second gate was taller than the first gate.

I loved the smell of the wood. Was there another scent? Incense? Fire?

I knelt and sat on my heels. Prayed again. It seemed easier than trying to pray in the first building and a lot easier than praying down below in the dust and ashes and bones.

"But next time," I whispered, "next time, Lord willing, you'll bring someone across my path who knows Japanese and American, a guy who can explain everything up here to me. Or you'll give me a Shinto monk who can converse."

Still, it was enough just to be there and away from the death and the melted bodies, not all of which had been pulled free of the ruins. I did not move for an hour. Finally, I put my socks and boots back on, stopped and picked up my belt, and started down the mountain. I did not see the monk.

I spotted a knot of Marines and Japanese near the battered school that served as barracks for my squad. The lady that served me tea was in the middle of it, trying to explain something in a shrill voice. At her feet was a dead Japanese man. Young, maybe twenty. Someone had disemboweled him.

A katana had been unleashed on him. No knife or bayonet made a wide, slick cut like that. I had seen enough disemboweling from Guadalcanal to Japan. So had most other Marines. Military police were using an interpreter to make sense of what the lady was saying. They were swabbies, sailors in white, Shore Patrol, the ones who always policed the Marines because the Marines were U.S.N., which none of them liked being reminded of. I pushed in and saw a young Japanese woman guarded by two Marines. Her sudden beauty in the middle of this mess threw me back.

It was not regular run of the mill good looks, if any good looks were. She was stunning. Even more so because she was wearing a vividly colored kimono, navy set off with cherry blossoms. And at her waist was a *katana*, sheathed in a wooden scabbard or *saya*, also navy with cherry blossoms, along with the short sword that traditionally accompanied the *katana*, the *wakizashi*. The pairing was called a *daisho*. I knew that much.

She looked like a Samurai. Our eyes met for a moment. Hers were dark, fierce and impenetrable. Yet they lingered on me. A surge of heat burned through my blood and heart. What the hell? I see a beautiful woman in the carnage of Nagasaki and she overthrows me with one look from her eyes? But I could not pull away. She'd snared me without even trying. When she realized that, realized there was a struggle in me she caused, she smiled. The smile, I thought, was both attractive and full of the devil. She was used to having a powerful effect on men, and she enjoyed afflicting them with her powers.

"Well, all right," the sailor leading the police detail growled. "I have enough Marine Corps witnesses. It was self-defense. He beats up the old lady and is stealing her money. Before any Marine can intervene, this dame with the swords shows up and tries to stop him. He attacks her with a large knife, the one we picked up by his body. He slashes three or four times. Cuts her robe. She draws her sword, opens him up like a can of beans, wipes the blood off on his shirt and sheathes the sword. Then we find out she's the old lady's daughter. Okay, I'm done with this. No brig time for Miss Errol Flynn. But I can't have her waltzing all over Nagasaki, disemboweling men. She needs to surrender those swords."

When the interpreter explained this to both mother and daughter, their eyes flew wide in horror and the daughter's face quickly went from horror to fury. She clutched her swords, and I thought she was going to draw them and lop off both guards' heads at the same time. I felt the only thing that stopped her was the fact she'd have to flee and go into hiding and she didn't want to leave her mother. The interpretation of her words didn't surprise me. "These swords have been in our family for three hundred years. It would heap shame and disgrace on us if we gave them up. The gods would judge us most harshly. And those who took them would be cursed. NO!"

The Shore Patrol leader snapped his jaws as if he were biting off the head of a fish. "Honor! Shame! Banzai! No surrender! Hail the Emperor! I'm sick of it! Okay, you tell her, she makes sushi out of another guy and she loses the swords and her freedom! Now get her and her mother out of my sight! And you two Marines, get that body out of my sight too! Cripes, we should be back home in America by now!"

The young woman and her mother hurried off.

I shrugged, wandered to the war-torn building where they served up the grub, took my plate and sat with Johnny Strange, who'd already cleaned up his chow.

"What's this?" I asked.

Johnny had a pencil and paper on the table by his coffee. "Aww, trying to write a good letter home. I mean, a really good letter home the censors won't cut to pieces."

"You can tell her you love her and the kid."

"Yeah, that's about all I can tell her. Can't even describe the weather except to say it pours and then it's sunny. The humidity is like a gag down your throat. Can't even tell her I'm gonna take a trip to see Fujiyama. You going?"

"When?"

"Truck's leaving Saturday at 0700."

"What about guard duty?"

Johnny shrugged. "First twenty go to Fuji. The rest do the grunt work."

"I'll think about it."

"Don't think too long. Only five spots left." Johnny sipped from his mug. "Hey, you hear about that ruckus on the street?

Some crazy Nip gal cuts up her boyfriend or something with a sword?"

"Yeah. I heard about it. It wasn't her boyfriend. The guy was beating on her mother and stealing her money. You know the tea lady?"

"Sure."

"Her. That's who he was beating up. The sword girl was her daughter."

"No kidding. So, they let her off?"

"Self-defense. He pulled a knife on sword girl and she defended herself."

Johnny shook his head. "Walking around wearing a sword. Acting like she's some sort of samurai. Is there such a thing as a woman samurai?"

"No idea."

"Hedges said she wasn't half bad looking."

I lit up a cigarette as he finished my plate. "Never noticed."

21

PUNISH AND REFORM
JOHNNY STRANGE

I LOOKED UP AT THE BLUE SKY. AMERICAN AIRCRAFT BUZZED overhead and American troops were everywhere—which seemed surreal to me because I was in Nagasaki, Japan, on the island of Kyushu. I shook my head in wonder. After Okinawa, the Marines went back to Saipan and started training. Me and a million other fighting men knew what we were training for, and we honestly expected to train to the hilt, say our prayers, and then load onto the transports for the invasion that would result in most of us dying on the beaches of Japan.

The last months on Saipan had been very tense. Discipline was hard to maintain because men were either paralyzed with fear or wired up to the point of explosion. We all knew it would be a bloodbath when we hit the beaches of Japan. We all knew that every single Japanese on all four of their cruddy little islands would wait for us at those beaches, armed with guns, knives, swords, sticks, fingernails and rocks. Not a pretty picture.

Most of us stayed in our tents every night writing what we assumed would be our last letters home, or sat in bars drinking ourselves stupid to blank out the pictures springing into our minds every minute of every day—pictures of death, destruction, horror.

There were some who argued for peace negotiations, like Billy. He just wouldn't let it go and his constant harangue was wearing thin. It was August 6, 1945. The three of us Mennos sat together that night in our favorite establishment, about six beers in, and Billy started up again.

"We've got the little slant-eyes against the wall. Why don't we contact them and tell them we have more than enough guns and men and equipment to crush their little empire back to the stone age. We don't have to keep burning everything down, killing all those women and children..."

I just stared at Billy for a long time while he went on. Finally, I'd had enough. I slammed my fist down on the table. A great anger rose in me.

"Look, Billy, you're my friend, but I gotta tell you. I am so sick of you whining about the poor Japs. Those slant-eyed creeps have been killing my friends for the last three years. Blowing them to pieces, shooting their heads off, hacking them with swords. Dear Lord, Billy! Don't you remember the 'chutists they overran at Bloody Ridge and tortured to death while we all sat up on that hill and listened to our guys screaming? Did you forget about Nanking so easily, or the Death March, or Tarawa? These people are nuts, flat out nuts, and they have to be beaten so bad that most of their men are dead. If we try to negotiate peace now, they, in their supreme arrogance, will see it as a sign of weakness, and there will be those among them who will rise up and keep fighting." I took a pull on my beer. "I know you got a soft spot for the kids, but I gotta tell you, if you don't stop with this crap, I'm going to kick your butt."

Billy stood up. "Yeah, you and what army, Pretty Boy?"

Man, he couldn't have flicked a bigger switch. I came out of my chair and before Billy could even move, I planted a wicked left into his wind and then stretched him out with a right that came all the way from Tarawa.

As Billy struggled to get up, Bud jumped in between us. "Hey! You guys knock it off. Now is not the time to be fighting with each other. Billy, you are a complete jerk for calling him that, and Johnny, you seem to forget that your hands are lethal weapons. Now, back off."

Billy had gotten up and tried to get at me, but suddenly found himself in the steel grip of his very big friend. Bud looked Billy in the eye. "Don't mess with me, Gyrene." He turned to me. "Now you boys shake hands and apologize."

I looked at Billy, who was wiping a bloody lip. "I will, if he will."

Billy just glared at me and then turned and walked out of the bar.

THE NEXT AFTERNOON, Crandall called his platoon leaders into his office. He had been fighting alongside some of us since Guadalcanal.

"Sit down, men." Crandall cleared his throat. "Yesterday, a single B-29 piloted by Colonel Paul Tibbets, flew to the Island of Honshu and dropped a new weapon, an atomic bomb, on the city of Hiroshima. Initial reports say that the devastation in the city was enormous. When they detonated the bomb, the pilots reported a brilliant flash of light, followed by a gigantic shock-wave that almost blew their plane out of the sky. Reports from our observation planes say that the entire center of the city is leveled and still burning."

There was complete silence. Then I heard Billy say, "Dear God." Crandall stood. "Gentlemen, I think we may be close to the end. Dismissed."

We started filing out of the room. Crandall called out. "Strange, stay put for a minute."

I waited.

Crandall sat down at his desk. "I hear you and Sniper had a go-round the other night."

"Yeah, we did."

"You still friends?"

In my heart, I wondered a little but I put on a bold front. "Yeah, Captain. That won't change. But he's pretty pissed at me. Knowing Billy, it will take a while, but he'll come around."

"I heard you clocked him pretty good."

"He shouldn't have said what he said." I left it at that.

"Well, I'm going to give you boys time to cool off. I'm putting you in different platoons. I think things are going to change and this bomb is the difference maker. If those little slant-eyes don't get the message, we'll probably send another. Which means I'm pretty sure we'll be thinking about occupation instead of invasion."

A great surge of relief flowed through my guts. "You think so, Captain?"

"Pretty sure, Johnny. But I'm not just putting you in a different platoon to keep you guys apart. I'm going to need some tough guys leading all my shore patrol squads, guys I trust and know I can depend on. You've been a corporal way too long for a guy who's seen as much action as you have." Crandall reached in his desk. "These are yours, by order of Major General Leroy Hunt, Commanding General, 2nd Marine Division, USMC." He handed me two emblems—three golden chevrons stitched together— sergeant's stripes.

I took them. "Thank you, Sir."

Crandall grinned and came out from behind his desk. He took my hand in his. "Strange, we've been together a long time. It's been a total honor to serve with you, and I am glad that I'm going to be the one that sends you home to your wife and little boy. You'll be a platoon sergeant under Lieutenant Ryerson. Billy will be in Jacobs' platoon. That's all."

I turned to go.

"Oh, Johnny."

"Yes, Sir."

"I'd really hate to see you guys end this war badly. Do what you can to make up with Billy, okay? It's important to me... as a friend to both of you."

I nodded. "Okay, Captain. I'll give it a try."

Two days later, another B-29 dropped a bomb on the city of Nagasaki. Reports from the observers were the same—total destruction of the center of the city. Crandall was right. On August 15, the Emperor of Japan went on radio and told his people that he had decided to surrender unconditionally to the allied armies. Within three weeks, on September 2, 1945, MacArthur was in Japan and the official surrender took place on the deck of the Battleship Missouri in Tokyo harbor. The war was over.

Now I was part of the 2nd Division occupation forces stationed in the city of Nagasaki. Bud got shipped home and Billy was sulking in his tent most of the time. We came ashore on Sunday, September 23, in Nagasaki harbor. The Marines loaded off the transports and climbed into the same assortment of landing craft we used on Tarawa and Saipan and Okinawa. But this time there were no bullets killing rows of Marines wading through the surf. There were no accurately registered 75 mm guns hurling death in batches from the hills above the harbor. There were no machine-gun nests, concealed and waiting to dish out bloody destruction.

No, this time we rode up to the docks like Daddy Warbucks in a limousine. All around us, on the streets and on the housetops, curious Japanese people watched as the long-feared American devils marched onto the sacred soil of Japan. They set quartermasters up on the docks, handing out C-Rations. The men formed up on De Jima Wharf and loaded into trucks.

The first few nights we had bedded down in the Mitsubishi factory. When the bomb went off downtown, it blew all the windows out on the side of the building that pointed toward Nagasaki. Me and my squad spent two days cleaning up the mess.

The rest of the time, we were out patrolling the city. We had orders not to go into the central part of town because of the lingering radiation, but we went everywhere else. MacArthur had given strict orders: no Allied personnel were to assault Japanese people or eat the scarce Japanese food. Flying the *Hinomaru,* the rising sun flag, was strictly forbidden. Crandall had briefed us on their two primary objectives; eliminating Japan's war potential and turning Japan into a democratic nation. The guys in my squad referred to the policy as "punish and reform."

The Japanese people were completely different from what I had expected. The first few weeks we saw very few women, except for some old ladies peddling vegetables. We heard that the men sent their wives and daughters into the hills to keep us from getting at them. I guess that was smart thinking. But aside from a few bumps in the first couple of weeks, things went smoothly. My primary job was keeping some of the more bitter Americans from assaulting the Japanese or harming the women. Other than that, the people seemed polite and respectful, and gradually, as they saw that most of us were just regular guys, we saw more women on the streets.

Three weeks after we landed, I was surprised to see Bud come sauntering into our new barracks. Actually, barracks was an overreach because there were no pipes, no water, and no heat. It was good to see Bud.

"Hey, Philoooo, whaddaya know?" I grinned and grabbed Bud's hand. "What are you doing back here?"

Bud shook his head. "To be honest, Menno boy, I don't really know. Here I was, settling down in my old room in the house in Ritzville, waiting for Kalasia to arrive from Tonga, when I get a call from Crandall. He practically begged me to come back. Said I was the best corpsman, and he needed me, or some such BS."

"What's he got you doing?"

"Helping the boys that we liberated from the stinking Jap camps. Some of these guys are in sad shape. I'm leaving for Hokkaido tomorrow." Bud paused and pulled out a Chesterfield. He offered one to me. "You seen Billy?"

"Yeah, around."

"You talked to him?"

"No."

Bud took a drag. "This is bull, Strange. You and Billy are best friends. Two guys couldn't be any closer. You gotta work this out."

"Yeah, Crandall said that, too."

"Well, don't mind me for sticking my oar in, but I'm gonna take charge of the situation."

"Yeah, what are you gonna do?"

Bud smiled. "Already done it. Sniper!"

A head poked around the door jamb leading into the barracks. It was Billy. He grinned sheepishly and stepped into the room. I backed up and took a fighter's stance. "If you're here to take up where we left off, Sniper, I'm good with that."

Billy spread his hands. "Nah, Johnny, I'm here to apologize. I opened my big mouth way too far, and I deserved everything I got." He rubbed his jaw. "My face still hurts."

So, I dropped my hands. I was sorry, too. "I shouldn't have bucked you. I can't tell you what to feel. We both see this whole situation differently, but we're still friends, right?"

Billy nodded. "You guys are the only friends I got."

22

CHERRY BLOSSOMS
BUD, THE CORPSMAN

IT SEEMED TO ME I'D HAD A HEADACHE SINCE I SET FOOT IN Nagasaki and each day was worse than the day before.

Helping with the Marine POWs in Japan was hard enough. They were in sad shape from illness and worms and malnutrition. I worked with the docs and nurses and other corpsmen to get them back on their feet. It would take a while. My migraines didn't come from that, ugly as their conditions were.

Interviewing the civilians. That was the horror story. That was the Bela Lugosi. When I finally persuaded some of them to talk to me, at first, I thought a lot of them were lying to get back at America for dropping the bombs on Japan. But too many had versions of the same story. And it wasn't just the Japanese. The POWs had stories to tell, too. Without knowing it, they corroborated what the Japs had said. It made my head spin. And people I got to know kept dying.

Bricks hadn't hit them. Fire hadn't burned them. They had nothing to tell me about the force of the blast the day Fat Boy hit Hiroshima, picking them up and throwing them a couple of hundred feet. They just died. I'd interview them a couple of times and three weeks later, they were dead. Others died in a month.

Two months. They kept dropping, some with blood bursting out of their noses and ears and eyes. Some never woke up. Not a mark on their bodies. They just never woke up.

I made careful notes. Talked with other men who were conducting interviews. We compared what we'd found. One doc, Thompson, pulled me aside and checked to be sure no one was listening before he opened his mouth.

"You know what's happening," he said quietly, but his eyes were hard.

"I don't know what's happening," I responded.

Which wasn't quite true. It wasn't like we hadn't been briefed about this. There had been accidents when nuclear fission was being explored and accidents when the bombs were being built. It's just that no one talked about it.

"I swear it's radiation, Bud."

I'd had the same worry myself. "You think it's in their blood?"

"I think it's in their blood, their brains, their intestines, their bowels, their saliva. I think it's been killing them since August 9 when they were exposed. Of course, it killed some Japanese outright. But others died a day later, three days, a week, two weeks..."

I cut him off, my head pounding. "Okay, doc, I get it."

"God knows how many are carrying slow death inside them, Bud. Maybe half of the survivors. Maybe more. And there's nothing we can do to stop it. There's no cure for radiation poisoning. Does the brass want to hear this? The governors and congressmen and senators back home? Do the American people want to hear this? That we dropped a bomb on Nagasaki that keeps on killing years after the war is over and we've made peace with our enemy? That we dropped some kind of weird vengeance bomb that never stops wreaking havoc and never stops feeding on human life? It makes us look like monsters. It makes us look like the frigging Nazis with their death camps and poison gas. No one wants America to look like the Third

Reich. Who in the world is going to want to hear what we have to say?"

I tossed and turned that night. I didn't want Thompson to be right, but no other explanation fit. Even if they didn't have radiation burns, men and women and children were still getting sick, their hair coming out in handfuls, their bowels gushing blood and pus, crying out in agony, dying miserable deaths. All the morphine in the world couldn't ease their pain. I never knew anyone it happened to, but it wouldn't have surprised me, given the openness to ritual suicide in their culture, like the seppuku of the samurai, if many Japanese didn't end their lives to stop the agony that began August 9th. Imagine counting yourself lucky you'd survived only to begin vomiting and battling diarrhea and feeling too weak to get out of bed a month later. You'd thought you'd cheated death only to find out you hadn't. Death had cheated you.

And I figured Doc Thompson was right about the other thing, too. Nobody would want to hear about what we were finding out except the U.S. war machine. The rest of America wanted to hear the bomb was dropped, that it killed like any other bomb, that it killed the same as the bombs at Pearl Harbor, that it ended the war, that it saved lives by ending the war, that it was over and done, we were the heroes, we would help Japan get back on their feet, the sun would shine, we'd have a Thanksgiving and Christmas free of war, and 1946 would open on the best year the world had experienced in a long time. What those of us interviewing the Japanese survivors were finding out, especially about why we were losing so many of them going into September, and October, and November, was not information that was good news and it would not be welcome.

I got up at four that night, my blankets twisted around me, and went outside. What was I going to do? Lie about everything? No, I wouldn't do that. I'd lay it all out on the table. If the brass didn't like it, or other medical men, or Crandall, even if

Thompson clammed up, too damn bad. My church roots went deep, no matter how much the war had damaged them. They were still there. Still intact. My faith didn't die on Tarawa or Saipan, though maybe it came close sometimes. I would tell the truth. Even if no one wanted to hear it or deal with it.

I smoked two packs between four and six. Watched the sun come up, no haze to obscure it. At the back of my mind, I remembered Billy had wanted to take me up a mountain to a Shinto shrine he'd discovered, so I could explain what that religion was all about. Bud the Encyclopedia. But, yeah, I knew about the Shinto faith. I'd been reading everything I could get my hands on about Japan since their war against Manchuria and China in the 1930s. Billy would have to beg off whatever policing assignment they had given him for Thursday. I'd have to set aside my interviews. We were going to climb into the sky and into the sacred. I hoped my stinking migraines would go away when I walked from this unholy world into the holy one I could not see.

The Torii gates were damaged, but still profound. Thirty-foot-high posts bracketed the entryways into the sacred. A long, curved beam, curved like a katana, joined the posts together at the top.

I told Billy the path we walked after we entered the sacred space through the Torii gate was the *Sando*. In the Shinto faith, I explained as we explored, gods and supernatural entities and spirits were known as kami. They ruled over nature and dwelt in places of natural beauty. There were evil forces, too. I didn't talk about those.

One building, I said to him, pointing, was the *haiden*, which was set aside for ceremonies and worship. Another, the *heiden*, was a building for offerings and prayers. The *honden* building was the sanctuary. It contained an image of the shrine's kami. The *goshintai* was the holy object inside the *honden* which held within it the spirit of the kami. *Mikos* were shrine virgins who sold charms. I imagined there had been *mikos* at this shrine in the past, and probably would be again, but the buildings were empty and silent now. Typically, a head priest ran the shrine, a *guji*. A smaller shrine, by one of the shrine elders.

"I saw someone my first time here," Billy told me. "He never spoke. He wore one of those conical straw hats. I gave him an offering of money. He was friendly, but pretty subdued and stoic. I decided to call him a monk."

"Perhaps he was," I replied. "Or he may have been a priest in disguise. Some like to do that sort of thing."

"What about Buddhism? I see it everywhere down below."

"And we saw it on the islands where we fought. Buddhism and Shintoism used to be joined at the hip way back in the past. They were separated in the 1800s. Some favor one path over the other, but I think a lot of Japanese follow both religions."

We sat down outside the *honden*, the building that housed the kami. We were in the shade; the sun goldened the ground that was beyond the trees and bushes. I felt no need to keep talking, and neither did Billy, apparently. I wanted to empty my head of the plutonium bomb and all the havoc it had wrought—a biblical way of putting it. I also knew I needed to have a talk with Crandall, which I wasn't looking forward to. So, let the breezes blow, let the wind soothe its way through the pines. I just wanted peace. Perhaps we were in the presence of other gods and spirits. That didn't bother me. I had my own beliefs, and they comforted me on that hilltop. I'm pretty sure I heard Billy whispering Psalm 23. I didn't interrupt.

After about an hour, it began to rain. The rain was not harsh. Almost like a mist. I asked Billy if he wanted to go into one of the buildings. At first, he shook his head. When it changed from a mist into a downpour, we both got up and went into the *heiden*. This was where prayers were offered. We stepped in and removed our boots and socks. Bowed. Knelt after the fashion of resting on our heels as karate and judo practitioners did in their dojos.

Closed our eyes. But I heard a slight movement, like the rustle of clothing.

Not next to me, where Billy was. In a corner or by a far wall. I risked a look, not wishing to offend, in case someone was in deep prayer or contemplation and did not want a hated American staring at them. It might be Billy's monk. I opened my eyes, saw what I saw, and closed them again. But not fast enough.

There was a young woman in a navy kimono that was decorated with cherry blossoms. She was slender, but obviously athletic and muscular, the folds of the kimono not hiding the strength in her arms or legs. The woman wore swords and was kneeling just like we were kneeling. Her eyes pierced mine as soon as I opened them. Fierce. As if she hurled black *shuriken*, the *Ninjutsu* throwing stars. Snapping my eyes shut did not save me. She was angry we were in the building and furious that I had studied her.

I tapped Billy on the shoulder and got up.

Without looking at the woman, I moved back to the entrance, bowed, stepped out, put on my socks and boots, and walked into the rain. Billy was right behind me. "What's the matter, Bud? Why are we leaving?"

"We don't have to leave the sacred space," I replied. "But I take it you saw the swordswoman in there?"

"I did."

"Well, she didn't seem to be too happy we were in there while she was trying to pray. She stared daggers at me. And I only glanced at her for a heartbeat. So, I don't want an incident. The last thing we need are more complaints about the Marines in Nagasaki, right? Let's go to another part of the shrine."

"I don't want to go anywhere, Bud."

I looked at him. "What? Did you hear anything I've just told you?"

"I heard all of it and I'm staying put. I'm going to wait until she finishes her prayers and leaves the building. I want to talk with her."

I felt like Billy had dropped a mortar bomb on me. "Are you crazy? Talk to her? She'll never say a word to you. Your charm won't work here. This is holy ground."

"I know what it is, Bud. And she will talk to me. I know her. I've seen her before. I even know her mother."

"What are you talking about, Billy?" I snapped.

"Her name is Sakura. Her mother told me. That means…"

I was growing angry. "I know what it means. My Japanese is better than yours. Cherry blossom."

"I've bought tea from her mother. She knows that. Bud, she gave me a smile, a ghost of a smile. So, I'm staying here till hell freezes over. I'm going to talk with that girl."

"You're nuts. She was wearing swords. Do you know what that means?"

"What does it mean, Bud?" he bit back. "Since you're Almighty God and know all things?"

"She's Samurai. Either *onna-bugeisha*, which means she's a defender who protects her family, her clan, and her home. Or she's *onna-musha*, which means she will guard her people by going after the enemy and attacking him. Either way, she is skilled with the weapons at her waist. She smiled, did she? Probably because she knows she could take your head off in the blink of an eye, Billy. And she probably will."

2 3

BEAUTIFUL SURVIVOR
BILLY MARTENS

I DON'T KNOW WHAT GOT INTO ME. BUD THOUGHT I WAS OFF MY rocker. But I wasn't going to leave the shrine until I'd spoken with Sakura. Maybe she'd ignore me. Maybe it would just be a polite hello and goodbye. But something was eating me. I had to make an effort to converse with her.

Things didn't go according to plan. Not my plan, anyway. Sakura came out of the building in the rain, put on her shoes, and moved quickly past me. I'm standing there soaked in my uniform, Bud was sitting nearby on a stone bench under a tree. She didn't acknowledge either of us. She passed through the Torii gate, not looking back, ghost of a smile or not, and Bud and I followed her as she passed through the other Torii gate and began to head down the mountain.

"Told you," Bud said to me. "You're a Yankee devil, Billy Boy. No way she's going to consort with you. Just as well. You'd probably wind up with your throat cut."

"She wouldn't do that."

"No?"

"Her mother likes me."

"Maybe so. But there are plenty of other Japs hot under the

collar that we've dared to occupy the holy island of Japan. In their eyes, we've desecrated their soil. They see you getting cute with one of their women, a Samurai no less? They'll gut you like a tuna."

I didn't see Sakura again for a few days. Her mother was still brewing tea and I still bought one or two cups a day, sometimes three, and paid her well. Maybe too well, but I wanted Sakura to notice. I also made sure that two Marines from my squad were stationed in the neighborhood where they could keep an eye on the mother while they went about their other duties. I didn't want Sakura descending on us like a wrathful goddess and disemboweling or decapitating anyone else and winding up in prison. When she did show up, it had nothing to do with wrath or swordplay. But she did make me jump.

I was actually giving her mother a couple of packs of Player's at the time. I noticed the little lady liked to smoke while she brewed her tea. Bolo asked me why I didn't just pay her in cigarettes instead of giving her tobacco and cash both. But, nah, I had my plan. So, I'm handing over the cigarettes, she's bowing and smiling, and there's someone right behind me, I never heard them come up.

"It won't make any difference, you know," a woman said to me with a very polished British accent. I had heard the voice before after she'd cut a man in half without a hint of remorse. "It is impossible, Marine Sergeant. You have killed my people for too many years for it to be forgotten quickly."

I turned. It was Sakura. Right at my back. How tall she was, scarcely below my eyes. Her beauty was staggering that close. Her eyes, perfect. Her figure, powerful and feminine at the same time. In the middle of all this death and desolation, she carried the smell of fresh flowers, flowers like my mom planted around the ranch house in the spring. My beautiful survivor.

I took off my wedge cap and bowed.

She had no choice but to bow back.

"Your people killed my people too, Sakura," I replied.

She hesitated a moment. "What is your name?"

"Bill. Billy."

"Billy. William. I appreciate your buying tea from my mother. You were doing that before we met, but I knew about it. Nevertheless, it is impossible. You are American, I am Japanese. We have just fought a long war against one another. You are still the enemy. It is impossible."

"What is impossible?"

"You know what is impossible."

"What if it were possible?"

"It isn't, William." She sighed. "My mother has asked me to ask you to tea. I cannot deny her. It is her way of thanking you."

"Are you asking me too?"

"My mother is asking you," she insisted.

I repeated myself. "But are you asking me too, Sakura?"

She sighed again. "Yes, have it your way, Marine Sergeant. I am asking you as well. But there is no use getting your hopes up. Will you come? At four?"

"Yes. It would be an honor."

A wisp of a smile to go with her clipped accent. "Thank you. My mother will be pleased." She handed me a slip of paper. "I drew you a map to our home. Soldiers like maps, don't they?"

"Marines and soldiers like maps. I'll be there at four. Will you be pleased, Sakura?"

She rolled her eyes. "My god, William. You never give up. Yes. I'll be pleased when you arrive for tea. I'll be pleased for my mother's sake."

"Will you be pleased for your own sake?"

"Stop it, William. We cannot take this any further after today. Unless mother makes tea with you a weekly thing which would be just like her." Her third sigh. "But that's all we can be, William, you and me. Two people who drink tea together."

"And never talk?"

"Of course, we can talk."

"About the weather?"

"Yes. The weather."

"Mount Fuji?"

"Mount Fuji? Yes, we can talk about Mount Fuji."

"The Samurai," I said. "Can you explain to me about the Samurai?"

She did not respond.

"Sakura?" I prodded.

Another sigh. "I see where this is going, Marine Sergeant. Yes, I can explain the way of the Samurai to you. I can explain Bushido. But don't think you can fool me into talking about myself. I won't, you know. I learned to be very clever about this sort of thing when I took schooling in England."

"What sort of thing?"

"Women and men sort of thing."

"You smiled at me at the shrine, Sakura."

"I did not."

"Yes. You did. My question is, what does a smile from Sakura mean?"

She bowed. "We will see you at four."

I bowed in return. "I will be early."

I caught the briefest hint of a smile, but it was there as she replied: "The door will be locked until four, Marine Sergeant."

I shook my head. "You will not lock the door on a guest. That is not the Japanese way."

"Perhaps it is the way of the Samurai."

"I don't think it is their way either."

"We will see you at four, Marine Sergeant William."

She turned to her mother, spoke a few words. Her mother grinned at me and nodded. Then Sakura left, swords swaying gently on her hips. She moved like water moved. Slow water that had a plan and a place to go.

My plan was to arrive on time, not make a fool of myself, keep the mother on my side, and hope to win a few more smiles from Sakura. I didn't arrive on time; I had trouble finding the address, locals didn't want to help me out, but I finally made it about ten minutes past the hour. Sakura opened the door—it was one of their sliding panels, *shoji*, rice paper set in a wooden frame, that couldn't be locked—bowed, and ushered me in.

Bud had begged me to keep my mouth shut. He reinforced that Japan was nothing close to American society. It would be considered an insult if I asked where the father was, if Sakura was married and, if so, where the husband was now. For all we knew, both had been killed in the war or by the bomb. Sakura's husband could have been a kamikaze pilot or a soldier on Tarawa, Saipan or Okinawa.

"Just sit tight," Bud had warned, "be polite, enjoy the tea ceremony, talk about the weather, but do not ask personal questions. If you do, I guarantee you'll never see Sakura again. If you take it easy, maybe the day will come when she will converse with you in the privacy of her home. Even that is dicey for her, though. The hotheads will eventually find out and might kill you both and burn down her house. None of that rage will go away until the Emperor personally commands the renegades out there to quit."

So, I knelt, watched Sakura move about like a gentle dancer in a vivid gold and orange kimono, spreading everything on the low table, took three cups of green tea (something I'd never had before), ate the small cakes she had prepared which lacked a decent amount of sugar, ate the almost-stale cookies which were like vanilla wafers back home, and which I'd had my share of from Jap stores on Saipan and Okinawa. Bud was right. I enjoyed the tea ceremony with Sakura and her mother, but there wasn't anything to talk about. Most topics had the potential to take us through a very tricky minefield.

On the street, I had thought the mother to be in her seventies or eighties. But here in her home, which was far enough away to have been spared heavy damage from the blast, with its images on the walls of cherry blossoms in bloom or manmade waterfalls flowing in perfectly landscaped parks and gardens, she appeared much younger. She wore a beautiful sky-blue kimono with petals decorating it. Her hair had been done up nicely. She smiled frequently. Now she looked to be more in her fifties. And what conversation we had, she directed.

She wanted to know about my family and where I lived in America. When would I be leaving Japan and going home? How my mother must miss me! But there was nothing about her family and Sakura contributed nothing to the conversation. After an hour, I got to my feet, bowed to them both, thanked them, and made my way to the door, sliding it open. Sakura followed.

"Thank you for having me," I said, smiling.

She smiled back. It lit her face like a candle. "Thank you for honoring our home."

"Perhaps we can do this again."

"Perhaps. It will depend on my mother. But you made a favorable impression."

"Well, that's something." I placed my wedge cap back on my head and squared my uniform away. "Here's till next time, Sakura. At least I'll see your mother at her tea stand."

"Ah. Thank you for making sure she is safe."

"That's one reason we're here. Don't worry. The Marines won't be in Japan forever."

Her eyes flickered. "No?"

"No. Goodnight, Sakura."

"Goodnight, William."

That might have been it. I knew not to push it. I kept buying tea from her mother. My squad worked to keep the neighborhood safe. I did not see Sakura again for several weeks when she suddenly appeared behind me on the street, unheard and unexpected, and invited me to tea again. I accepted, and we went through the whole tea ceremony thing a second time, with the same sort of mother-led conversation: What was Montana like?

How tall were the mountains? What sort of creatures lived in them? How cold was it in winter? How deep was the snowfall in January? Then I went to the door again and Sakura saw me out with a bow.

It was the fourth tea ceremony, and we were well into a Nagasaki autumn, when things changed. Outside, trees turned amber and gold, the Japanese maple or *momiji*, and the gingko tree or *unchou*. I taught myself this from a book from the library. The leaves filled the trees and filled the ponds and covered the wreckage of the city, creating a strange but welcome beauty. I thought of the yellow aspens back home, so bright it was like each leaf was a small sun.

Inside, Sakura or her mother, or both, had made table arrangements with the colorful fall leaves. They used pottery bowls full of water where the golden leaves floated. They placed the leaves in random but precise patterns on the tabletop. They filled several vases with the red leaves of the maple, which had been the first to color before the gold arrived. I complimented them on the way they had decorated their home. The two of them murmured their thanks, and I left it at that, sipping my green tea. That's when Sakura spoke up, looking at me directly.

"We both feel it is time to tell you about our family, William-san," she said. "The season has turned."

24

A BRINGER OF NEW THINGS

JOHNNY STRANGE

OCTOBER 4, 1945

My Dearest Marjean,

I'm here in Nagasaki, Japan. It is so strange for me to be writing this. The only way I ever thought I would come to the Japanese home-land was in the first wave of a million men who would give their lives on the beaches of Tokyo Bay. But it's over, Marjean. This stinking war is over and I'm coming home soon—home to you and John Albert. Home. I can't wait.

How's your dad doing? I was worried when you said he had a mild heart attack. I sure am glad he's been there for you and J.A. while I've been gone, and I hope he's doing okay. Tell J.A. I miss him terribly and I'm pretty sure we will all be coming home soon, at least the 2nd Div guys who have been out here in the Pacific since Cactus. Some of the new recruits will have to stay longer, but Crandall told us that his guys will most likely rotate home first, probably in the next three to four months.

Oh, I forgot to tell you. I'm a sergeant now, three chevrons on my sleeve. That means a bigger check coming in the mail every month, and a little more respect around the quad out here. Ha, ha!

I'm a squad leader in a different platoon than Billy, though. He and

I have been a little on the outs since I clocked him a good one back on Saipan. Oh, we made up and everything, but it hasn't been the same with him since I got back from the states a married man. Ever since then, Billy's been acting strange, but I think Bud has figured him out.

Part of it has to do with Chamorra, his Saipan girlfriend. They broke up and Cham started going with a jerk of a pilot who laughs about firebombing the civilians of Japan. Billy felt terrible for the women and kids that were getting burned up every night and to tell you the truth, so did I. That doesn't discount the fact that the Japs started this whole brawl and now they are reaping what they sowed.

Anyway, the nightly fire-bombing raids and the fact that Cham was going out with this guy really put Billy on edge. To tell the truth, Billy hasn't really been the same since after we cleaned up Guadalcanal. When I first met him, he seemed to have all the answers. I mean, he had been reading the papers about what the Japs were doing in Manchuria and China, and he was on a holy mission to drive them back to their islands. But the more we fought, the more his standards switched around. I think it had to do with the fact that his dad disowned him for joining the Marines and he never really got square with that. So, while he's out shooting Japs, his insides are getting torn up by a lot of conflicting stuff. He's real private, and it takes a lot to dig things out of him, but I haven't given up. He's my pard, as they say in the west, and I'll never forget that.

Me, when I came out here, I was just a crazy kid with a gut-full of hate and a head screwed on backwards. It took a lot to get me turned around. The biggest thing that did it for me was after I figured out that you really loved me and you were my girl and nobody else's, I came around to seeing that if you could love me, maybe I wasn't such a bad guy after all. And when you married me and I saw the look in your eyes, I knew that you and me were good to go, forever. I sure love you, Jean.

Anyway, I'm working with Crandall and Bud. There were a lot of prisoners in camps here in Japan and the Japs didn't treat them so well. A lot of the guards and Jap commanders did extremely brutal stuff to our guys, so they put Crandall in charge of sorting that out. He's interviewing a lot of Gyrenes and G.I.s and getting the skinny on some of the worst of these guys. Me and my boys, once we get a name from Crandall, it's our job to root out these slime bags and bring them in for trial. So, I'm getting to see a lot of the countryside.

Bud, he's as steady as ever. He says to say hi. He can't wait to get back to the states because then Kalasia will come up from Tonga and they will get married. Bud has decided he wants to be a doctor, so he said to tell your dad thanks for all the help and encouragement.

One thing I can't talk about yet in my letters is what we found in Nagasaki after they dropped the bomb here. I can tell you it was horrible, but I'll have to save the rest until the medical people and the brass sort it all out.

Keep me in your prayers. There are still some Japs out there who haven't given up yet, so we need to be careful, even though the Emperor has commanded all his people to lay down their arms. Before MacArthur got here, they had several go-rounds where the young Jap Army guys killed some of their generals because they thought their leaders had lied to the Emperor and that's why he surrendered. And the Jap navy pilots all wanted to have one last go as Kamikazes and attack our fleet, even after the official day of surrender. There were a bunch of them who took off from Oita Airfield to go on one last suicide mission. The leader, Admiral Ugaki, sent one last message and then the entire group just vanished. Nobody reported any attacks, no planes sighted by any of our ships. The Jap Kamikazes just disappeared. That's just one of the many strange things about being here in Japan.

Another strange thing is how the ordinary Japanese behave. Here, for almost five years, we faced this brutal enemy that killed men, woman and children just as easily as killing a fly. When they captured our boys, they tortured them or cut their heads off. Now, when you meet them on the street, they are polite and courteous, and you'd think we never ever fought a war. I just don't get it and to tell you the truth, I wouldn't trust any of them as far as I could throw them. But that's just me. A lot of our guys already have Japanese girlfriends, but the brass really frowns on that because there are still some nut jobs out there that think death is far better than surrender or fraternization with the enemy.

Anyway, I'll go now but I'll write soon.

I love you more than you will ever know.

Johnny

P.S. I've enclosed a letter for Gerald King's father. You can read it. It tells how Gerald died and that I was there with him. Please let Mr. King know I will come to see him when I am home.

OCTOBER 10, 1945

My beloved husband,

Oh, how I love saying that.

I got your letter, and I wanted to tell you my dad is doing better. He had a blockage in one of the blood vessels in his heart. Fortunately, he had a friend who has pioneered a new heart surgery that restores the flow of blood. It was kind of experimental, but they are pretty sure they cleared his vein. He needs to take it easy, which means he will retire soon. And he must watch his diet. Cecelia has taken over managing what he eats, and he doesn't like it one bit. J.A. feels sorry for his grandpa, but I enlisted him in the managed care program, so we are all looking out for Dad. He doesn't like it much, and he keeps saying he can't wait for you to get home so the odds will be a bit more even and he won't be ganged up on so much.

I took your letter to Gerald's dad. He has been heartbroken, of course, but he is also very proud that Gerald stood up to him and took a stand for his country. He is also very grateful that it was you who was with Gerald at the end and that his son didn't just die in some horrible cave all by himself. I told him you would come to see him and he kind of got teary and thanked me. He said something very nice. He said, "Johnny was a little wild, but I always really liked him and was glad that he was Gerald's friend." I think that was nice, don't you?

Okay, so I've been saving this part for last, because I've been a little scared to tell you. We're going to have another baby. There, I said it.

I hope it's okay and that you will be happy to hear the news. When we were together after we got married, I felt like we connected so deeply and so amazingly that a child could be the only possible result of such deep love. When you left, I think I already knew in my heart that I was pregnant. Sure enough, when I missed my monthly, I asked my dad to check me out and he confirmed it.

I hope it's a little girl and I hope you want another baby. If you are coming home in three or four months, I think that will let you be here when the baby is born. And you'll at least get to see me when I'm ugly and fat, and then you can decide if you really love me after all.

But then, I know you do, and I know I love you with all my being.

Johnny, Johnny, Johnny, my heart is so full of love for you, sometimes I think it's going to burst. Sometimes I just sit down and catch my breath when I think about you. I can't wait for you to be here all the time. I know our life will be wonderful.

So, I've told you my news. I'll be waiting for your next letter on pins and needles.

Your girl, your wife, your lover forever.

Marjean.

October 22nd, 1945

My wonderful, dearest, incredible Marjean.

I am so excited. Another baby. How great is that? I told Bud and Billy and the guys and Crandall produced some cigars, even though he doesn't smoke them anymore, and we celebrated. Crandall said he will make sure I get home before the baby is born. Billy just shook his head and grinned. I think he's coming back around. Bud says he has a Japanese girl that he likes and I think that's good. He can work out his concern for the Japanese civilians and maybe take a load off his conscience. I think that's what it is with Billy—his conscience.

War does terrible things to you if you let it. When you go to war as a boy, you have a grand illusion of immortality. Other people get killed, not you... Then when you see your friends get killed the first time you lose that illusion and you know it can happen to you. War does something to your soul, and that's the part that is hard to deal with.

For some people, war makes it impossible to go home again. Billy is like that. He came to war from a real home and he lost it all. Me, I never had a real home and now I do. Funny how those things work out.

I think Billy is embarrassed by the words sacred, glorious, and sacrifice. We hear people say those words all the time, and we have read them on posters and in newspapers, and I think that Billy no longer sees anything sacred in war, and the things called glorious have no glory, and the sacrifices became meaningless when the only thing we could do was bury our friends and go on.

For Billy, words like glory, honor, courage, have become obscene beside the burned-out cities, and the dead innocents, and the reality of war. He is the best friend a man could have and I worry about him. I can see these things hanging on him like dark shadows.

All we can do is pray for him and let God take care of him.

Sorry for rambling on, little mother. I will be home soon and by the way, no matter how pregnant you get, you will always be beautiful to me.

Your Husband,
Johnny

25

WAR'S END

BUD, THE CORPSMAN

THIS IS BAD, TERRIBLE.

I GOT the call from Crandall at 0200.

"Bud, Johnny's hurt. He's hurt bad."

"What! What happened, Captain?"

"I sent him out to round up some guys on the war criminal list, and he got into a firefight. Seems there are a bunch of these Nips who won't give up. Johnny got shot up good."

"No! Where is he?"

"He's at the local Prefecture Hospital. They don't think he's going to make it."

"What?"

"I'm telling you, Bud, he took five to the chest. Two of his squad are dead."

"I thought the war was over, Captain."

"Yeah, that's what they told us. Everything is hunky-dory. We do our stint here, get these bastards back in line, and then go home. What they didn't tell us is that there is a sizeable group of Jap patriots who have not, I repeat, have not surrendered. Even before we got here, they were killing each other over the Emperor's proclamation."

"But, Captain. I thought these little ants always did what the Emperor said."

"Well, from what I heard from my intel, a bunch of them believe that the peace party kidnapped Hirohito and forced him to make the proclamation. Some of them even took over the palace for a while, but in that case, saner heads prevailed. But they were still out there and Johnny walked right into a nest of them. Bud, I need you over there now. I got a jeep on the way. If anyone can help Johnny pull through, it's you. I'll see you there."

I was already tying my shoelaces.

So, is this how it ends? Me and my two buddies fight through hell on Cactus, Helen, Saipan, and Okinawa. We dodge every bullet on Bloody ridge; we wade through the lagoon on Tarawa untouched while all around us Marines are having their heads taken off by 50-cal machine-gun shells. Billy and Johnny march right down the main street of Garapan with bullets flying everywhere and them dealing death with their BARs. We get into a British Square on Saipan and fight through the last Banzai of WWII. And then they send us to hell on earth on Okinawa and we somehow survive?

And then the war is over and they send us to Japan to help these people come back to some semblance of humanity and what do they do? Shoot Johnny down. This just doesn't make sense.

I'm prayin' in the jeep, prayin' hard as we race through the dark streets of Nagasaki. I always said I had an inside track and now I'm layin' all my chips down on the table. God, this can't be. Johnny's got too much going for him. He's got a life back in the States, Marjean, J.A. and a new baby on the way. God, I know that a lot of guys have died in this man's war, but not Johnny—please, not Johnny.

WE PULL up and I run in the door. Crandall's in the hallway. He grabs me and we head for Johnny's room. There's a young lieutenant, probably one of the guys they sent over to run the Jap health facilities, and several nurses in the room. Johnny's on the bed. He does not look good. His skin is pale, and he's got tubes everywhere. Crandall tells the guy who I am, and he looks relieved.

"I'm glad you're here, Corpsman..."

"Bud. Just Bud."

"Okay, Bud."

"So where are we, Doctor?"

The kid tells me. So far, Johnny's lucky. Young as he looks, this guy knows what he's doing. Turns out he's from Chicago and he worked in a clinic out by the projects. He's seen a lot of gunshot wounds. Answered prayer number one.

His primary survey is spot on. He got Johnny's airway open and applied high-flow oxygen by face mask. Then he inserted a drain because it's clear there is damage to the lungs and chest wall.

"Have you checked for the entrance and exit wounds?"

"Yes. He's got five. The bad news is that he took two in the right lung and two through the liver. The last one tore his hip up pretty good, but it deflected off the bone and went through."

"What's the good news?"

"The bullets were small caliber—maybe a 38 caliber, but more likely a 22. Not a lot of collateral damage, but I'm having trouble getting his systolic BP up to where I want it."

"Blood?"

"I already cross-matched six units and I got more being

tested. I placed two large bore IV cannulae and we are getting fluid into him. He'd lost a lot of blood by the time he got here."

The kid is good... very good. He did everything right. Maybe Johnny's got a chance.

"Damage to the heart, Lieutenant?"

"I don't think so, Bud. His BP is low, but steady, so his heart seems to be functioning. I'm monitoring his vital signs, blood gas, CXR and ECG. I've got a team of really excellent nurses."

He pointed to one. "This is 2nd Lieutenant Williams. She's the chief nurse here. She saw battlefield action on Okinawa. We are lucky to have her."

A battlefield nurse. Answered prayer number two.

I did a quick check on Johnny. Everything that could have been done to stabilize him has been done. Answered prayer number three. I motioned to the doctor, and we stepped out into the hall. Crandall was there. I heard a commotion down the hall. Two guards were stopping someone from coming down. Billy!

Crandall saw him at the same time. He shouted down the hall. "Corporal, let that man through!"

Billy walked up. "What's going on? Is he alive?"

"Alive, but just barely. He was lucky. The Lieutenant..." I turned to the doctor.

"Krawiec, Bud. Lieutenant Robert Krawiec."

"Lieutenant Krawiec did everything right. He probably saved Johnny's life."

"So, what's next?"

"We keep monitoring him and stay with him 24/7."

Crandall put his hand on the doctor's shoulder. "What are his odds, Doctor?"

Lieutenant Krawiec shook his head. "I don't know, Captain. I'd say about twenty-five seventy-five, he makes it. If he does, it will be a miracle."

The nurse stepped out. "Doctor, he's trying to say something."

I go in with Krawiec. Johnny was mumbling. "Lift his mask, Doctor."

Krawiec lifted his mask and Johnny's lips moved. I knew exactly what he was saying.

Marjean.

I STAYED at the hospital all night. Billy was with me. I checked in on Johnny every ten minutes. Billy sat in one of the uncomfortable hallway chairs and caught a few winks. I'm worried. Johnny's alive, but just barely. Krawiec has done everything, but the odds are not in Strange's favor. He needs something. He needs Marjean. I know him. Marjean was the only thing that kept him going during boot camp, through the bloody early battles, and through the last big ones. At 0600 I go down to the office and ask to use the phone. I give Crandall a ring.

"How's our boy?"

"Not good, Captain. Not good. He keeps asking for Marjean, when he's conscious. Is there any way..."

"Already working on it, Bud. I called Marjean as soon as I got back from the hospital. I asked her if I could make a way, could she come? She said that her dad would take care of J.A. and she'd be on the next plane if I could work it out."

"How are you going to do that, Captain? She's a civilian."

"Remember what we talked about when I asked you to come back?"

"Yeah, the POW reparations and..."

"The other part, Bud."

"About interviewing bomb victims?"

"Yeah, that part. I have teams coming here and it seems Marjean could fit right in. She's a trained stenographer, uses the steno and graduated top of her class. We need several of them on the team to record the conversations with the bomb victims. I called in some favors and she'll be here in twenty hours. She already left Spokane."

Answered prayer number four. Marjean's coming.

So that is how I welcomed Marjean Strange to Japan. One of the first civilians to arrive during the occupation and on the most important mercy mission of her life. I gotta tell you some heads turned when that doll stepped off the plane. If I didn't know what she was here for, I would have guessed USO show. Crandall and I are waiting at the bottom of the steps with a jeep right behind us.

Marjean is all class. That beautiful blonde hair, those deep blues, the little smile. I'm telling you, the Japanese that are working the airbase must have thought she was one of their goddesses come to earth. They are all standing there with their chins on the ground. She sees me and gives me a big hug. "Bud, how is he?"

"Well, I think he will have a fighting chance now that you're here."

Then she turns to Crandall. "You're Captain Crandall. Johnny has told me all about you. I am so glad that you have been with him all these years. He couldn't have had a better officer to take care of him. Thank you for helping me get here."

Well, Crandall turns beet red and even redder when she gives him a big hug and a kiss on the cheek. "Thank you, ma'am..."

"Marjean, Captain. And I hope I can call you Jamison."

"Yes ma'am, I mean Marjean."

Crandall sees the crowd forming around them and barks an order. "All right, you jimmies! Get back to work. This is not a sideshow!" Everyone hustles off and we get Marjean and her things into the jeep. She leans on me and puts her head on my shoulder.

"I'm so worried, Bud. What if he doesn't make it?"

"Johnny's strong and tough, Marjean. If anybody can pull this off, he can. God put a bright young doctor in his way and the kid did everything right in the first two hours he had Johnny. Besides God, if anybody gets credit that Johnny is still alive, it's Lieutenant Krawiec."

We pull up at the hospital and Crandall helps Marjean out. "I've got a small house arranged for you to stay in with a Japanese girl to help you. Her name is Himari. I've vetted her, and she's got great references. I hope that's okay."

Marjean nodded. "That's fine Jamison. I appreciate it."

He turned to me. "Keep me on the hot line, Bud. I want to know any changes, good or bad."

"Yes, Sir!"

Crandall drove off, and we went in. Down the hall, a sergeant was asleep in a chair. When he heard us coming, he woke. When he saw us, he stood. "Bud and… Marjean?"

She walked up and put her arms around Billy. "Billy. I would have known you anywhere. I feel like I've known you for a hundred years."

Billy hugged her back. When he pulled away, I saw tears.

"How's he doing?"

"The same, Bud. He hasn't opened his eyes and every so often he calls for Marjean."

Lieutenant Krawiec came out of the room. When he saw Marjean, he stopped in his tracks. "Are you Marjean… I mean Mrs. Strange?"

"Yes, Doctor. And you must be Lieutenant Krawiec. Bud told me what you did for Johnny."

"Good training, ma'am. It just kind of kicked in when I got him."

Marjean walked over. "Well, I will thank God for the rest of my life that you did get him." She put her hand on his shoulder and gave him a kiss on the cheek. "Thank you, Doctor, for saving his life."

Boy, if Crandall turned red, you should have seen this kid. He started to stammer an answer and Marjean, ever gracious, helped him out. "Can I see him?"

"Yes, ma'am," the kid says gratefully. "This way." He points to the room.

Billy and I and the doctor follow Marjean in for just a moment. She sits down in the chair next to Johnny's bed and puts her hand on his. She looks at his face for a long time. Then I hear her whisper.

"Johnny Strange, you come back to me. I need you."

26

THE DRAGON KIMONO
BILLY MARTENS

SSAKURA AND HER MOTHER HAD NOTHING TO SAY TO ME UNTIL I told them where I'd fought during the war. There was no point in holding back. They listened, hanging on every one of my words: Guadalcanal, Tarawa, Saipan, Okinawa.

"Nowhere else?" asked Sakura.

"Nowhere else."

She waited a few moments.

Her mother spoke.

Sakura translated.

"My husband, Sakura's father, was at Pearl Harbor. He flew many combat missions after that. Eventually, he was stationed on Iwo Jima and assigned to attack your bombers. That is where he was killed."

I looked at her mother and bowed my head and held it bowed for a ten count. "I am very sorry."

Sakura continued to translate. "I had four sons. One was a pilot like his father. Another in the Navy. The other two were soldiers. One soldier son died long ago in China. The other died on Peleliu. My pilot son was in the Philippines. We do not know what happened to him. His plane did not return to base. As for my naval son, he went down with his ship at the battle at Midway. He was on the carrier Kaga. Do you know about Midway, William-san?"

I kept my head down as Sakura's mother listed all her losses. It was too many, too much. "Yes. I know about Midway. I'm very sorry for the loss of your sons."

There was a silence.

I kept my eyes on the floor.

I felt there was something else. Someone else.

Sakura translated again. "I had another daughter. My youngest. I can barely speak about her. It is too painful to even mention her name. She was killed the night of the fires your bombs started in Tokyo."

My head remained down. "I am sorry. I did not agree with the bombings. I thought they were wrong."

A long silence took place after my words.

Then Sakura spoke softly. "It is best you leave us now, William-san."

I got up and bowed to them both. Sakura did not see me to the door. I did not expect to hear from them again. Why would I? America had wiped their family out. At the same time, it was also true the Japanese had wiped American families out. And families in the Philippines and on Saipan. Had their father and husband bombed the Arizona? How many Chinese had the one son killed? How many Marines had the other son killed on Peleliu? And then our B29s had destroyed her daughter, Sakura's sister, filling her young body with flame.

What a mess wars made. I'd been a crazy Montana boy to think I could ever have any kind of relationship with a Japanese woman, as if 1941-1945 could just be swept under the rug and forgotten in a couple of months. I smoked a deck of Lucky Stripes after that tea and tried to think and pray it all through, but there were no easy answers. Or any answers at all.

I was back and forth about going to the mother at her kiosk

on the street. I made sure there was a Marine there at all times to keep her safe, but other than that I tried to put her and Sakura out of my mind. What was there to say? What could I do to ease their grief? Bring a father and husband and five children, Sakura's siblings, back to life?

You'd think it wouldn't sting to let go. Sakura was just a cowboy's dream, nothing real had ever been there, we barely knew one another. But I felt it. When I had the time, I'd head up to the shrine. I found some measure of peace there, like I always had.

And I'd go to Johnny. He was in the worst of ways. He could barely speak. I'd give Marjean a hug and sit by Johnny's bed in the hospital, my hand resting on his arm. I'd talk about nothing. But one day he was more alert than he usually was and asked about Sakura. He kept pressing, so I told him everything. He nodded, but it was hardly even a nod, more like a ghost of a nod.

"I am sure she'll talk to you again, buddy," Johnny whispered. "But you gotta keep your eyes peeled. The Japs hate us and won't like you wooing one of their women. They'll kill both of you, if they can. Don't let your guard down."

"Maybe I should just leave off and be done with the whole affair," I replied. "*Sayonara* to mother and daughter and leave well enough alone."

Johnny mustered the thinnest line of a smile. "You always liked strong women. Who's stronger than a female samurai? Don't give up just yet, buddy. You may have to fight for her, but don't call it quits too soon."

I listened to Johnny. And what was cooking inside me? After about five days, I bought some green tea from the mother again. There was nothing to lose, I figured, since it felt to me I'd already lost Sakura, anyway. It surprised me the mother was friendly, bowing and offering the tea without a complaint or a scowl. So, I went back the next morning and bought tea from her again. This time she handed me a note: *My mother would*

like you to join us for tea at four this afternoon if you are free.
Sakura.

I wish she'd said something about her wanting me there, too.
But, of course, I was going to go. Autumn was still with us, so the
colored leaves were placed around the table and in vases again.
Sakura did not have a face of stone. Now and then she offered a
smile and eye contact. They invited me back the next afternoon.
And the next. Suddenly, it became an everyday event.

It became more than tea. At their request, I arrived early one
afternoon and Sakura escorted me into the yard behind their
house. There were small bridges and stone Buddhas and a small
waterfall that spilled into a pond. It had sustained little war
damage. She asked if I would like to help her restore the gardens
and pond. I must have been too eager, for she lowered her face to
hide her smile at my enthusiastic response. Now every day I had
dirt under my fingernails. Johnny said I had started whistling and
I swear I don't even remember whistling at the hospital. He just
gave me a tired wink and spoke in a tired voice: "One day at a
time, cowboy. Don't rush the cherry blossoms. It's not spring."

She laughed when I fumbled around in the pond. I was trying
to find out what was blocking the flow, making it only a trickle. I
fell in headfirst. One hand covered her mouth, but the laughter
rang through her fingers like chimes. "Oh, William-san, you are
so amusing. Why didn't you just lean over and use a shovel?"

I'd never heard her laugh before. It was distracting. "No, I
need to feel my way with my hands."

"Are you coming out?"

"I'm not. I have to finish the job."

"But you're soaked."

"So what if I'm soaked? Plenty of times I've worked in the rain.
(I was careful not to mention that plenty of times I'd fought in the
rain too.) Back home, you just shrug it off and work the cattle. Of
course, I have a rain slick to put on when I do that. And I'm
wearing a Stetson as well."

"What are those things, William-san?"

"What things?" I was digging silt and stones up with my hands. "Oh, the slick is like a raincoat, but it goes all the way to your boots to keep your pants dry. And a Stetson is ... is a cowboy hat..."

"Ah. I've seen those hats in movies before the..." She stopped. "Well, are you coming out or not?"

"Once the waterfall is a waterfall again."

"You are covered in water and leaves."

"And I look beautiful, don't I? I'm the very picture of tranquility."

Her dark eyes glittered. "Ah. Very much so. A picture of tranquility." Her British accent. "You look like a tall tree. Perhaps not. A tall sapling."

"Isn't it running better now?"

She examined the waterfall, hands on the hips of her scarlet kimono, the hilts of her two swords nudging her palms. "Somewhat."

"Somewhat?"

"It could be a stronger flow, that's all."

"All right. Jump in and lend a hand."

She arched a perfect eyebrow. "Jump in?"

"Go grab your Wellies or whatever you call them, your rain boots, and your umbrella or parasol, and help me out."

She backed away from the pond. "Now you're being silly, William-san. Climb into the pond in one of my best kimonos? And don't get any ideas about dragging me in. That would not be appropriate. I'm not one of your American girls."

I went back to work. "I know that, Sakura. I need a few more minutes. Then I'll haul myself out and head back to our barracks to clean up. Not that the water there has any great flow either. But it will be sufficient. After that, I'll be back for tea. I won't be that late."

Sakura seemed to steel herself. "Not so, William-san!" She

blurted out the words. I looked at her, surprised by the strength in her voice. "That will not do. It would be rude of me not to offer you cleansing when you have become dirty working on our behalf. No, it would not be right. It is not our way. Our bath is still working well. You must bathe here."

"Sakura..."

"You must bathe here, please."

I felt pretty awkward about the whole thing. It took some time for her to heat water and bring buckets of it to me, but there was no point in arguing. My refusing the bath would have been considered an insult. She set each bucket outside the door and I opened it just enough to pull them in. I poured the first over my head and body, then soaped up with the bar she'd given me, and poured another bucket. I was instructed to soap up again. After that, there were two more buckets. She left a towel for me. Sandals. Even a kimono of black with golden dragons chasing one another over the silk.

I knew it was silk without being told. Mom had a few silk scarves back in Montana and I remembered how smooth they were. What bugged me was that the kimono was big enough for me, so one of their men had been tall. Who? Father? Pilot? The sailor? One of the soldiers? There was no point in asking. They were not going to tell me. It was something that would not be spoken about. Sakura and her mother had decided and chosen the kimono I would wear. I had to accept that.

It felt soft against my skin. When I walked into the tea room they both stood and bowed. I bowed in return. They could not hide the tears, but it was up to me to pretend I did not see them. I bent over and removed my sandals. We sat and Sakura served. It was a quiet tea ceremony, but not unhappy. After an hour, it was as if a weight had disappeared from the room. Sakura said softly. "You honor us by wearing our family's robe. It will be here for you every time you return."

"You've cleansed me and clothed me and fed me, Sakura. I

give my thanks to you and your mother," I responded. "May I return tomorrow afternoon to continue to help you with the gardens? There is work we should begin on the house as well."

Sakura gave me a full smile, nothing hidden. "You are welcome here every day, William-san. Your uniform is hanging by the bath. You may leave the dragon kimono in its place. You will find that your uniform is quite dry."

I looked at her. "Dry? How could you accomplish that so quickly while we had tea? It was only a short time, Sakura."

Then she teased me for the first time. "I am full of secrets, Marine Sergeant Martens."

27

DREAMS OF HOME
JOHNNY STRANGE

How in God's green earth did this happen?

Crandall sent me out on a routine roundup. Looking for a bunch of characters that were guards at Fukouka Prison. There's a lot of ass-covering going on in Japan these days. One lowlife from the prison ratted his buddies out. It seems that right after the Emperor announced surrender, the slime bags at Fukouka had hauled eight of our captured airmen out to a place called Aburayama, several miles from the prison.

They dug pits in front of our guys in a field surrounded by brush. Then, one by one, they forced our guys to their knees and cut their heads off. When the sixth prisoner came forward, they lashed his arms behind him and then took turns running at him and smashing him in the stomach with karate chops. The flier slumped, but they pulled him erect for more blows. When he did not die, they cut his head off. They tortured the seventh man in the same way. One of the Japs got so worked up he kicked our guy in the testicles. Then they pulled him up to a kneeling position and argued about how to kill him. They settled on *kesajiri*. Another sword glinted in the sun over the bowed form and cut down through his left shoulder into the lungs. Our guy died in a froth of blood.

Number eight was the worst. After watching all his buddies slashed to pieces by the blood-crazed Japs, they pushed him into the center of a circle of maddened Japs, who made him sit down on the ground with his hands tied behind him. Ten feet away, an officer raised a bow, placed an arrow in it, sighted on the prisoner and let the arrow go. The arrow just missed his head. The Jap did it three more times and the third time hit him in the eye. Blood sprayed everywhere. Tired of the sport, his captors forced him into the kneeling position and chopped his head from his body. Eight headless torsos stained the meadow grass on the field of Aburayama.

But that wasn't all. Four days later, the officers of the Western Army Headquarters listened as the Emperor broadcast the decree of surrender to all his fighting forces. The officers fell into a rage and, after a short meeting, decided to execute all the remaining captive fliers. Since Japan had surrendered, the executions were to be secret.

Crandall's stoolie told him that the Japs killed the rest of the fliers because they knew too much. They could testify that the first group of murdered POWs had been alive just before the war ended.

Once again there was a deadly caravan down the road to Aburayama. In the back of the truck, sixteen of our guys sat surrounded by guards. None of them knew the war was over. In the field where the Japs murdered their eight friends, they stripped the men and formed them into a ragged line. The commander of the Japanese execution squad stood nearby with his girlfriend, as if they were at a circus. He shouted an order and several men dragged the first prisoner into the woods and fell upon him with swords.

The Japs repeated the brutal scene again, and again on the dwindling group of captives as individually, or in groups of twos and threes, they dragged the fliers into the woods and cut them to pieces. Unlike the first organized execution, this was an orgy of blood-letting, a frenzied destruction of our guys. While crowds of happy Americans roamed the streets of New Orleans, San Francisco and other cities celebrating VJ day, the bastards dumped our guys into hastily dug pits and buried them. The men who killed them returned to headquarters and burned every record pertaining to the whereabouts of the fliers.

What the killers didn't count on was that we rounded up one of their crew in a dragnet and identified him as a guard at the prison. When pressured about the missing fliers, he broke down and sang like a canary. Not only did he tell the story of the murders, but he pinpointed the location where the rest of his buddies were hiding out. So, Crandall sent me and fifteen of my squad members out to a little village close to the killing field to round them up.

I guess I took too much for granted because the war was over. You'd think a guy like me who had survived the hell of Cactus, Tarawa, Saipan and Okinawa would have been a little more on the ball. But I blew it. Big time.

When we got to the house where most of the guards were staying, I sent half my guys around to the back of the house and then instead of just tossing a grenade in and busting down the door, I waltz in thinking the little slant-eyes would panic and fall down, just begging to kiss my heinie.

Boy, was I wrong.

A fat slope was sitting at a table with three other guys, and they did not even hesitate. He gives me the stank-eye, and then, in a split second, he pulled a pistol and let me have three in the brisket without blinking an eye while his buddies cut loose with some subs. I went down, and the lights started to go out.

Hell! They shot me! Not a little pass-through in the shoulder, but three good ones in the chest. And then, as I'm blacking out, the fat guy gives me two more for good luck. As I'm fading, I can't believe it. What about Marjean, what about J.A.? What about the baby? I'm Johnny Strange, I'm a survivor. I made it through the friggin' war from beginning to end.

The war is over, but I'm lying on the floor of some filthy shack in Japan and my life is slipping out through five bullet holes. I'm gonna die! Holy crap, I'm gonna die!

Like I said, how in God's green earth did this happen?

DEATH IS DARKNESS. I always thought it was light. I always thought your loved ones were waiting on the far shore of a sparkling stream or across a green meadow. Not so. Maybe I should have gotten my act together with God a little sooner. Maybe I should have listened to Bud more. Maybe what I believe is not what saves you from hell, or blackness, or whatever this is.

Bud used to talk about Charon's barge taking the dead to the underworld. Is that where I am? On some stinking black boat stacked with the shredded remains of dead men and women, kids, white people, black people, yellow people, redmen? Cerberus, who's Cerberus? Something about a dog…

Are those sparkling things the radioactive atoms of the Japs who got vaporized at Hiroshima and Nagasaki?

There's a face I know.

Eddie Kremer.

The first guy in our group to die. The stupid kid who got excited, pulled the cord on a satchel charge and held it too long, blew his arm off at the shoulder and the life out of his insides like a candle in the wind.

"Hi 'ya, Johnny. Where you been? It's nice here in the dark. No bullets, no blood, no Japs to hunt you down…"

Another face. The Jap pilot I machine-gunned as he was standing on the wing of his plane twenty yards short of the transport off Cactus and pissed because he didn't quite get his plane into our ammo stores. He sure looks surprised as those .50s take him apart.

Mist and fog. Screaming in the dark. One of the chutists in a foxhole on Bloody Ridge getting a Katana between the ribs.

Scene shift.

Bodies bobbing in the blue lagoon. If I'm dead, shouldn't there be angels? Shouldn't there be some kind of music? Why bobbing bodies? They are all awake, bobbing in the water, bloody faces and bodies, bobbing like corks in a sea of blood.

I don't think I'm in heaven.

And now it's dark and I'm locked inside a room and I'm looking at the biggest Jap I've ever seen. He's covered with dirt and blood, and he has a sick grin on his face. "Want to pray with me, Maline?"

I look at the Jap. The big man has no weapon in his hand, but he doesn't need one. Somebody has been feeding this gorilla...

And then I'm in a tent and I feel Jenkin's hands on me and then he's rolling me over and I smell his stinking breath and I know what he wants to do to me and the bile rushes up in my mouth and then I'm off the cot and I have a knife in my hand and there's a trickle of blood down his arm where I cut him and that's when hate is born and he's begging me not to say anything and I'm telling him if he ever touches me again I'll gut him like a catfish...

Dark again, endless waves. Am I going to the land of shadows or the place where unbelievers go?

Something really hurts in my chest and I think I hear voices and it's the voice of an angel and I know if I can just reach out and touch the angel I'll be saved...

But shouldn't angels be men? This angel has a soft, sweet voice, but I can't see her. I have to see her...

Then it's dark again, and there's another face. Gerald King. He's shot to ragdolls, and he's smiling and he's thanking me and then he gets up off the filthy floor of the cave and walks down the tunnel and the light at the end is so bright and I want to go there but I'm stuck here in the dark.

I can't feel anything, but I hear the angel again and I know that voice.

Marjean.

Marjean, come save me, I'm dying but I'm not ready to die. There's too much to do, too much life to live. I never knew love and now I feel it slipping away.

Marjean.

It's dark again and then I'm walking toward the light, the same light Gerald walked into. But there's someone standing there.

Rudy Rudebaker.

I go toward him, but there's like a line on the floor of the cave, just before the light, and I can't get past. He's standing there in the light and I can't step into it. It's like there's a wall there.

"Hi, ya, Johnny. What's the skinny?"

"I think I'm supposed to die, Captain. I don't want to, but I think I'm supposed to come in where you and the guys are."

Rudy smiles at me. There's somebody standing behind Rudy, but I can't make him out. He whispers something to Rudy. I know just across that line there is peace and love and joy and I can't get in. The places I got shot don't hurt anymore. I have to get in there. But I can't.

Is this what happens if your faith isn't big enough?

"No, Johnny, that's not what this is about. You can't come in because it's not your time."

"But I'm dead, Rudy."

"Not yet, Johnny, not yet. You have a very big life to live. Go back. People are waiting for you."

"But where you are, there's no more of this pain in my guts."

"You're a tough guy, Strange. You'll handle it."

"But how do I get back?"

"Just listen to the voice. Just follow the voice."

And then the light goes out and I'm back in the dark. I take a breath and stay real still. Then I hear something. Something sweet and soft. I can't quite make it out. I turn and take a few steps toward the sound. Each step I take makes the places I got shot hurt more. They're burning, but the sweet something pulls me. I'm going, but each step has become agony. There. Now I can hear it better. It's a voice. Quiet, soft, drawing me back to the world.

Like being underwater for a long time in the darkness and now I'm going up and way up above me there is a little circle of light and I'm swimming up and up and I don't know if I can hold my breath and then I hear it, real clear and I think I'm going to live.

"Johnny Strange, you come back to me. I need you."

Marjean.

TATAKAI

BUD, THE CORPSMAN

I DID NOT EXPECT IT TO HAPPEN LIKE IT DID.

That it not only might happen, but would happen, unless the Emperor intervened, I had no doubt.

Not wanting to exhaust Johnny, it was me Billy came to when he hungered to talk about how his romance with Sakura the Samurai was developing—I called her that—and it was developing fast. I tried to get Billy to slow down, as usual, feeling like the grandfather of the platoon, reminding him this was Japan, not Saipan, not L.A. But apparently Sakura and her mother had grown as enthusiastic about Billy as he had about them. So, if Sakura wasn't going to slow Billy down, I sure wasn't going to make any headway.

He swore they hadn't kissed. Swore there had been no hanky-panky. I believed him. I knew he wouldn't do anything to dishonor Sakura or her mother. The kisses would come once Sakura invited them. Anything else would come with marriage, if there was a marriage. The trouble was, looks were deceiving. I knew nothing was going on between Billy and Sakura because he told me so. Few others would see it that way.

Billy was at their house seven days a week and if he could

have squeezed another day out of God, he'd have been there eight. The neighbors saw it and gossiped. The gossip was everywhere. Marines heard it on the streets they guarded, in the alleyways, in the shops. And the Marines themselves were gossiping about Billy's big romance with a gorgeous Japanese girl. It didn't matter what I said to change their minds. My arguments carried no weight. Player winked after one of my long rants about Billy's innocence: "We all know you love him, Bud. You two and Johnny have been to hell and back together more than once. It's okay if you want to cut him some slack. Just make sure you're there the day the Rising Sun comes looking for blood. You know it can happen."

Yeah, I knew it could happen. Knew it could happen, but prayed it wouldn't.

That's why I had a watch kept on the house, even when Billy wasn't there. Who knew what the Japs of the IJA, the Imperial Japanese Army, would do to Sakura and her mother? The renegades who refused to surrender would be no different from the Japs we'd had to battle on every island where we'd fought. They would show the mother and daughter who, in their eyes, had betrayed Japan, no mercy. If they got their hands on Billy, I knew death would not come quickly. Decapitation and disemboweling did not cause enough suffering. So, instead, they'd kill him slowly with bayonet thrusts. Maybe they'd put rope around his neck and take their own sweet time strangling him. Maybe they'd crucify him and let him die in agony from suffocation and blood loss. Like Jesus. I had no idea what they'd come up with. I did not dwell on it much because I had no intention of allowing it to happen.

We all have stories about prayers answered and the many prayers not answered. That's when we don't understand God's ways. At least this time, I could say God made sure Billy wasn't alone at the moment of reckoning. I didn't hear about it an hour too late. I wasn't conducting an interview with another survivor of the plutonium bomb that struck Nagasaki in early August. I wasn't helping at the hospital. I wasn't at the shrine up the hill. I wasn't grabbing some shut eye—just like the war, I never felt I got enough sleep. No. I was right there. Because, at the request of Sakura and her mother, Billy invited me to join them for the tea ceremony at four. I was on time and I made sure Bolo, Player and Gyprock were nearby and out of sight. No M1 Garands. I had insisted all three carry Thompson submachine guns. If it came to battle—*tatakai*—it would be mean and dirty. They needed the firepower.

Billy had been there since noon, fixing a wooden fence that ran around the small property. When I showed up, he was just emerging from the bath in the black and gold dragon kimono they had lent him. He looked sharp, as youthful and fresh as I remembered him at boot camp in California in '42.

I bowed to Sakura and her mother. I told them it was an honor. In flawless Japanese. I'd even picked up the Nagasaki dialect. They knew, and both smiled, bowing low and welcoming me. Of course, Sakura's swords were at her waist. I wondered if she checked them every day, the way a Marine checks his firearm to be sure it's in working order. I wondered if she kept them sharp. Then I felt like kicking myself. As if a Samurai would let her swords rust in their scabbards. As if she would leave them blunt or let them be stained and pitted by the blood of the man she'd slain who had assaulted her mother. No, the two blades, her *Daisho*, were clean and honed like razors. If she needed them, they'd be ready.

Everything was perfect. The green tea hot and spicy and good. The conversation light and polite. The mother wanted to know about me. My home town. Was I married? What about children? I took several of the cookies I remembered from Guadalcanal and the Jap supplies we liberated. Like vanilla wafers. Time passed easily. I grew so relaxed I could have curled up on the futon and cat napped.

Three things happened at the same time, or almost the same time, maybe four. There was a fast crackling of machine gun fire from the street. It made me spill my tea and scald my hand. My shooting hand. Sakura sprang to her feet. Drew her long sword, her *katana*. Shouted at Billy to take her father's sword off the display stand where it lay in its scabbard painted just like the dragon kimono—she knew he had stopped wearing his sidearm to their house out of respect. Two men crashed through the wall of the house and screamed at us: "You devils! You all deserve death!"

Two men jumped in after them. All four were in officer uniforms. One fired a shot from his pistol. The leader of the group yelled at him and I understood every word: "Put it away! They only have swords! That is how we will kill them! Sword against sword! Do not dishonor us!"

Sakura leaped at them like a great cat. She leaped so high and she leaped so far. I only saw her blade flash. I did not see it make contact, but the officer who had fired at us stood without a head. A second flicker of light and another officer cried out, his stomach slashed open, his guts falling into his hands. Billy ran up beside her and swung at the leader. The man had drawn his sword and met Billy's attack steel on steel. Two more officers crashed through the wall. They were also brandishing swords.

I fumbled for my pistol, but it was no use. I could not flex my fingers or close my fist. There was still the short sword on the stand where the long sword had been, the wakizashi. I had no choice. I had to use it and I had to fight. I could not let Sakura and her mother and Billy be slaughtered. There was more firing from the street. An officer hurtled through the front door behind me. I had to swing the wakizashi with my left hand and I was clumsy. He laughed and swatted it aside, using the flat of his hand.

"I killed plenty of Marines on Bataan," he sneered. "You will add to my glory."

He smacked my blade to the floor with his own.

Then he coiled with a gloat and poised his katana above his right shoulder, ready to slice down onto my head and neck.

All I could think of was to tackle him. As if he were the opposing team's quarterback, ready to throw a pass that would devastate us. And I didn't even really think. Just crouched and dove at his knees. I hit him just as he swung. He missed me as I knocked him on his butt. Then I pounced. Just as if I were dealing with a banzai charge on Saipan and had wounded men to protect. I wrapped my hands around his scrawny throat and bore down with all my weight, swords ringing behind me. He had acted tough, but he did not last long. I took his life quickly. War had changed me from one man to another kind of man.

I got up, but was smashed from behind and fell. I saw an officer above me with a small blade in his fist. A tanto. He dropped onto me as hard as he could and rammed his knee into my stomach. All the air left my body as I gasped in pain. I could not draw another breath. I choked for oxygen. He pressed the point of the tanto into my throat, ready to take a swipe and cut my neck wide open. There was nothing I could do. I had no strength left to seize his knife hand or throw him off me.

Even before he opened me up, I would be unconscious. His knee thrust into me with all his body weight behind it, and my mind swirled in dark, tight, concentric circles. I could not save myself. And Billy couldn't save me, either. Nor Sakura. Far off, I heard them grunting and shouting and fighting, steel cracking into steel.

It was the mother who was the heroine in my *tatakai*—my battle.

Yes, the mother, who was far more powerful than she let on, and far younger too—though she made out she was in her seventies. She struck the officer from behind with a Bo, a long hardwood fighting staff, and emitted a shout. *Ki-yii!* He went sprawling, stunned. Half gone, half there, I watched her stand over him and suddenly she seemed ten feet tall; her face a mask of fury and might, arms I'd thought frail, rippling with muscle. She thrust the Bo down into his neck, spearing him with what looked like all the power she possessed, clearly the equal of any strong man's. I heard his neck snap and saw blood shoot up through his mouth. Then she spun, swinging out at two officers behind her, cutting one off at the knees with her Bo, cracking the other across his throat, smashing bone and cartilage. The one she had hit on the knees lay squirming and moaning on the floor. She let out her yell and speared him just as she had the first man, ending him with one blow.

No wonder Sakura was Samurai. Her mother had raised her that way because she was Samurai too. I raised myself up on one elbow and groped for my wakizashi. I would fight beside her. Even as I got to my feet, she dealt with yet another foe who did not take her seriously. He grabbed her from behind, roaring, wrapping his brawny arms about her and lifting her off the ground. Mother kicked backwards viciously, caught him, and he dropped her, bent over in agony. I thought she would use her Bo on him, but she picked him up, held him over her head, then drove him headfirst into the floor. How did she have the strength to do that? She glanced down at him, saw by the angle of his neck she had snapped it, then looked at me. My shock must have remained on my face from watching her battle like a twenty-year-old. She smiled, happy with my surprise and her fighting prowess I had witnessed.

Behind her, Billy was swiping the father's katana savagely across a large man's chest, the last Japanese man standing in the house, a shattered house now, but no more shattered than the attackers who lay strewn about it, two of them headless. The man fell backwards, his heart pumping out his blood. Sakura rose from a man she had knelt over and straddled, raining blows upon his head with her fists until she broke him, rage twisting her pretty face and darkening her cherry blossom softness. She pulled his body by the feet from the house to the yard, still snarling: "Get them out, get them all out, they bring evil into my home."

I turned back to Sakura's mother, who I now viewed as someone from a Japanese legend. "May I ask your name?"

She bowed, sprinkles of blood like freckles on her face. "I am Kana."

"That means the one who has power."

She bowed again.

"You are Samurai, Kana."

"Women have been Samurai in my bloodline for many generations."

"Yet you act as if you are seventy or older. Bent over. Walking with a stoop. Taking baby steps. Using a cane."

She grinned like a schoolgirl. "All part of the act. Do you know what is *ninja* or *shinobi*?"

"No."

"Warriors who are invisible. Many Samurai consider them and their ways undignified and dishonorable. So, I live and fight in secret."

"You could have killed that man who harassed you at your kiosk months ago."

"With my bare hands, yes. But then everyone would have known what I truly am."

"And here you have killed three men. With ease."

"Five." She shrugged. "It does not bother me. They were fated to die by my power."

"How old are you really, Kana?" I asked.

Her smile grew. "A gentleman does not ask. A woman does not tell. Not even a Samurai woman. Especially not a ninja."

29

LOVERS

BILLY MARTENS

CRANDALL GOT THE ENGINEERS TO SHORE UP SAKURA'S AND KANA'S house and make it as good as new. Not that hard. Like many of the traditional homes, they had built it using wooden frames and shoji—rice paper made from paddy field grass called *katori*. It was durable, but thin. Easy to crash through if murder is on your mind. But it's used because it brings in the sunlight, filtering the rays through its whiteness, making the whole house glow. I'd always liked that.

The guys gave the inside rooms a facelift too, adding shoji walls and screens that hadn't been there before. All the rooms had been *washitsu*, traditional, which were enhanced by the gentle light *shoji* produced. The screens could be moved around. They each had three panels. A swell grunt from Milwaukee painted cherry blossoms on one of those screens. I swear his work was like the painting of a Japanese master. Kana and Sakura were amazed.

A week after the attack, the Emperor had had enough. He gathered the rogue officers and their following and told them the raids and killing must cease or they dishonored him and all Japan. The Americans would not be on the island forever. They must waste no time while they were. It was time to restore what had been lost. The American doctors had been helping Japan by healing its people. It was time for all Japanese to do the same. Heal the land. Heal the people. Serve the gods. Honor the Emperor.

The attacks ceased. They laid their weapons down.

It was well understood by Bud and me that nothing was to be said about who and what Sakura's mother really was. But we both looked at her in a different light from then on. I couldn't believe how she could transform herself into a woman who seemed without strength or the ability to move easily or even to straighten her back. However, she no longer kept up the pretense when Bud or I had tea with them. She sat erect, her eyes shone. She served us with suppleness and grace. Bud had her at fifty-one or fifty-five. I figured forty-eight or less. She knew we wondered and were trying to puzzle it out. She smiled like a young woman might smile who was teasing the boys. And kept her secrets.

Things changed between Sakura and me. In the best of ways. A couple of weeks after the attack, when the house was well on its way to becoming a home again, her mother kind of disappeared after tea. It was like she did her ninja routine and went invisible on us. I asked where she'd disappeared to and Sakura only smiled her quiet smile and asked me to walk with her into the garden. The days were shorter now as winter approached. The moon was just rising in the east and a few early stars sprinkled the dark. Her hand slipped into mine.

I didn't know what to do. She'd never taken my hand before. It was warm, soft, and strong all at the same time. She drew closer to me and the warmth of her body and the scent of her skin just about knocked me out. I guess I hesitated too long. She brushed her lips against my cheek and ear: "I am Samurai. I don't have to wait. Samurai make their own choices. I choose you. My mother approves. But I am the one who decides. Open to me, Marine.

Open to me like a blossom, William-san. Do not fear me or my power. I will only do you good."

Her kiss was soft and slow at first. My whole body jumped at the contact of her lips on my mouth. I could hear the waterfall splashing. I could hear her murmuring in Japanese. Then she gripped my face firmly in her two hands and took control. Her kiss went deep and long and it was like having flames cross over from her to me. I did not know where this was going to lead in our American-Japanese lives, but I wasn't going to stop the flow so I could think about it. I put my arms around her and kissed back as hard as I could. It still wasn't as strong as her kisses. She slipped her hands inside my kimono and ran them over my chest. Between her kisses and her touches, she rendered me weak and helpless in no time, and she knew it. I just wanted more and more of her.

And she gave me more and more of her. Sakura's hair was always up, her hair like shining raven wings. She tugged it down and directed my lips until they pressed against the fall that went past her shoulders, down past her waist and down past her knees. I kissed it, her miraculous hair, her neck, her shoulder, my face pushing past her kimono. There was no protest from her. "More, William-san," she whispered. "Much more."

It wasn't as if I'd never prepared against the day and moment, hoping she might initiate a romance between us. I'd gone to Bud, and he'd given me a few phrases to memorize. I tried one as my lips touched her hair and ear: *"Hana no youni kirei." You're as beautiful as a flower.*

She laughed softly. "Oh, am I? A tough Samurai girl like me? That's very good. But shouldn't you say I'm as beautiful as a sword?"

"You are as beautiful as a sword and just as deadly. But right now, I can only think of you as a beautiful flower."

"Ah. And do you find me as beautiful as your American girls?"

"You're as beautiful as anyone."

"Am I? Truly? Aren't I more like one of your tomboys? Or one of your rough and tough Montana cowgirls?"

"I like tomboys. I like rough and tough Montana cowgirls. I like Samurai women with their power and their speed. *Kimi ni muchu nanda, Sakura." I'm crazy about you, Sakura.*

"Oh." She drew back to look at me. The moon was caught in her hair and I just wanted to kiss it. I wasn't interested in talking. "You are not."

"Of course I am."

"How can you be crazy about me overnight?"

"I'm not crazy about you overnight. I've liked you from the start. Even when you were ignoring me."

"You did not say anything."

"How could I say anything? There are too many rules I don't understand. I didn't want to blow it."

She looked confused.

"Make a mistake and mess everything up," I explained. "So, I didn't say a thing. But I thought about you all the time. Going back to when I saw you at the shrine."

"Yes. I understand. There are many rules and customs and Samurai are bound to much of it. But come." She drew me to the grass and knelt. "Put your head on my lap."

I hesitated.

"Don't worry, I'm not going to decapitate you." Her teeth flashed. "Come, William-san." She patted her lap. "I wish to romance you."

I got down and lay my head on her lap. I was looking up at Sakura. Her hair tumbled over me. For a long time, I took in her wonderful scents while she traced patterns on my face. Then she sang in Japanese. It sounded like a lullaby, though she told me later it was a love song. She thought she'd never sing the song because it had never been in her heart to fall in love. I did not understand the words, but she stroked my face in the gentlest way as she sang.

After a while, she leaned over and kissed me again. Each kiss began as if she didn't want to hurt me. Then it grew into the kind of kiss that overwhelms everything else. For a few moments at a time, you do not even remember your own name or what city you are in or the reason you are in the city to begin with. I pulled her down beside me. There was nothing else I could do. She created such desire in me. Her warmth came through her kimono.

"Oh, Sakura," I moaned, "you are so much good."

"I'm glad, William-san. I feel treasured by you. Do I give you joy?"

"Yes, God, yes."

"Just my kisses and my touch are enough happiness for now?"

"Yes."

"In time, there can be more. If you want me enough. If you want me as your wife."

"Sakura, I—"

She pressed her lips onto mine to silence me. "Shh. I don't want you to answer me. Not now. Let's just kiss and snuggle and not think about hard things and big things. Just enjoy each other."

"It's not a hard thing."

"Mm. But it is a big thing. So, let's wait a bit. You haven't kissed me enough."

"You haven't kissed me enough either."

"Ah. You don't think so? Let's see what I can do about that."

This was the first of many nights. I guess I ought to say it was the first night of every night. Tea with her mother. Her mother vanishes into thin air. We walk to the garden in our kimonos. We kiss standing up. She kneels, and I lay my head in her lap. We kiss some more. After a long time, I sit up and ask to brush out her hair. She brings the brush out of a pocket. I stroke her long, thick, glossy black hair.

I do well enough for a few minutes. Then it is too much. She is too beautiful. She has too much power over me. My ache for her is too painful. I sink my face into her hair, dropping the brush in the grass. I breathe in all her glory and wonder, all her fragrance, all the warmth that runs through her. I turn her over in my arms. I kiss her neck and shoulders; I kiss her eyes, and I take my time at it, saving the best for the last. Her perfect mouth. Her perfect mouth, like flower petals, like cherry blossoms, pink and fresh and spilling with life, unbelievably sweet. It's as if we absorb one another through our kisses. The stars are gone; the moon is gone, even the happy splashing waterfall is gone. Sakura is the only thing that matters in the entire earth.

She loved to trace patterns on my face. Sometimes they were paintings she imagined, she told me, similar to art done of trees, houses, hills, rice paddies and farmers for hundreds of years. She often did drawings of Samurai. Samurai art was ancient. A lot of it she had memorized. Other times she traced Japanese characters, kanji, and worked haiku on my forehead. Haiku were poems with only seventeen syllables. She would do one in Japanese and the next in English.

I walk seeing just sky and loneliness. Look! You are on the same path!

"I have been lonely," she confessed one night when the moon was full to bursting. "Crushingly lonely. I had my siblings to keep me amused. We did everything together. When I realized not even one of them was coming back, it almost broke my spirit, though Samurai are not supposed to ever break."

"I'm sorry, Sakura. Does our friendship help?"

"Yes, of course it helps. And you should know better than to call it a friendship."

"Aren't we friends?" I asked, knowing how she'd answer, but wanting to hear it.

"Oh, you know very well what I mean." She stopped. Her eyebrows fascinated me. She indulged me, but rolled her eyes as I began rubbing them. "Don't distract me. You can be a most infuriating and annoying man when you want to be. We are friends and far more than friends, William-san. You are my lover. The only lover I've ever had." She gripped my head in her hands and her grip was steel. "Tomorrow we are going to Mount Fujiyama. I want to get married to you there. I doubt very much you are going to say no."

30

THE WAY BACK
JOHNNY STRANGE

A COOL TOUCH, A SOFT VOICE, A GOLDEN GLOW AROUND THE FACE from my dreams.

Marjean.

I know now I'm in heaven because Marjean is in Sandpoint, Idaho, with my boy and I'm dead in Japan. Well, I think I'm dead. I couldn't be anything else. That Jap shot me up close and personal. I felt every one of those bullets hit me and every one headed for vital parts.

"Johnny Strange, wake up."

I'm having trouble with this. I can't seem to move and there is something over my mouth and nose. But the face is still there. It must be an angel because I'm dead...

Aren't I?

"Johnny Strange, you come back to me. I need you."

I was wandering in the dark. It seemed like for a long, long time. I was on a boat, on a deep river and I sailed past lands where people live in darkness and mist and the sun never pierces, neither when it rises, nor when it sets. I beached the boat on black sand and waited.

What was I waiting for?

I saw people, people that are dead or from a hated past. They crowd around. Ghosts, shades, empty of life.

"Hi ya, Johnny."

Malena!

"How did you get here? You disappeared. We thought a croc got you."

"You were right. A real FUBAR. I got so sick of the mud and the slime and the blood that I just needed to get clean. That's all I wanted. To get clean. I took off my clothes and waded in. The water was cool, and I just wanted to get clean."

Tony was crying.

"Yeah, we found your stuff on the bank. What happened?"

"I didn't even see him. I'm just sitting in the water, dreaming about a cold Miller High Life, when something grabs me from behind and pulls me under. Like a vise, but with teeth."

"Jeez, Malena, that's bad luck."

"Yeah, stupid. They told us about the crocs, but I didn't listen..."

He faded away and more ghosts came, more faces.

I know I'm dead because this is hell, right?

"Johnny, come back."

There's the voice again and the cool hand on my face. I try real hard... harder... I have got to go where the voice is, where the face is, because if I do, I won't die, but I'll live...

"Open your eyes again, Johnny. Try."

I never thought this would be so hard. But Marjean is here, and she's calling me back.

There!

I got them open.

I'm not dead. There is a plain white room with a bed in it. I'm in the bed.

I got a tube down my throat and some in my arms. And she's sitting by me with her hand on mine.

Marjean, oh Marjean!

She smiles at me.

"Hello, my darling. Welcome back."

She turns around and says something and another face swims into view.

Bud!

He smiles, but it's not the sad smile. He's glad to see me. "Hey, Strange, whaddaya know?"

"Hey, Philo..." I croak, with a tube in the corner of my face. "Just got back from a vaudeville show. And boy, what a show."

Bud laughs, and Marjean puts her head down on my chest and cries. I try to get my arm around her, but it's hard and then Bud leans down and does it for me.

Another face.

Sniper!

He's grinning like a Cheshire cat. "C'mon, Strange. How long you gonna lie here and goof off? I'm getting married and I need you on your feet."

"Married?" But with the stuff in my mouth, it sounds like "Mawwied?"

Billy laughs. "You sound like Elmer Fudd."

Marjean looks up and the tears are running down her face. Dear God, she is so beautiful. Thank you, God.

<hr>

IT TURNS out I've been down for five days. Crandall was so worried I wouldn't make it, he got Marjean over here to be with me. When I made a turn for the better, he got her set up in a house just down the road. As soon as I get a little more stable, they are going to let me out of here and instead of sending me home, I'll rehab right here in Japan. I guess Marjean's working for Crandall with Bud on some project that's pretty hush-hush, so that's why we're staying. Marjean talked to Al and J.A. back in Sandpoint to let them know I'm doing better.

Today when she came to see me, I noticed the big baby bump for the first time. Holy cow, I forgot all about that. We're going to have another baby. Let's see. I went home from Saipan in October and got married in November. Back to Saipan in March of 1945. Marjean says that we made the baby the night before I left. So, she's about six months. We might have a new addition to the Strange family by Christmas.

Bud tells me I came close, very close to cashing in my chips. Yeah, well, I knew that because I felt the slugs go in. I'm sure glad that Jap only had a .22 caliber suicide pistol instead of a .45 or I would be dancing with the angels.

THERE'S a lot to think about when you're lying in a bed and you can't get up. I guess while I was out of it, Marjean slept on one of those Japanese futons beside my bed. But now that Bud and Dr. Krawiec have me on the good side of the hill, she's been going back to our place at night. So I've had a lot of time to think, in the small hours before the dawn. And I've been thinking about what a long strange journey this has been. The stuff that happened to me as a kid, my dad's refusal to take my side or believe me, the anger and pain I felt inside and especially... the fear I felt inside that I wasn't really a man. So from the day I walked out of my dad's door, got in my car, drove to the King's cabin and found the best thing that ever happened to me, it's been remarkable.

Marjean.

I remember when I took her out in my boat that day I met her. We were pounding down the lake as fast as we could go. I glanced over and there was a look on her face I had never seen on a girl. She looked like a beautiful wild animal. Her lips were parted, and she bared her eyeteeth, like a wolf. Her hands were clenching and unclenching, and her face was alive. She threw back her head and laughed and the sound was bells and ice.

I remember what happened in the boathouse when we got back and how from that moment on I somehow knew nothing would separate us, except death, and even then...

I think about going to war, all my friends who died. In the darkness of my hospital room, it's like a Movietone reel at the picture house. Guadalcanal, New Zealand, Hawaii, Tarawa, Saipan, and finally the worst of all, Okinawa. I became a killer, a boxer, a leader, a man. I had a son; I got married and somehow, somewhere, I found the faith I left behind in Bonners Ferry, Idaho. The faith I left lying on the floor in that confrontation with my father, when I knew he would defend his reputation before he would defend his son. I don't know if it was in the jungles of Cactus, or the mountains of New Zealand. I don't know if it was in the sweat lodge in Hawaii where my code-talker buddies showed me that the pain you feel inside is not who you are. It's just the grindstone that sharpens you. But somewhere, I found that faith again.

I think about Bud and Billy. I wonder in these dark hours how God knew they would be my friends: a Menno cowboy from Montana and a big lunk from Ritzville, Washington. How does God do that?

Bud, who never gave up on me, who talked me through the dark times in the barracks at boot camp. Bud, who picked up the crumpled-up letter I wrote to Marjean, telling her for the first time that I loved her and wanted to be with me. And then I wadded it up and threw it on the floor, doubting my manhood and wondering what a girl like her could ever see in me. I think about how he carefully flattened it out, smiled at me and told me to get my ass down to the post office and mail it or there would be serious consequences. Somehow Bud always knew the real me. He knew I needed Marjean; he knew I wasn't a sissy and in time I saw he had a direct link. I knew that he prayed for me and that it changed things.

And Billy. The guy who seemed to have all the answers and

yet the most lost of the three of us. A guy I could ride the river with the rest of my life, but a guy with a dark place inside, a place where there were more questions than answers, a place where the swagger and bravado and skill disappeared, leaving only doubts.

So now Billy has this Japanese girl. I saw her a couple of times before I got shot. She's definitely a real beauty. But Billy, once again, has put himself in the middle of a mess. From what Bud says, Crandall is fit to be tied. A Jap girl and a Marine? Man, we just got done spending four years killing every Jap we saw and now Billy's in love with one?

Me? I don't trust any of them as far as I could throw them. I mean, how does a whole nation go from being a blood-thirsty, murderous horde of monsters, raping and burning their way through Asia, with their sights set on conquering the entire world for their Emperor—how does a country like that suddenly become a polite, ah-so, 'me like Amelicans', nice and friendly, invite them over for tea kind of group? It doesn't make sense to me.

Those guys in that house out by the prison camp had not surrendered, not by a long shot. I came in the door and they didn't even hesitate. I remember the look in the fat boy's eyes as he put five into me. He hated my guts. There was no way in hell that this character would ever stop hating me.

I've seen too many of my buddies shot to pieces, heads gone, guts in the sand, arms and legs blown off. I've seen too much of that to make a one-hundred-eighty degree turn and walk it back. No, Billy may have a love affair going with this gal, Sakura, but I don't trust it. I don't trust her and I think Billy's just headed for more heartache.

Will I stand up with him? If my legs work, damn straight I'll stand up with him. But I won't like it.

Me, I'm glad we dropped the bomb on these little bugs. Billy's been pissing and moaning about it since it happened. But what about the one million guys that would have turned Tokyo bay red with their blood if we tried to come ashore in Japan? Me, Bud, Billy, we'd all be lying dead in the sand along with all of our men and most of the nutcases on these insane islands. I mean, these people are whack jobs.

I don't know how this will work out. It's probably something that will be between me and Billy for a long time. But... I hope it works out. I hope I can get to like his wife. Someday, I hope, we can all sit down to dinner and forget about everything that happened between her country and mine. I hope that the sight of her yellow skin and slanted eyes doesn't make me want to pull out my .45 and put three into that lovely face.

This is going to be hard. Damned hard.

31

TWO FACES OF LOVE
BUD, THE CORPSMAN

MAN, OH MAN. WHAT A KERFUFFLE.

I thought we were all done with the battles, with the danger, with the turmoil. War out there is easy to handle. You just get behind a rock, shoot your gun and then the corpsman goes around and cleans everything up. Oh yeah, there's blood and death and mayhem, but at least you know what it is. It's when you deal with the war that goes on inside people, that's when it gets hard. For example, I got three, maybe four battles on my hands in spite of the fact that Japan surrendered. What's up with this?

After getting the insides shot out of him, Strange has finally turned away from death's door. Thanks mostly to God, Lieutenant Krawiec, and most of all, Marjean. I honestly didn't think he would make it. When they brought him in, in my mind I said, "stick a fork in Strange, he's done."

I mean, for the first time with my Menno boys I got a brass heaven, even though I almost wore out my knees. I did not know what the outcome would be, and God didn't help me out one bit. For four days I'm in the dark.

I'm not hearing, Billy's not really praying, and Krawiec is mostly an interested observer. I think the only one who didn't give up was Marjean. That girl held her man in this world by the slimmest of threads. She never once let go. She sat there for four days, calling him back.

And Johnny must have heard, and he must have asked God to help him while he was out there, or at least he made his peace. Because here he is, alive and well and taking nourishment, and I didn't have a thing to do with it.

I guess that shows me I can't ride herd on these guys all their lives. I've been the go-to guy since boot camp, but now I'm learning these guys have to grow up—all the way up. That means at some point they pick up the slack and ask God their own questions.

Meanwhile, Billy is driving the whole Marine Corps nuts. He's got this Japanese girlfriend, and he swears he's going to marry her. Crandall is fit to be tied. I mean, I haven't heard the Lord's name taken in vain so much since we showed up at Camp Tarawa on the high and windswept plains between Mauna Loa and Mauna Kea, and all that was there was a pile of canvas, some wooden slats, a sea of mud and the bitterest mountain wind that ever carved a volcanic rock. I had never heard such professional cussing and have yet to—until Billy told Crandall he's marrying Sakura, his Japanese Samurai. So, it's a mess.

The reason it's a mess is that I don't think Johnny is up for it. He and Sniper had some bitter go-rounds on Saipan when we were burning down Tokyo and Billy got a soft spot for the civilians. Johnny, on the other hand, thinks that everybody in Japan signed up for the big show. They all got in line and they all were thrilled when their army burned down China and bombed Pearl back to the stone age. At one point, Billy made the mistake of taking a swing at Johnny. He never saw that right hand coming back at him and I think the little birds are still flying around his head, tweeting. Why else would he take up with a Jap girl? If he's not careful, Johnny may put his head back on straight.

The other thing I got going is the detail Crandall has me on.

When I went home after Okinawa, I thought I was there for good. I mean, we had done Saipan, Johnny was married, I got right with my dad; I survived the last big battle and now I was home, waiting for Kalasia to come from Tonga. Me and my dad were spending time together, my mom was fattening me up, and I did not have a care in the world—well I was worried about Billy, but just because his Chamorran girl-friend dumped him and he was wandering around Japan in a daze. But I figured he would work it out. At that point I did not know what lengths he would go to work it out, but I was pretty sure Sniper would pull it together.

Well, anyway, I'm sitting there in hog heaven in the old digs in Ritzville, WA, and I get the call from Crandall. I put my Tongan Princess off for another three to five months and back I go to Japan.

The deal was, when they dropped the bomb on Hiroshima and Nagasaki, the big brains behind it had no idea what the effects on the human body would be. For the most part, when you take an enormous blast of gamma rays to your body, it affects you in different ways. The unit of measure that accounts for these factors is the sievert, which measures absorption of radioactive energy multiplied by a quality factor that changes depending on whether the radiation being measured is alpha particles, beta particles or gamma. Now I know this sounds pretty heady, but I'm just filling you in.

Most people get two to three milli-sieverts a year. One sievert will cause nausea, vomiting and hemorrhaging, but not death. The people at ground zero in Nagasaki took an enormous blast of gamma rays, like one hundred and fifty sieverts or something, and the resulting sickness was instantaneous and horrible. First off, around forty thousand people died immediately. They were the lucky ones. Of those who survived the initial blast, many had their eyes literally melted in their sockets by the heat and the blinding light. Then the radiation kicked in. Skin sloughed off, and people walked around or lay on the ground begging for water. People's faces hung down, melted, and their hair and clothes were burnt right off their bodies. These people died within minutes or hours.

But many survived, and those were the ones I was interviewing. What we discovered was there were many, many people who had been exposed to one or two sieverts and died days, weeks or even months after being exposed to the radiation. Folks who got a minor dose had their initial symptoms, like nausea, diarrhea, headache, fever and even, in severe cases, loss of consciousness, fade within a few days. Then they would go along with absolutely no symptoms until suddenly, the body would just implode and within a few hours, they were dead. They called the symptom-free time the latent period. The sad thing was, you could not tell, or even diagnose, who would die. And even if you could, there was no treatment. The radiation was a silent killer.

After the latent period, the actual damage became clear. The radiation just worked its evil and took apart cells and structures inside the body. Most vulnerable was bone marrow, where stem cells produce blood cells. Damaged marrow can't produce enough red or white blood cells, leaving the body anemic and susceptible to infections. Radiation also damaged the cells that line the digestive system, not only preventing that system from functioning properly but allowing bacteria to migrate from the digestive tract into the blood, causing more infections.

So, one day, a person could be fine, and the next, they were dead.

There were a few who overcame the radiation and survived. I met a guy like that in the hospital in Nagasaki. His name was Tsutoma Yamaguchi. The amazing thing was he survived both bombs. He was in Hiroshima for a special job for his company, Mitsubishi. He spent the summer there. On August 6, he was walking on his morning commute to work. He heard the roar from a big plane, then watched a bomb fall, and a parachute opened. Then the sky flashed with a blinding light. He dove into a ditch and the shock wave… *shi omaki ko nada*… engulfed him.

When he woke up hours later, his skin was burned black. He made his way to an air raid shelter and spent the night. There was nothing left of Hiroshima. The next morning, he went to the railroad station to get back to his home in Nagasaki. The bridge across the river was blown down, and he had to swim the river. He swam through a raft of dead bodies.

He got back to Nagasaki just in time for the second bomb. When they finally got him to the hospital, his arms were gangrenous. I asked the doctor in the Nagasaki Hospital what his chances were. They were very surprised that he was even alive. But he was and slowly fighting back from the effects. That's how I found out there were some who survived the radiation, but they were the exceptions.

As I do my interviews, I find many people who have lost loved ones they did not know were sick. I think that for many months and even years, we will see them dying.

And that's part of my problem. On the one hand, Billy was right. How could a nation that calls itself civilized do this to other human beings? The guys who built the bomb must have known it would produce such deadly energy. When they tested it in New Mexico, they saw its power. This bomb was hell in a steel casing. The guys who dropped it were so amazed at the monstrous thing they released, all they could do was stare.

When I signed up to be a medic, this is not what I signed on for. I learned about the damage a bullet or a shell or a bomb can wreak on the human body, but when you are in action on the battlefield, it's right there in front of you. You learn to deal with it, because you not only studied it, but you face up to it every day. But this radiation sickness is something else. To watch a little child just waste away and die, a kid who was playing and laughing a few days before, well, that is something you have to see with Billy Martens' eyes.

But Johnny's right too. When we were back on Saipan after Okinawa, every one of us had finally seen what the Japanese were capable of when it came to defending their homeland. We killed one hundred thousand of them in that fight and few of them surrendered, mostly Okinawan civilians. The Jap army boys didn't even consider surrender as an option. They had their honor to consider. When we were cleaning up, we would find Japs with their arm gone and their guts blown out. They would pull the pin on a grenade and hold it against their chests, rather than let us capture them. The guys who shot Johnny were the same way. It didn't matter what the Emperor said, they never surrendered. And Japan is filled with people like that. I heard they gave the women sticks and told them that if any Americans tried to come ashore, they were to attack them. Are you kidding?

So, if we tried to come ashore anywhere on the main islands, it was guaranteed that one million of our boys would die and probably four million of their people. A stinking blood bath, the worst in the history of the world. I can't even wrap my head around numbers like that. On the one hand, you got hundreds of thousands of people burnt to a crisp or getting sick and dying after the fact, and you weigh that against five million people killing each other with guns and bombs and sticks and swords.

The battle for Japan—the bomb or the bullet. Which way is the way of love? Kill a few to save the many, or kill many to spare the few the most horrible fate ever seen on the face of this planet? You tell me. I don't have the answer.

Billy sees it one way, Johnny another. And I don't think they are going to work it out for a while. Not this week, that's for sure.

3 2

PETALS

BILLY MARTENS

I THINK SAKURA WAS USED TO GETTING HER WAY THROUGHOUT HER life, at least in the things she could wrestle under her control. She wanted Mount Fuji to be the site for her wedding because it was such an important symbol of Japan. But her mother pleaded with her to have our marriage performed at the shrine on the hill: "The ashes of your brothers and sisters and father are here, not on Mount Fujiyama. Your grandparents and great-grandparents and on down through the centuries. Do not dishonor them. Do not betray them. For their sake, for my sake, remember the gods and marry here."

Sakura bowed to her mother's wishes. There was no way out of it. Unless she wanted to bring shame on her family and her ancestors and that, of course, was something she would not do. We made arrangements for both a Buddhist priest and a Shinto priest to be involved. The Buddhist priest agreed to perform a ceremony in Sakura's and her mother's garden. The Shinto priest would perform another at the shrine. And then there was the United States Marine Corps.

Crandall raised bloody hell. The marriage could not happen, would not happen. It would be too controversial, and the top brass agreed with him. However, I pointed out to Crandall that blocking the wedding would be construed as a tremendous insult, and the ripple effect would disrupt the entire Nagasaki community. Everyone knew the four sons and their father had been killed serving Japan. They knew one son's ashes had never made it home because his body and plane had gone missing in the Philippines and never been found. They were well aware the youngest daughter had been killed in the Tokyo firebombing in March. Now the Americans were going to refuse to let the surviving daughter be married? How did he think that was going to play out?

"I don't give a flying rat's ass how it plays out," Crandall fumed. "We will not have a Japanese-American Marine Corps wedding ceremony, Martens. Tensions are still running too high. What's gotten into you? Why wasn't that beautiful Saipan girl good enough for you?"

"She was good enough for me, skipper. I wasn't good enough for her. Anyway, it doesn't matter now. If she wrote me a letter tomorrow, I wouldn't answer it. I'm head over heels with Sakura."

"Head over heels, are you?" he snarled. "Too fricking bad. I'm shipping you out on the next boat that floats."

"Bad idea, skipper."

"Don't presume on our wartime camaraderie too much, Martens. I'll bust you down to private and take your stripes."

"Take my silver star too, skipper?"

"Shut your stinking mouth. Get outta my sight."

"You ought to know there are some big names connected to this wedding, skipper."

"Like who? Harry S. Truman? I still wouldn't let it go ahead even if he showed up with the whole Congress and the U.S. Senate."

"How about the Emperor, skipper?"

"What? What about the Emperor?"

"Sakura's family has always enjoyed relations with the royal family. One of the Emperor's uncles knew Sakura's father. The Emperor is well aware of the sacrifice the family made for Japan. He is sending representatives."

I thought Crandall would blow a gasket. "Representatives! Godamn it, Martens! Now, what have you got us into? An international incident?"

"Not if you give the wedding the go ahead, skipper. Otherwise, Sakura and her mother will have to tell the royal family the wedding is off. The Emperor actually thought it might be good for Japan. Especially if we raised our family here as a symbol of peace and hope."

"Bloody hell, Martens! You've ambushed me! Did you set this up?"

"No, skipper. Sakura made all the arrangements."

"You've gone over my head, Martens, and that really pisses me off. You're more trouble than the entire Pacific War."

"And it was a lot of trouble, skipper."

"Damn right it was. We won the fricking thing and now this. This!"

There was no way the brass were going to get into the Emperor's bad books. So, Crandall cussed his way right up to the wedding ceremonies. A goddamnit in the garden by the pond. Another at the Shinto shrine. And a third the USMC threw in to make sure the marriage was USA official and Gyrene approved. A professional job, if I ever heard one.

Johnny and Marjean and Bud were at all three along with Bolo, Player and Gyprock. We still looked slick in our uniforms. Not that it had been that long since we'd worn our combat fatigues for real.

Several relatives and friends of Sakura and her mother attended as well. Not all of them. The Japanese liked their wedding ceremonies small. The reception in a hall that had been rebuilt was another thing. That would be crammed.

Sakura wore the white kimono her mother had worn, called a

shiromuku, along with a large fancy headpiece. This was for the Shinto ceremony, not the Buddhist one. I wore a black kimono with a black jacket and pants, all of which had been the father's, and that was for the Shinto ceremony as well. At the shrine on the hill we were blessed, the Shinto priest prayed to the kami, we drank three ritual or nuptial cups of sake each, small cups—that was called *san san ku do*. We made our vows again, having made them first by the pond in the garden. Back down the hill, a Protestant padre, I think he was Baptist, had us do our vows once again. He pronounced us man and wife after reading First Corinthians 13 from the Bible, the love chapter. I heard Crandall grumble the third time was the charm and that now we were married for damn sure. I lost him in the crush of the crowd at the celebration, downing sake and clutching a plate of sushi. I lost everyone. I just wanted to be alone with Sakura. Hours later, she gifted me with herself by our pond.

All alone. Nagasaki is quiet. The moon in hiding like a ninja. Only the stars. Their shine was quiet too. Sakura opened my kimono, and I opened hers. I drew in her strength and beauty like breath. "How happy you are, my American man," she said in her British accent, smiling playfully. "I will make you happier yet."

We held each other and kissed slowly. I didn't want anything to be rushed. Her body trembled. It was cool. I'd heard Mount Fuji had much more snow already. I wrapped her in my black kimono and carried her into the house and into her own room. I laid her on her futon, which her mother had opened and spread with silk sheets and warm blankets. We snuggled underneath it all. She giggled. "This is more fun than I thought it would be."

"What did you think it would be?"

"I don't know. Scary."

"Scary?"

"Yes."

"But you are Samurai."

She did her tracing on my forehead with one perfectly manicured finger. "I may be Samurai, my husband, but I've never had one of you in my bed before. I've never been in love before. I hadn't even been kissed before you showed up. This is all unfamiliar territory for me. Unless we wrestle, my fighting skills are no good under these blankets."

"You will learn new skills then, Petals."

It was my new name for her. She liked it.

She kept tracing. I'm sure she was writing a haiku. "Oh? New skills? What will they be?"

"Let's find out," I murmured, kissing her delicate ears. "I am so in love with you, Sakura. I'm helpless and hopeless."

She laughed. "Are you? I think not. I am sure it will be a long, happy night for both of us." She pulled me down beside her. "Here is my poem for you, my beautiful husband. *Dark night, weary, I go to my bed, ah! A husband is already there!*"

I laughed too. "Surprise! Here I am!"

Sakura was so supple. She wrapped herself completely around me, arm and legs and body, like a vine, like a lovely perfumed growing plant. There was nothing more to say. I adored her. She was moonlight in my arms. We became one flesh.

There was nowhere we wished to go but under the blankets of the futon, so that is where we stayed for several days. We had tea with Kana at four every afternoon. Then Kana would vanish and so would we. We had all become ninjas.

Finally, we wanted to stretch our "just married" legs. It seemed only natural that we'd walk up to the shrine, pass through the gates onto holy ground and sit together, staying very close, whether inside the shrine or outside on a bench. Neither of us made a whisper. We were conscious of the Shinto priest, who had married us the Shinto way, hovering around. Perhaps he thought we might kiss and cuddle, or worse. We just sat quietly and thought our million thoughts.

The war already felt like it had happened in another century or that it had happened to other people, not to me. How quickly the body could shovel everything far below in the coal shaft of the mind. Sure, I could bring the memories back if I wanted to. Otherwise, they didn't intrude much. I'd heard of guys going nuts over their combat experiences. How they followed them home and, like a ravenous beast, ate up what was left of their lives. I prayed that wouldn't be my fate. I had a strong hunch it would never happen, could never happen, so long as Petals was in my arms and her warm cherry blossom lips kissed not only my mouth and my face but my heart.

Yeah, Petals brought me peace. I slept so well next to her, wound up in her strong, healthy body. I doubt I'd slept that well since New Zealand. There were no dark moments, and I had no fears. Dad never showed up to chastise me for the millions of war dead, military and civilians both, of all nations. I thought those dreams would probably come back. But for the time being, it was like the good sleeps I had in Montana under the white stars, a campfire dying nearby, the embers glowing red and gold. Maybe a few coyotes yipping. Deer barking in the brush. A light mountain breeze moving over my face since I rarely used a tent. Sakura's love and presence could do all that for me as if she were the mountains, as if she were the night, as if she were the air I breathed and that moved all around me and over me. There weren't any bad days, really. Only if she pushed me on the chest, not a weak push either, and basically threw me out of bed: "No more futon time, Billy. Let's get up and get cracking."

Her use of American slang made me laugh, but she kept on with it, anyway. Things were swell. I was cooking with gas. If she didn't like something, she'd say, "It stinks." If we spoke about U.S. dollars, they were bucks: "Do you have a sawbuck, Billy, or maybe two bits?" When she got thirsty, she was "dry as a bone." From someone, somewhere, somehow, she got her hands on a Batman comic, brand new, read it aloud to me and went looking for another. Fuel wasn't the Brit petrol any longer, it was gas. A car's bonnet became a hood, and the boot became the trunk. She took up smoking as an American thing, even though every country smoked, insisted on Marlboros, and always seemed to get her hands on them. Instead of a torch, it was a flashlight, instead of sweets it was now candy, no longer 'cheers,' it was 'see ya.'

"Billy," she told me one night after we'd made love a number of times, "you give me goose bumps."

Of course, I went back to the Marine Corps and did my duty by Nagasaki. But every evening I was back with Sakura and her mom where Sakura finally kept a wedding night promise and taught me bushido, the path of the warrior. She lent me her father's sword for that: "It only makes sense, Billy. You've already drawn blood with it. My father would be most pleased."

We were in our kimonos by the pond. We both held our katanas in their scabbards. It was dark, but it was dark inside the house too. Half the time, the electricity flickered off and on. Her mother came out and hung lanterns with kanji on them. Sakura bowed, and I bowed. Then she launched a sudden attack, knocked me down and swiftly beheaded me. Or would have if she'd shucked her scabbard and used the naked blade.

Sakura bowed. "Never let your guard down, Billy. Always keep your eyes on your opponent. On their face." She actually lit a Marlboro. "Let me say a few things about that fight. You were brave and bold. But you swung wildly. Fortunately, you swung into your foes' bodies most of the time. If you had watched me, you would have seen I rarely parry and never edge to edge. Mostly I was ducking and dodging their blows, and then I would strike when I had an opening. There is no time for sword fighting in a true battle. You want to kill as quickly and cleanly as possible. Otherwise, don't draw your blade to begin with."

We trained for two hours every night, no matter how cold it was. Then we had our bath together, which was, I suppose, the reward. After about ten sessions, she wanted me to try cutting Tatami mats. The cutting was called *Tameshigiri*. The mats were the same as they used on the floor in the house, but rolled up and placed on a pole that was stuck in the ground.

"You must slice at the angle I teach you, Billy," she said before my first attempt at cutting. "The grip must be so. The alignment of your edge—exactly like this." She stopped. "Why are you smiling?"

"You look cute," I said.

"I look cute? I'm teaching you how to be a Samurai and I look cute?"

"Should I use another word?"

"What other word?"

"There is nothing to be upset about. You're a beautiful woman. You are also a natural warrior. When you are teaching the way of the warrior, you become very intense. This brings color into your cheeks and a glitter into your eyes. So, if possible, you become even more beautiful. It's also cute. Not in a way that makes me take you less seriously. In a way, that makes me want to ask you to marry me again."

I saw her shoulders relax under her navy kimono with the cherry blossoms. "So." She smiled. "You find me beautiful, do you, American man?"

"As if you don't know that. As if I haven't told you a thousand times."

Her smile grew. "Perhaps two thousand. I'll let you know when I tire of hearing you say it."

"You are an excellent teacher. I feel sure my first cut will be just right."

"You think so? I can help."

"You can help?"

"I see you are tense. You wish to please me. You also wish not to humiliate yourself before me. So, yes, Billy, I can help."

"How?"

"Oh, it is no great Samurai secret. Keep a close eye on my face." She approached and slipped her long, elegant arms around my neck. "Now, pay careful attention to my lips." She saw delight rush into my eyes and laughed softly at how eager I was. "Many weeks married and still my young happy girl-crazy Marine." She began the kiss, taking her time. "I guarantee every muscle in your body will relax. The looser you are, the better you will swing the sword. Not swing like a baseball bat, no. The slice, just as I have taught you. By the way, did you know I saw Babe Ruth and Lou Gehrig when I was a girl ten years ago? Oh, yes, they were here, playing our best ball players. Father loved baseball and formed a team that girls and boys could play on together. I outhit all the boys. I did. Would you play catch with me, Billy?"

She had caught me by surprise. "Baseball, Petals?"

"Oh, yes, we Japanese love it. We have been playing it for fifty years. Now, make your cut. Baseball on Saturday."

"What about the rest of my kiss?"

"Oh, you don't need more than I already gave you."

"I might debate that."

"Shh. Don't be silly. Swing your sword and we will have fun in the bath to celebrate."

I felt pretty loose. I made the cut, sliced the bundled mats just right. She laughed and hugged me and pulled me into the house. We had our bath and had our bed, and on Saturday she got us up early to throw a baseball.

They had bats, and leather gloves that someone had kept oiled and soft, ball caps, even cleats. I thought playing catch was all she had on her mind. She had a good arm. She could send that ball sizzling into my glove. But pretty soon she wanted me to pitch to her: "I will show you how good I am at this, Billy."

"I believe you, Petals."

"No. I want to show you."

So, I pitched, and she hit a fast grounder to first, if we'd had a first, and I told her she was out. She made a face and said I was not an umpire, just the pitcher, and that she wanted me to send her good balls. My fourth pitch she whaled the ball high and far.

I had to run down the street after it while she jumped up and down and declared it was a Bambino homer. A Marine actually caught the hit, I never told her that, and tossed the ball to me: "She's sure got arms on her, Sarge."

We did it for a couple of hours. She blasted that ball so hard I thought the cover would come off. She loved it, of course, and loved surprising me. Kind of shocking me, really. "See, Billy," she teased, "you married Superman." I didn't get up to bat once. "The Samurai Baseball Team has trounced you 55 to 0," she crowed. "You have been destroyed. Soon it's your Christmas, isn't it? We'll have a tournament, really play a game. I'll pick my team and you can pick yours from the Marines, and I'll trounce you again. Ho, ho, ho, Santa Claus will say."

I remember I noticed tufts of her black hair on the street where she had been standing at bat and striking the ball. I thought nothing of it. Just that she had been energetic. I was back talking with Crandall about the neighborhood patrols when Bolo came tearing in, no salute, no by your leave, and yelled, "Sarge, you gottta come quick! Something's wrong at your house!" He had a Willie jeep and Crandall and I jumped in. What? Another attack? The Emperor was supposed to have put an end to that.

Bud was already there, standing just outside the door. A bunch of docs and nurses and corpsmen were with him. Bud was covered in blood. I thought they had shot him. I leaped out, snatching a Thompson from the jeep, and went running towards him. "What is it, Bud? What's up? Where's Sakura? Where's her mom?"

Bud blocked me. "You're not going in there, Billy."

I exploded. "I'm not going in there? The hell I'm not!" About six guys jumped me and I started thrashing and punching. "Get your frigging hands off me!"

Bud got in my face. "Remember her as she was, Billy!"

"What the hell are you talking about? Let me see my wife!

Dammit, let go of me, you big apes, or I swear I'll kill every man jack of you!"

"It's radiation sickness, Billy!" Bud thundered. "You know what that does! You know what that's like! Let her be! Let her go! There's nothing you can do! She doesn't want you to see her like this! I mean it, Billy! Let her go in peace!"

"Let her go in peace?" I roared. "How can anyone with radiation poisoning go in peace? Let me go! I have to see her! I have to!"

I don't know if the guys let up, or Bud gave them the nod, or maybe it was Crandall, but I broke free and tore into the house, frantic, racing to our bedroom and throwing open the door. I looked and everything hurt suddenly, the pain stormed through my body, tears were cutting down my cheeks like fire, and I cried at the top of my lungs, "God, no! Please, God, no! NO! NO! NO!"

33

HONOR

JOHNNY STRANGE

Sniper's married.

Billy and I have walked through tough times. I've stood shoulder to shoulder with him in the heat of battle. I've seen him become a demi-god in combat. This guy, Billy Martens, is one of the most intense men I have ever known. I've seen him do a lot of astonishing things. I've heard him say a lot of perplexing words. But in all of that, the last thing I ever thought I would see him do is stand up in a Shinto Temple in a black dragon kimono next to the most beautiful Japanese girl I've ever seen and marry her.

Oh, yeah. Sniper is married. The whole Marine Corps brass is spitting nails about it. Crandall is so mad he wants to put Billy in cuffs and send him back to Leavenworth, Kansas, to rot in a solitary cell until the downtown area of Nagasaki stops glowing. But Sakura's family is related to the Emperor or has a direct line to him because before Crandall could ship Billy out the word came from the top, I mean the White House, that Billy marrying Sakura might do a lot to ease the tensions and get Japan and the U.S. back on some kind of friendly footing.

Personally, I think if Billy married the Emperor's daughter, it wouldn't do a stinking bit of good. I've seen how these guys operate. I remember the Jap who spoke perfect English, who would sneak over and lay up next to our fox holes on Cactus and pick up the names of some of our guys while they were talking. Then he would go out in the jungle and act like a dying Marine. I almost fell for it once. I'm in the foxhole with Sergeant Brown, and I hear someone out there calling me.

"Johnny, Johnny, I'm shot. Come get me, man."

Well, like a dumbass, I stood up and started to climb out of the hole. If Brown hadn't jerked me back down, the Nambu that opened up on me would have cut me in half.

Brown pulled out a grenade, popped the pin and uncorked a Cy Young fastball over my head. The explosion didn't drown out the screams of the Jap squad that had been lying out there not thirty feet away. He got shot doing it, but he lived. That's the crap they pulled.

On Okinawa, about one hundred of them stuck a white flag out of a cave entrance and started yelling *Kuppuku suru! Kuppuku suru!* I found out later it meant "I submit." Our boys let them come out of the cave and every one of them had a grenade in his belt. They started getting excited and pulled those grenades out. The price they paid was one hundred dead Japs shot to pieces, but they killed some of our guys, too. After three years dealing with this kind of crap, you get a feel for the way these little sand-bugs think.

It was awkward. Billy really wanted me to stand up with him and I said I would, but I am still a little under the weather, if you know what I mean. It's only been three weeks since the gunfight at the OK Corral and even though the slugs were only .22 caliber, they still messed me up a bit. And I'm still a little put off by the Jap stuff, so we compromised. They had their little deal up at some temple and then Sakura got dressed up in a fancy Jap getup and they got married again. I waited until they did the official USMC marriage ceremony with a real American padre until Marjean and I went. We were all in our dress blues and Sakura was in a western dress. Except for the skin and eyes, she could have been getting married at the Methodist church in Anywhere, USA. Bud wheeled me into the hall in a wheelchair, Marjean at my side. Bolo and Gyprock and Player were there too. When it came time to do their vows, Bud hauled me to my feet, and we all stood up for Billy.

I'm glad for Billy, I really am, but there is something eating at me. He looked really happy for the first time in a long time and I hope that we all can get through the next two or three years and put all this stuff behind us. I would really like to feel good about Sakura. But somehow, I don't think I ever will. You can't fight a people for four years in the most brutal way and then just stack your weapons and line dance together. Something inside me will never trust the Japanese.

AFTER THE WEDDING and the reception, Billy and Sakura vanished. One minute I was shaking his hand and the next he was gone. I don't blame him. Sakura really is beautiful and I remember when I got married all I wanted to do was brush off the gaggle of admiring friends and just get alone with the most beautiful girl in the world. After they left, we all hung around. Crandall took the edge off his anger with a couple of bottles of *Saké*. The last time I saw him before Jean and I took off, he and Bakar were off in a corner about three sheets to the wind, remembering the good old days of the Spanish Civil War where they fought white people who at least behaved like gentlemen.

Marjean got me home, at least what we called home. A nice little place a few blocks from the hospital. It was kind of a combination of Japanese and western architecture with a little garden in the middle. The pond had these big carp in it, what the locals called *Koi*, big fat bottom feeders that I wouldn't eat for a hundred bucks. Not good ol' cutthroat trout by a longshot. But I enjoyed sitting out in the garden when it was warm. We were heading into late November now, and it could get nippy. Nagasaki is about the same latitude as north Mexico, but you have the North Pacific and the Bering Sea close by and that affects the weather.

I like this house. It's set up to create peace. That's the only way I can describe it. There are little trees in the garden. They call them *Bonsai.* They're like the giant pines in the mountains of Idaho, only they are two feet tall. I can wheel out into the garden and just sit for a long time. Very peaceful, quiet. The little pond has a waterfall at one end and the sound of the water running over some rocks into the pool soothes me. That's the only way I can put it.

See, that's one thing that really bug me. What is it about these Japs? They can go out and butcher ten thousand people and then come home to their little garden, sip some *Saké,* and enjoy the peace and quiet. I think these people must have split person-alities.

And another thing. I don't like Hamari. That's the gal Cran-dall got to help around the place. She's like a fricking ghost. She must know that I don't like Japs much because she just pussy-foots around like she's walking on eggshells. Marjean is a lot better with her than I am. But that's because Jean never sat in a rain-filled hole in the stinking jungles of Guadalcanal, hearing the scream of one of her buddies who just took a knife between the ribs about three holes down. And Hamari's got this guy that she has come over once every couple of days to tend the garden. His name is Akira. He's an old guy, and he never says a word. But he's got this look on his face like he's got dog crap on his upper lip. One day I'm in the garden and he's cutting away at the little trees, a snip here and a snip there. And he looks like his dog died and his truck broke down and his wife left him all on the same day. So, I brace him.

"Hey, Akira. If you're going to work here, at least make a

happy face from time to time. You're really buggin' me with the sorrowful looks. What's up with you, anyway?"

He looks at me for a long time and then he says, get this, "You would also be sad if you lost your honor."

Somehow, that doesn't sit right with me. "Lost your honor? How did you lose your honor?"

"We lost our honor when we surrendered, when we lost the war. Japan has never been conquered."

Okay, that did it for me and I cut loose on the little creep.

"Honor? You lost your honor when you surrendered? You little scumbag. You lost your honor when you invaded Manchuria, even though your Emperor didn't want you to. When you massacred the civilians, raped the women and enslaved the rest, you lost your honor?

"Honor? You talk about honor and you marched our men from Corregidor up through the Bataan peninsula, shooting the wounded, and bayonetting the weak who couldn't keep up? Then you shoved the rest into rat-infested camps and starved them to death?"

"Every country you invaded, you strutted around like the arrogant little pricks that you are, and those countries will hate you for a thousand years."

His face has gone white and his hands are trembling. So I finish him.

"You make me sick. You sit here whining about your honor when you are the lowest kind of human being. Your sick little Bushido code and your Samurai posturing didn't get you shit. You lost and now we sit here occupying the great Empire of Japan. The great shithole of Japan is more like it. Don't give me that crap about honor. You don't even know what honor is."

Hamari comes rushing in. First time I see her move quick. She takes Akira by the arm and helps him to a bench. He's white as a ghost and trembling like a leaf. Hamari has tears in her eyes.

"Please, Mr. Johnny, please."

"Well, he's got a lot of nerve talking to me about honor."

"You do not know him, Mr. Johnny, who he is."

"What has that got to do with it?"

For the first time, Akira spoke to me. "Not all Japanese supported the war, Mr. Johnny. In your country, you have Democrats and Republicans. They believe in completely different things. If you looked at many American white people together, you could not tell which party they belonged to."

Well, that kind of pulled me up short. "Go on, Akira. What are you trying to tell me?"

Hamari sat down next to Akira. "My grandfather was a top officer in the Imperial Japanese Army in 1938. There were two major factions in the army, somewhat like your political parties. My grandfather was a leader of the *Kōdō-ha*, the Imperial Way. They were in conflict with *Tōsei-ha*, the 'Control' faction. The *Kōdō-ha* believed in the importance of our culture, spiritual purity over material quality, and they believed that our greatest enemy was the communists of the Soviet Union. The *Tōsei-ha* believed in the total war theory that Japan should rule the world, starting with our great rival, China." She looked at her grandfather.

Akira spoke again. "A group of foolish young officers in our faction decided the only way to save Japan from the threat of global war was a coup d'état. On February 26, 1938, they assassinated several leading officials and occupied the government center of Tokyo. They did not seize the imperial palace. The Emperor was furious with them and sent the *Tōsei-ha* to quell the rebellion. After that, they consigned our faction to the shadows and the war party took over the military. They invaded Manchuria, and the war began."

Well, I didn't know that, so I was interested. "Go on."

"I had no more influence. When I heard of the plans to bomb Pearl Harbor, I went to Yamamoto and begged him not to do it. He sat me down and told me he no longer controlled the army or the navy, but Tojo was in control. He had no choice but to follow orders. He hoped that by destroying your fleet he would give Japan enough time to negotiate a peace."

I looked at him. "Yeah, well, I guess he didn't figure that we would never give up. He poked the wrong tiger with that little stick."

Akira smiled for the first time. "An apt picture, Mr. Johnny."

Hamari spoke again. "My grandfather lost two sons and a grandson, my husband, in the war. He worked tirelessly to convince the civilian leaders that it was a lost cause. He was treated like the prophet Jeremiah of your Bible. They threw him into prison, where he was beaten and tortured."

Akira waved his hand to quiet her. "So, you see Mr. Johnny, I know what honor is. I am not talking about the honor of the army. I, too, am ashamed of the things we did in the name of the empire. But I weep for my country. I weep because we have lost everything—our homeland, our culture, the Japanese way of life. No matter what happens, Japan will never be the same. And I weep for that, because our life is gone, and with it our *Kuni no meiyo o sonchō suru,* our national honor and respect. Among the nations, we cannot hold up our head."

I looked at him for a long time and I think maybe the penny dropped. Finally, I spoke. "I am sorry, Akira... Maybe because so many of my friends died, maybe because I saw so much of the horror of war, I have a grudge against all Japanese. I think I need to ask my God to help me understand."

He looked up.

I took a breath. "Akira, will you come and tell me more? I once found the way of peace with some Navajo Indian friends. You don't look much different from them. If you will come maybe, together we might find a different path."

There. That wasn't so hard.

He smiled again. "Yes, Mr. Johnny, I will come."

Just then, I heard the front door burst open, and Marjean's

voice calling to me. "Johnny, where are you?" There was something in her voice…

"In here, honey. I'm talking with…"

Marjean burst out the door into the garden. "Johnny, you've got to come. It's Sakura. She's dying."

34

THE SHIP HOME
BUD, THE CORPSMAN

It was a hell of a thing.

I said that to God. That was my prayer. It was a hell of a thing.

Billy was a lot stronger than I thought he'd be. Stronger than I'd have been.

He asked me and Johnny and Marjean to join him at the house. Sakura's mother put the urn with her daughter's ashes in the garden right by the pond and waterfall. There was a Buddhist priest. Even in winter, the little garden was beautiful. A place you'd go to collect your thoughts. I imagined the mother would go there often.

She was all alone. All her family was gone. Billy tried to persuade her to return to the U.S. with him. I doubt he'd have gotten official permission, but he tried to talk her into it. I know he would have done right by her. Made sure she had her own rooms wherever he wound up living, enough to eat, spending money, whatever she wanted and needed.

But her family's ashes were in Japan. All her memories. All the life she had lived, the lives her husband and children had lived, the lives her ancestors had lived. Her sisters and brothers, her kith and kin, no matter how far away, in different niches and corners of the country, were all in Japan. I could have told Billy to save his breath. Sakura's mom wasn't going anywhere. She was *ninja*, for heaven's sake.

And, of course, that's how it worked out. She bowed politely, thanked Billy, and refused to leave with him. Tears ran fast down both their faces. I had to look away.

Billy tried to return the sword, the katana that had belonged to Sakura's father, the one he had fought with and defended Sakura's home with. But the mother was having none of it. She knew her husband's spirit approved of how Billy had used his sword. It was his to honor and protect and, should the need arise again, use against his foes. This was the will of the gods. She wrapped it in a black silk bag with tigers on it, tied the cords tight, and handed it to him. Billy accepted the sword with his own bow.

We all had our goodbyes to make. Not just Billy. I never would have guessed it. Going back to '41 and '42, I saw us winning the war, whatever that took and whatever that looked like, and then being back home with green grass that was well mowed, white picket fences and gates, morning coffee and the newspaper—no gunfire, no bombs bursting, no danger. I never thought we'd end up living in Japan. And I'm dead sure Billy never saw himself falling in love with a Japanese woman.

It was a winter sea, but we had lots of sunny days. Billy would wind up at the rail with me and Johnny and Marjean. It didn't take long before he was talking about Sakura and Japan. We didn't mind. We knew he had to get it off his chest. We all had a lot to get off our chests before we docked in the States, too.

He talked about the little things. How Sakura poured the tea. The few times she would let him watch as she pinned up her hair. Mucking about in the garden together after it rained. Did we know she played a Japanese flute or *fue*, of very old bamboo, the *shakuhachi*? That she could make it sound like a wind moving through the trees? Water rippling in the pond? Many evenings he had fallen asleep to her playing. She was able to push the war farther and farther away for both of them. Even learning how to use the katana properly, and the Bo, the fighting staff, did that.

"Did she teach you the flute?" I asked.

"The shakuhachi?" he responded, acting surprised I'd brought it up. "Yes, Bud, yes, she did. I wasn't her best pupil."

I played a hunch. "Where is it?"

"Where is what?"

"The flute she taught you on. Did you leave it with her mother?"

"It's stashed with the sword," he replied.

Marjean spoke up. "I'd like to hear it, Billy, if you don't mind."

Billy hesitated. "Like I said, I wasn't her best pupil. I'll drive the swabbies and the Marines nuts."

Johnny laughed. "Heck, the swabbies need a good laugh and the Marines are all tone deaf from the mortar and artillery blasts during the war. They'll think you're a genius."

So, Billy went to his bunk and brought back the flute, except he never called it a flute, just a *shakuhachi*. It was a beautiful-looking thing, my style of beauty anyway, rugged, with nice lines, the way I'd describe a Chevy pickup. He leaned over the side, which I didn't think was a great idea with the sea churning past, but I saw Johnny shake his head at me, so I didn't say a thing, just let Billy blow.

At first, it was pretty bad, like he warned us it would be. The flute squeaked and whistled or didn't produce any sound at all. I heard some Marines jeer and wondered who would go over and ring their bells first, me or Johnny. If it had been '42 or '43, hands down, Johnny. Now? '45, '46? I wasn't so sure.

But Billy suddenly got into it. Some really nice long notes came out. Then a few more. And a few more after that. The Marines shut up and started listening. I don't know what others were hearing, but I was back on a favorite hiking trail stateside. There was this boulder I always sat on after being hard at it for three or four hours. It was the turning point. I'd head back down the trail after an hour or so. I'd angle myself to get the sun on my face, lean back, sometimes hunker down and use the boulder for a headrest. Then I'd listen.

I'd hear the sparrows, the loud shouts of the jays, whistles, and calls I didn't even recognize. Sometimes the huff or bark of a mule deer. Farther off, several coyotes yipping and crying. Back of it all, the boughs of evergreens talking. That's what it sounded like. Pines and firs and spruces whispering and making movements with their hands. I always felt they were saying something. I could never write it down.

So, that's what Billy gave me. It wasn't picture perfect. But it was like Sakura was playing through him and that was enough. I heard the sea rushing past, heard gulls, heard the sun—crazy as that sounds—heard the air and sky. And that pushed my war far away too. Not just the island battles and the plasma and morphine and the frightened men. It pushed the bomb away too, both bombs, and all that had happened with them, the radiation poisoning, the destruction, the scars on beasts and humans. When Billy finished playing, apologizing for being awkward and fat fingered, I laughed, so did Johnny and Marjean.

Johnny said, "Don't sweat it, Billy. You gave us some dream time."

It helped rinse me. I needed more. Yeah, I'd been back to the States on leave and enjoyed Johnny's wedding. But since then I'd been through the savage fighting on Okinawa, the high casualties, the atomic bomb and the plutonium bomb, the Japanese surrender, the occupation of Nagasaki, interviewing the survivors. I'd watched Sakura explode in a shower of blood—her ears, her nose, her eyes, her mouth, Lord have mercy, every opening the blood could find. No, I wasn't ready for America and my lady just yet. I wasn't ready for peacetime. I needed more rinsing. A lot more.

I wrote a letter to Kalasia, crumpled it up and started another. Johnny at least had Marjean with him. They'd had weeks to talk things over. I just had paper and pencil. Billy had less than that. That's why we didn't care if, some days, he went on and on about Sakura. Other times, he was as quiet as the grave and that bugged me. What was going on inside? Was he going to pitch himself off the ship into the sea? We'd never be able to save him if he did.

Johnny said he'd heard Billy got mail delivered to him in Nagasaki. From Saipan. If that were true, Billy hadn't said a thing about it. We had to assume Chamorra had written him, if anyone had written him at all. Suppose he had got a letter from her? Was it a Dear John, closing that door for good? Or did she want to renew the relationship and ditch all her B29 pilots and colonels? I couldn't imagine Billy writing her once he'd fallen for Sakura. All his energy had gone there for months. But he might write a letter to Saipan now. Maybe. Or he might think that was betraying Sakura's memory. Even her spirit, if he believed God granted her the ability to roam around and touch his heart.

We made it to Pearl in good time. Left for America in pretty short order after a few days in Hawaii. Had some purple cloud storms and other days the ocean was a plate of glass. I think we were maybe three days out of San Francisco when Billy talked about the final time he'd gone up to the Shinto shrine with Sakura. Though of course no one had any idea it was a last time and this happens a lot in life, doesn't it? I thought of several Marines I was sure I'd have a coffee with after an island battle, whether it was Tarawa, Saipan or Okinawa, always assuming we'd all make it, but I never saw them again. Billy and Sakura had asked for a blessing from a monk, prayed side by side in one of the halls, gone walking over the hilltop, kissed forbidden kisses knowing the priests and monks would not only frown on that but might ban them from the shrine.

According to him, she always said to Billy, "Human love is just as important as love from the gods. It is just as spiritual. Just as divine. And who made it so? Us? Mortals? It is the spirits who have made it so. Kami has made it so. Why shouldn't we kiss in a scared place? Our love for each other is holy too, not just our love for one god or another. Human kisses are blessings."

He looked at Johnny and Marjean and me, his eyes dark, almost hollow, like caverns. "Look. I know I've been shooting my mouth off. I don't know what else to do. But once we dock, I'm done. Sakura's ashes are in Japan, a big piece of my heart is there too and always will be. I won't talk about her again, not to you three, not to anybody. I don't know if life will be normal or not. What is normal going to look like for us? I'll try to get to the family ranch in Montana. Whether my father will let me on the property is another thing. I doubt it. Which means I'll need to find another place to live. No, I'm not asking to move in with any of you, so don't make the offer. The one thing that is for sure is me and Sakura—don't bring her up after we set foot in California. Don't remind me of her. Don't ask me how I feel about her and Japan. I'm keeping all that locked inside. Of course, I'm going to go there in my head. Probably a lot. But I'm going there alone, okay? A lot of things are over now. The war, Nagasaki, my marriage, probably the family ranch too. I'll deal with it. It's the cards God and life have handed me. I'm not leaving the table. I'll play it out. But it's like Sakura and me never were."

"Okay, Billy," I said.

35

WHERE NICODEMUS TOOK ME
BILLY MARTENS

I TOOK A BUS INTO MONTANA AND THE CLOSEST TOWN TO THE
Martens Circle Bar Ranch. Then I hitchhiked, lugging my duffle
with USMC stenciled on it, to Old Man Nikkel's place, which was
only a couple of miles from ours. The air was crisp, in-between
late winter and early spring, still snow on the ground. I'd gone
soft after four years in the Pacific. Had to put on everything the
Marines left me to stop the shivering.

Mr. Nikkels and his wife welcomed me like a son. Their boy
James had made it back from the war in Europe months before
and had a good job in Whitefish managing a resort. We sat, drank
coffee, ate huckleberry pie and laughed a heck of a lot. I don't
know what we had to laugh about. Neighbors on both sides of
them had lost children. Four altogether. One of them was Francie
Abbots, a true Montana beauty I'd always wanted to take out for a
milkshake and a movie. She'd signed up with the Marines,
became a nurse, there had been some kind of accident. It didn't
seem right. But then, none of it seemed right. Johnny was
supposed to come marching home again. Jane too.

"I wouldn't advise heading on into your family ranch, Billy,"
Mr. Nikkels warned in a voice like gravel tumbling out of a dump

truck. "Your pa has made it plenty clear to all around that the war was the work of the devil and anyone who got involved in it was doing the devil's work. He had nothing good to say, and plenty bad, about families that let their young 'uns go off to fight. Four or five families found him so insulting they left the church. They are attending Pastor Kettles' log one at the foot of the mountain there instead."

"Are you and Mrs. Nikkels still with my father?" I asked.

He fidgeted with his coffee mug, pushing it back and forth. "No, Billy, we aren't. I understand about pacifism and conscientious objection. We're Mennonites too, just like you and your dad and your family. But I also know pacifism didn't free up those Nazi death camps or liberate Europe or the Philippines. It took soldiers and all the rest of them with guns. That's just the way of it. We're on the far side of heaven here and the business end of hell. Were you at Iwo?"

"No, Sir, I wasn't. Everywhere else, it seemed." I glanced at Mrs. Nikkels. "Have you seen my mother and sisters?"

She smiled a good, strong smile. "I have. The girls are all grown up and so pretty. Your mom speaks of you when your father isn't around. You know she loves you. She doesn't bear the grudge your father does. If you write a note out for her, I'll see she gets it. But I side with Mr. Nikkels on this—today is not the day to go to the ranch. There will just be a fight and he won't care who sees it or hears it, including your siblings."

"They need to know I'm alive."

"I agree with you. But they already know that, Billy. The postmaster gave your mom your letter from Japan on the sly—I think there was just the one. Well, you made her happy. Alive and well and setting things right in Japan, weren't you? Free as a mountain bluebird. It's a wonder you didn't marry and settle down there."

I got up. "I'm wondering if I might have the loan of a horse."

"Why, sure, son," Mr. Nikkels replied. "You know Nicodemus.

And there's a saddle that'll work for you hanging from the wall in the barn. The one with the three Xs carved into it."

"Yes, Sir, thank you, Sir. I won't be gone above three hours."

He shook his head. "You need what my boy James needed. A night on the range. It'll put God, the moon and the stars back in your eyes. If you're lucky, you might hear the coyotes or a wolf, who knows? You'll find a bedroll near by the saddles. Mother here will scrape some food together and I'll fetch you my Win 1886 and the .45-70 government cartridges."

I protested. "Whoa. You two don't need to go to all that trouble."

Mrs. Nikkels puffed her cheeks. "Poof. What's the trouble? The pie's already baked and sliced, the chicken is fried and there's a bit of baked ham too. Do you need a canteen?"

"I've got my USMC one."

"Better take three. James will not mind. I'll fetch his pair."

She brought the canteens from a closet and pumped water into them from the tap in the kitchen sink. They were in their canvas covers. He'd sewn a patch onto both of them. Eagles.

"I didn't know he was with the 101st," I said.

"Oh, he has stories to tell, James has. Wait till you two get together. I imagine you have stories to tell, too. You need to stay over the weekend. He's coming down from the resort to see us. He'll be tickled to find you here."

My plan was to look over my family's spread without them knowing it was me. I was glad Nico was an Appie because they'd see right off it was the Nikkels' horse and wouldn't dream I was sitting it. I went high and roamed about, following the hills that were strung out around our ranch.

Everything looked good. The cattle seemed fat enough coming out of a Rocky Mountain winter. The fencing was well-tended. The remuda had grown. They were spread out, finding some grass and grazing in our big fenced pasture. I saw a young black Morgan kicking up its heels in the corral.

A rider moved in among the Red Angus. Two riders. I saw right off one of them was my older brother, Jake, and the other, one of the girls. I squinted. Even from a distance, and a hat on her head, it had to be my tall, blonde sister, Nancy. She waved. I waved back. She had no idea. Probably thought I was James.

My throat went stiff, my eyes burned. It would take only five minutes to ride down and greet them. It wasn't right that I couldn't. But I was certain my father was hovering around somewhere. Probably like to load up Uncle Charlie with salt and have at me. Uncle Charlie was a ten-gauge shotgun, big as a bison, and my father called it that because that's who'd given him the gun. Uncle Charlie himself was long gone over the Great Divide.

I'd go down. It would be good. But then the others would need to know, mom and my other siblings, Bekka and Mike. Father would find out. He'd come raging and roaring. What if we came to blows? No need to turn everyone's day into a sour apple. I just had to pray something would come together a year or two from now. I pressed my knees gently into Nico's flanks. We moved on. *The Lord is my shepherd*, I thought to myself as we went. *I shall not want for anything.*

I took old trails but cut a few of my own too. Avoided the snow banks that were still hanging on. Hoped I wouldn't run into anyone I knew. Or anyone at all. Those war years, what Marine had ever been alone? There was always somebody at your elbow. Sometimes a good thing when we were fighting for our lives. Other times something you had to put up with. Now I had the big, wide, broad lonesome I needed to survive deep down in the well that was Billy Martens.

The peaks filled my eyes. Still white as chalk. Their sides purple and blue from where Nico and I stood. I always looked to see if I could spot a goat or ram or even a bear traversing those slopes. Had done it since I was a kid. I never had any luck then, and I didn't have any luck now. It didn't matter. It was the high vertical rock that made the difference.

Mount Fuji had been stunning, something done with fine brushes and watercolors, I used to tell Sakura. She was surprised. She had no idea I might have an eye for beauty that resembled the intricate lines of Japanese art. I smiled. Not for the first time, I had fooled Sakura about who I was. I remembered a kiss softer than silk after one such epiphany of hers about her American Marine. "All our greatest Samurai were poets and artists as well as warriors," she murmured, nestling into me.

I'd said I wouldn't talk about her after I'd set foot in the States. That didn't include me talking to me about her or remembering her pearl skin, her eyelashes dark as a long night, her kisses, the way she found her niche with my body and slept so soundly, sheets tugged up to her perfect chin. I didn't just tell Sakura she was beautiful. I told her often enough she was a work of art. That would make her lower her eyes. That would bring a soft, sunrise pink to her face. It lingered.

Sometimes I tortured myself, remembering what the bomb had taken from me. It was the same old debate in my head. The bomb saved lives because an invasion of Japan would not only have killed many more Americans who were safe at home now, but it would have killed far more Japanese than died in Hiroshima or Nagasaki. Maybe more than died in all the island fighting. More children, I was certain of that.

But the bomb had taken innocent life too. Incinerated nursing mothers with their infants at their breasts and their toddlers at their feet. Melted old men. Ignited the strong and weak alike, torched people who had been against Pearl Harbor and the war from the beginning. It was still killing. It killed Sakura. The thick, dark clouds of nuclear destruction hung over our world forever.

I set out my camp where old stones made a ring, but not a ring I remembered. Maybe Jake or Mike had made it. Maybe Bekka or Nancy. Or all four. Or a stranger from a ranch that was miles away. The sun still went down early but not quick like it did in the islands. Light stayed in the sky while I unwrapped the huckleberry pie. I pretty much cleaned that out first. Then I had some cold chicken and a slice of ham. Drained one of James's 101st canteens. Had a smoke. Nico did his own thing with the grass he could crop, and a thin strip of nearby water slaked his thirst. I placed the saddle on a boulder. Nico was never much for wandering. Human company suited him fine.

I drew in the smoke, held it, released it through my nostrils. It was nice to be able to take my time. The stars tumbled out. Robert Service had said that in one of his wilderness poems. My father had read those out loud to me when I was nine or ten. *The stars tumbled out neck and crop.*

Mrs. Nikkels was not a drinker, but her husband and James loved their brews. She'd been kind enough to pack me a few bottles and wrap them in a towel filled with ice. I had my Ka-Bar on my hip and used it to flip off the cap of one. It was cold and good. I sighed, my muscles, heart and mind unwinding. Maybe I was human after all.

I remembered the paper I'd balled up in my pocket just for this mountain rendezvous. I wasn't Bud, PhD. I didn't memorize things by the acre. I flattened the page and held it in my hand. I used my Zippo to read it.

*T*HOUGH MUCH IS TAKEN, *much abides; and though*
   We are not now that strength which in old days
   Moved earth and heaven, that which we are, we are,
   One equal temper of heroic hearts,
   Made weak by time and fate, but strong in will
   To strive, to seek, to find, and not to yield.

"I STILL GOT life to live, Sakura," I said out loud. "I'll do that for you."

3 6

THE LAST DAY
JOHNNY STRANGE

I'VE SEEN A LOT OF DEATH IN THIS MAN'S WAR. SO MUCH DEATH that I often wonder how I will live after I go home.

In the Pacific war, death was the measure of all things. You gauged each day a success if you were alive at the end of it. Midnight simply marked the next round, like a boxing match. The bell sounded. You picked up your BAR and your mags and stepped into the ring. When the end of the round came, you looked around to see who was going to go back to their corner.

Many didn't.

Time crept slowly from each sunrise to each sunset and you came to the end of it, conscious not of who was with you, but who was not.

Death ruled time, and the fear of death was the subtle undertone of each moment.

When the war ended, I thought that the light would turn back on, that me and my friends would shed the weight of the death we carried on our shoulders every day, that we would come back to life, like Lazarus from the grave. But it wasn't true.

When we came to Japan we saw more death, but this was death as king, death that had come in a blinding flash, searing heat, death that turned people back into the tiniest elements of their beings, floating in the air invisible, but still there.

———

WHEN I FIRST HEARD ABOUT the atomic bomb, I thought it was a great thing—a weapon that would kill our enemies in great swaths, mowing them down like wheat under the immense wheel of the combine. I thought of the many lives, the many men that would return home, back to their wives and kids, men who would survive because we killed more, faster, more horribly. I rejoiced in my living and exulted in the many enemies who were dead. The bomb was a great thing.

Until it killed my friend.

Oh, Billy's body isn't dead, but his heart is. And the bomb killed him just as dead as Kremer or Sharples or Rudy.

When Sakura died, Billy died, and the bomb killed him, because it killed her.

———

BUD TOLD me how it worked.

The people who died in the first seconds of the blast were the lucky ones. Because if you made it through that blast, the bomb came, like the angel of death, and marked you, like a sheep at the slaughterhouse, or a big pine in the forest, to be cut down and sent to the mill.

The bomb put death inside you, and death waited, incubating, searching out all your vital parts and digging itself into your very being, waiting for the bomb to call for the marked ones. And then, days later or weeks later or months later, your body just fell apart, and you were dead.

And that's how Sakura died, and that's how Billy died.

AND IT'S NOT FAIR, because Billy hated the bomb. He hated what it did. He stood up for the dead. The women, the children. The people on the streets. He spoke for them; he championed them. You'd think the bomb would have honored him, seen the tears on the lintel over his door, and passed him over, spared him. But the bomb is no respecter of persons.

The Japanese call it *Pika-don,* the blinding light, the boom. When Billy met Sakura, she told him about that day. How she walked through the streets of Nagasaki trying to help. How she saw men and women piled on top of each other, the ground beneath them soaked with the fat of their bodies. Ground that would never dry. She told him about seeing people wearing burnt rags, but when she approached them, she realized it was their skin and they were still alive, squirming on the ground. She told Billy she wondered if the radiation that showered her body would remain. It did.

BILLY TOLD us about Sakura on the boat when we were going home. He talked a lot, a dead man talking. I could see it in his eyes that he was dead. When she died, Billy Martens walked away from life. I don't know if he will return.

And that's what kills me, because Billy Martens beat the odds. It's like every day in the jungle of Cactus, or the sand dunes of Betio, or the cane fields of Saipan, or the tombs and caves of Okinawa. Every day, he beat the odds. One step ahead of the bullet with his name on it. One foot beyond the reach of the mortar shell that killed fifty guys around him. One leap beyond the Jap sniper's field of fire.

And it is as though death grew angry, and marked him with an unseen x on his back. And then waited, knowing that eventually, he would catch Billy with his guard down. Like he almost caught me when I walked into that room and they shot me to pieces. And then when Sakura came, death rubbed his hands together with glee and set the trap for Billy.

Death didn't want to kill Sakura—she was already dead. No, death wanted Billy. Because death felt cheated, because Billy was a hero, because Billy out-foxed him, because Billy made it through to the end, and that enraged death. So death killed Billy, and for death it was a glorious victory, because Billy is still walking around. He still gets up in the morning, has his coffee, eats with us in the mess, wanders the deck of the ship, stands at the rail, looking west, back, toward Japan.

But he's dead, because she's dead. And me and Bud can't help him. We just look at the body of our friend and mourn—with him and for him. So death won after all and it's a rotten shame.

———

WHEN WE WERE FIGHTING out there in the jungle, I could never picture what death was like. Oh, I had a fear of it, but I could never imagine myself dead. Living I knew. Living was the sun lifting just beyond the edge of the sea, breaking the steel gray of the pre-dawn. Living was Marjean, her warm arms around me, her golden hair spilling across my chest in the dark hours of the night. Living was J.A.—a life from me and Marjean. A boy with his own life, but so much me and her. Living was the baby growing inside her. Living was walking in the hills above Coeur d'Alene and watching the clouds form over the lake. Living was a trout stream in the hills of Montana with a lunker on the end of your line.

There are many ways to know life, but only one way to know death.

BEFORE WE LEFT JAPAN, I sat with Akira for many days, in the garden, in the peace. I learned I was wrong. I learned you can't hate people because their eyes are slanted or their skin is yellow. Bud told me that a long time ago, but amid all the death, and blood, and guts on the ground, I forgot.

I forgot that a Jap, the Jap that we fought in the jungles and on the beaches, and in the hills, is not a Jap because of what's on the outside, but what's on the inside. In his heart and in his mind. A Jap could be any color. We just called him Jap because he was Japanese. But he could be a Jap, a Kraut, or a Nazi, a Chink, a Russky or a Roman or a Greek. He could be any man who decided that he would impose his way on everybody else, and that decision was based on what he was inside and not on the color of his skin or the language he spoke.

Akira reminded me of this in our talks. One day he said something to me I won't forget.

"Mr. Johnny, where has it gone?"

"Where has what gone, Akira?"

"The dignity, Mr. Johnny, the dignity of human beings as being human?"

"I don't know, Akira."

He pointed toward Nagasaki. "It lies destroyed, Mr. Johnny. Destroyed and ruined out there, corpses in the atomic fields."

And I knew he wasn't just talking about the dead. He was talking about the dead, and the men who killed them.

He shook his head sadly. "For when human beings deal death to other human beings in such a manner, death strips the dignity from the killer and the killed. And laughs."

We sat silent for a long time. Hamari brought us tea.

Quiet, the Japanese are quiet. Japs may be loud, arrogant, boastful, murderous, but so are Nazis. Japanese are quiet.

We sit in the peace and it's almost like when my two Navajo friends put me in the sweat-house. When I sit with Akira, I remember what I learned. The darkness does not make us who we are. The things that we carry are just things that we carry. They don't tell us what to do or where to go.

Every man has a story. Most lives have good and bad. You can let the story be who you are, or you can make the story stay in its place—a signpost, a reminder, a guide. I hope to tell that to Billy. But I don't know if he's ready.

Billy is his story right now. He's the kid who got thrown off his ranch by a judgmental father. He's the boy who searched the jungles of Cactus trying to find the bones of our friends who were killed and buried in the ooze. He's the survivor who wandered the high mountains of New Zealand. He's the Chamorran warrior, running naked in the jungle with a yellow-haired, black-toothed goddess at his side. He's the killer of Japs, he's the traveler of Troy, he's the sniper, he's the hero… he's a dead man.

All these things have become him.

Bud said it once to me a long time ago. That poem, the one that followed us from Dago, the one we have lived by, as though it was written about us.

I am become a name;
    For always roaming with a hungry heart,
    Much have I seen and known; cities of men
    And manners, climates, councils, governments….
    Myself not least, but honor'd of them all;
    And drunk delight of battle with my peers,
    Far on the ringing plains of windy Troy.
    I am a part of all that I have met, both the living and the dead.

Billy has become a name, but he has forgotten about the living and right now he only bears the name of the dead. And I hurt for Billy Martens. More than I hurt for any of the friends I left behind, in swamp or oozing mud, or shallow grave in the sand of Tarawa, of an empty tomb in a shaded valley on Okinawa.

Though he stands beside me, and he laughs, and talks, and eats and sleeps, Billy is more dead than all of them.

AND SO I look toward home. Marjean and I stand together on the deck at dusk and the sea breeze smells of life and I see my future and it is full of peace. I hope we have taught the Japs and the Krauts a lesson they will not soon forget. I hope my son will live among less cruel people. I hope to live out my days, walking beside the dark, smooth Pend Oreille River, my hands held by those I love.

For these days have taught me much. I hope I will be a different man when I get home. I hope I can help others shed the weights they carry. I hope to live out my days in a world that has come to its senses.

I HOPE my friend finds his heart again.

THE THINGS WE LEFT BEHIND
BUD, THE CORPSMAN

So, that's it.

The end of the line, the story is over.

The mariners return to Ithaca, the ringing plains fall far behind, the fair wind takes us home across vast seas whose deep and sunless bottoms lie littered with sunken ships, mangled aircraft, and the rotted bones of thousands of men—friend and foe.

On those blood-soaked shores across the endless sea, the white Crosses and Stars of David line themselves in neat rows, marking the place where the winners lie. No one speaks of the losers, bulldozed into a pile, set ablaze and consigned to eternity as the forgotten ones, the enemy whose only resting place is in the hearts and memories of the mothers, fathers, wives and children of Japan.

The losers will only remain as actors in the faded photographs of young Imperial Army soldiers, grim faced and stiff, standing beside their brides—he in uniform with one hand holding a sword upright, she in a traditional Shinto wedding dress. A picture, that like the fierce present of the battle at that defining moment of berserker combat, will fade until it is a gray, meaningless, forgotten, a slip of paper in an unread book, some-where on a dusty shelf.

We went to war cloaked in ignorance—heroes, giants, demigods, saviors of the world. Our bugles blared and our flags snapped in the breeze. We "Sir, yes Sir'ed" our way across the parade grounds of countless camps, straining to catch the eye of a proud mother who would soon receive the yellow slip of paper from an uncaring, impersonal government.

What would we win?

What will we say to our children, our grandchildren? Will we tell them about spitting a Jap on the end of our bayonet and watching him scream and beg until the blood pouring from his mouth chokes off his beseeching words? Will we describe what a man who has taken a direct hit from a 60mm mortar shell looks like, how his blood, parts, and entrails make a kaleidoscope of colors on white coral sand? Or will we stay silent, trying to make it to the next morning without the dreams—the damned dreams?

We survived, but we are all going home wounded.

When we disembarked in Frisco, we looked like old men. Johnny leaning on his cane, still struggling with a hip bone nearly destroyed by a fusillade of bullets. Billy, eyes vacant, the quick smile and jest giving the lie to the grave dug deep in his soul. And me, Philo Parmalee, Bud the Corpsman, relatively unscathed on the outside but scarred forever in my being, haunted by the surprised look in the eyes of the Japs I killed on Saipan.

I swore I would never kill, but things get rearranged when the men you have promised to bring home in one piece are at the point of a knife, or about to be shredded by a grenade.

And that's the biggest thing for me. I promised to bring them home in one piece and I didn't. No matter how much I wanted to, how much I prayed, I couldn't keep them from the wounds of war.

We don't have the strength we had back in the halcyon days of

Camp Elliot, when we were the Hollywood Marines. We strutted on the parade ground, eyes right, shoulders back. We were going to war. We could move heaven and earth, afraid of nothing, snappy dress blues, trousers creased just right on a thousand pairs of pants. We were all the same, pre-heroes, strong in will, our eyes steely, resolute—win the war.

Then the first battle, no creases now. Just a thousand scum-caked faces and a thousand pairs of crapped dungarees. The pre-heroes forgot the cheers and the bands and the far-flung white hats. Survival became our name. And one by one, the heroes met their fate. Death came on a pale horse and the only thing we cared about was keeping our heads down and our guts inside our bodies. And yet... and yet...

We rose from trenches, from holes, from caves, and met the enemy. And though we left our youth behind, we found some-thing to replace it. We found what it means to be a man, to love your brothers, to go the last mile, to never give up until the job is done. A fiery crucible forged us, once straw men, now steel. We drank of life and emptied the glass. In the midst of death, we were more alive than ever before. Semper Fi was our shibboleth, the password into the world of men.

We found something out there in the Pacific, something none of us imagined. I think it might take all my life to understand how deep was the learning.

We toiled, we brought about great works; the Valkyries rode upon our shoulders, heroic hearts beat within us and it was as though two men stood erect in each single body—the one who was dying and the one who was learning to live. But, along with cast off magazines, canteens, packs and empty tins, we left much strewn behind us in the jungles, on the sands, in the hills.

If I had to make a list of the things I left behind, it would be long.

My youth, my dreams, my hope, my understanding of what is right and what is wrong. My belief that all men are the same,

God's children, created equal, blessed with certain rights, given the ability to pursue happiness, so much more this paper I write on cannot contain it all.

Now at the end of this war, I think none of it is true. This planet will not get better. This war solved nothing. I had hoped that my children would bask in the light of a different world. A realm where the problems of hate, and lust, and fear are banished. But I think not.

In Japan we found a people humbled, crushed, defeated, but not apologetic. They were sorry we defeated them, but when we challenged them about Pearl Harbor, about the death march, about Nanking, they stared at us in wonderment.

"That was the war," they would say. "We did our duty to the Emperor. We never ratified the Geneva Convention..."

As though that made sense.

What about the dead people, what about the shades wandering the Happy Isles, the ones who refused God until his enemy came to recruit them? Did they not warrant a chance? Did they deserve to be dispatched from this world, cut off in the blossom of their sin, no reckoning made, but sent to their account unshriven with all their imperfections upon their head?

Would they have died in such a way if the war machine of the Empire had not ground down upon them, seeking whom it could devour?

I would like this story to end on a better note. A high point, some great goal achieved, some precious thing preserved for all generations. I had hoped to be part of an epic adventure that ends with the hero coming to his rest in his comfortable chair, pipe in hand, children gathered at his knee, listening with rapt faces while the returned one tells of great deeds, and great victories.

But that is not life.

So, I'm writing these things down in a book and I will carry that book home. I will meet Kalasia on the wharf in San Francisco. We will be married, we may have children, proud Tongan warriors who might never go off to war. But I think not.

I think Billy will finish his life with a great scar. I think Johnny will never go home again, and I think Bud will never be the pacifist he signed up to be.

So that is what we left... over there.

What can I say or do to make sense of this great thing we have endured? What promise can I make to those coming behind me that will be kept? I hear moans around me, many voices, Kremer Sharples, Big Band, Teacher, Rudy...

Come my friends, is it too late to seek a better world?

Clamber aboard the ship once more, sail beyond the glimming sunset, and the realms of all the distant stars.

There must be something more, something of life and love, something that we can stumble upon, some greater nobler work.

Was the war noble? Were the acts of demented men struggling together with their humanity cast aside worthy to be entered into the book of life?

As the poem said, "Death closes all; but something yet may be done, not unbecoming men that strove with Gods."

We are those men. We fought the fight. We escaped the sting of death and the victory of the grave. We are the men who strove with Gods.

Will the world be better for what we've done?

Time will tell.

MURRAY PURA

Murray Andrew Pura writes in a number of genres for a variety of publishers including HarperCollins, Harlequin, Harvest House, Islands, Elk Lake, Baker, Barbour and MillerWords. He is the author of the award-winning series The Zoya Septet which includes the novels Zo, The White Birds of Morning, Beautiful Skin and A Sun Drenched Elsewhere. He makes his home in southwestern Alberta by the Montana border and Waterton-Glacier Peace Park.

PATRICK E. CRAIG

Patrick E. Craig is a lifelong writer and musician. After retiring from the ministry in 2007 he concentrated on writing and publishing fiction books. He has published six Amish novels, two YA mystery books, two World War II historical novels, a Civil War novella, an outdoor memoir and two anthologies of Amish stories. He has published with Harvest House, Harlequin, P&J Publishing, Elk Lake Publishing and Islands Publishing. He lives in Idaho with his wife Judy.